國際職場
溝通專書

Business
Communication
in English

商用英語

從自我介紹到海外考察，通通難不倒！

USER'S GUIDE 使用説明

以「情境式會話」編寫，模擬互動實境，
一步步打造自學最佳途徑！

1 實境會話，學習在現實中反饋！

從第一關面試開始，到接待客戶、
洽談生意、談判議價、出國考察等
等上班會遇到的各種應對情況，
翻開本書全都有，突發狀況也不擔
心！

😊 **情境會話** *Conversation*

Ⓐ Mr. Lawrence, I have something to *consult* with you about.
Ⓑ Oh, what's the matter?
Ⓐ Well, I wish I could work in *another* department.
Ⓑ Why do you want a *transfer*?
Ⓐ I want to *know* more about our company and *find out* more of my *latent capacity*.

2 重要詞彙，深入瞭解對話內容！

從每篇情境會話中，精選出重要關
鍵的單字、片語，幫助學習者更進
一步掌握用字關鍵，學習事半功
倍，效果更加倍！

😊 **關鍵單字&片語** *Words & Phrases*

discuss	[dɪ'skʌs]	動 討論
quite	[kwaɪt]	副 相當、頗
embarrassed	[ɪm'bærəst]	形 羞愧的
suddenly	['sʌdn̩lɪ]	副 突然地
request	[rɪ'kwɛst]	名 要求
raise	[rez]	名 加薪
inform	[ɪn'fɔrm]	動 告知
boss	[bɔs]	名 老闆
deserve	[dɪ'zɝv]	動 應受、該得

3 替換短句，靈活運用對話更生動！

每一情境之後，同時補充 10~12 句和實境相關的實用短句，讓學習者隨時可以替換運用在職場互動中，談話內容更豐富！

超實用精選短句 Useful Sentences

» Welcome to our company!
歡迎加入我們公司！

» Please try to relax yourself.
請試著放鬆自己。

» Do you like the working environment here?
你喜歡這裡的工作環境嗎？

» It seems that you are a little nervous.
你似乎有點緊張。

» Our coworkers are all very friendly and nice.
我們的同事都很友好的。

» I am glad that you could be a new member of our team.
我很高興你能成為我們團隊的新成員。

4 More Tips，讓你職場更如魚得水！

每一主題，皆補充相關你一定要知道的重要其他內容，例如：更多道地的英文表達和職場生存祕技，帶你避開英文陷阱，提升職場競爭力！

你一定要知道！ More Tips

為訪客或來賓大致介紹公司環境時，通常只要介紹幾個跟對方較有關的地方即可，如：「Let me introduce to you our newly built plant and research center.」（讓我為您介紹我們新建的工廠和研究中心。），或是「Let me show you around the headquarter building.」（容我帶您到總部大樓四處看看。）。

5 雙速語音檔，迅速提升聽説能力！

全書實境會話中英語全收錄。更特聘外師親自錄製雙速（唸慢1次／唸快1次）語音檔，先讓學習者聽清楚每一句子的單字組合，「再唸一次正常語速」使熟悉外國人説話速度，同步提升口語聽説力！

曾經聽某位企業高階主管說過：「工作想求上位，英文一定要會！」

這句話聽在大家的心裡一定都有不同的答案！

其實，我是認為，若是自己的工作或職涯裡確實沒有需要用到英文的地方，而自己對英文也沒什麼興趣，那倒是不必強迫自己一定要學英文。只是身處在全球化的時代，若是能夠擁有「外語」這項強有力的專長，相信在某些預料之外的場合或是必要的重要時刻，一定能有更多的機會展現自己，甚至有意想不到的收獲；即便是在本土企業工作，還是可能會有出國參展、出差拜訪的機會，這個時候，若是有基本的溝通能力，就能取得職場優勢。

我印象很深刻的一件事。我有一個在進出口公司工作的朋友跟我說：「即將有一個外國客戶要來台灣拜訪，老闆希望我能陪同一起去接待對方。雖然老闆說不用擔心英文，但一想到我的爛英文，若是當場結結巴巴或是說不出口，那不是很糗？害我壓力大到幾天睡不好！」其實就我了解，這個朋友的英文程度並不差，只是不常

有機會進行口說英語，因此一旦遇到要用的機會時，反而會害怕。相信有不少的讀者們，可能也有同樣的狀況。

因此，我希望這本書能夠有效地協助在職場工作的你，能夠將本身已經具備的英文能力實際地應用在職場中，從工作第一關的面試，進而到公司會議、客戶簡報，甚至在商務談判及電話溝通等等狀況，都能夠有足夠的英文能力去運用，讓自己更有競爭力，那麼不論是在薪資或職位升遷上，就能更順利了。

這本書，我結合了在職場上會遇到的各種情況，編寫成模擬會話，再加上補充的實用短句，讓學習者在交談的時候可輕鬆變換句型，練習多種用法。另外，特別從情境會話當中挑出了重要的必學單字、片語，只要掌握了關鍵字，即使無法完整理解整個句子，但是透過關鍵詞彙，亦能輕鬆猜出對方語意。

特別值得一提的是：本書收錄中英版本的音檔，英文採用雙語速的錄製方式，一次慢速讓學習者可以仔細地、逐字地聽；另一次則是正常語速，讓學習者可以習慣外國人平日的交談速度與音調起伏。跟著外籍老師學習正確發音，開口說英文時才會更自信、更道地喔！

希望藉由這本書的學習，能夠讓在職場努力打拚的人不僅能更輕鬆地學習英文、有效提升英文能力之外，同時也對求職或是想加薪升職的你都有幫助！

CONTENTS 目錄

新鮮人入社會

篇

→ Part 1 音檔連結 ←

因各家手機系統不同，若無法直接掃描，
仍可以至以下電腦雲端連結下載收聽。
（https://tinyurl.com/2chr9s7w）

01 通知面試者

📖 關鍵單字＆片語 Words & Phrases

corporation	[ˌkɔrpəˈreʃn]	名 股份（有限）公司
resume	[ˌrɛzjuˈme]	名 履歷表
interview	[ˈɪntɚvju]	名 面試
bring	[brɪŋ]	動 帶來
graduation certificate	[ˌgrædʒiˈeʃən səˈtɪfəkɪt]	名 畢業證書
as well as...	[æz wɛl æz]	片 也、和
detailed	[ˈdiˈteld]	形 詳細的

😊 情境會話 Conversation

A This is IDEA *Corporation*. We received your *resume* and hope to have an *interview* with you.

B Oh, I'd love to!

A Is it convenient for you to come between 2 p.m. and 5 p.m. next Monday?

B No problem! Is there anything I should *bring*?

A You need to bring a copy of your ID card and *graduation certificate* *as well as* one *detailed* resume.

B OK. Thank you very much. See you then!

A：我是 IDEA 公司。我們收到了你的簡歷，希望與你面談。
B：喔，我非常樂意！
A：您方便下週一下午兩點到五點之間過來嗎？
B：沒問題！我應該帶什麼東西去嗎？
A：是的，你需要帶身份證和畢業證書的影本以及一份更詳細的履歷。
B：我知道了。非常感謝。到時候見！

超實用精選短句 *Useful Sentences*

» This is JD Company. Is that Miss Lynn?
這裡是 JD 公司。請問您是林恩小姐嗎？

» We received your resume yesterday.
我們昨天收到了您的簡歷。

» Would you like to come for an interview?
你願意來參加面試嗎？

» I would welcome an opportunity to meet you for an interview.
我非常感激能有機會與您面談。

» Could you come over for an interview the day after tomorrow?
您後天能來參加面試嗎？

» What time is convenient for you?
您什麼時候方便呢？

» What should I bring with me?
我要帶什麼東西去呢？

» Only a detailed resume is enough.
只要一份詳細的履歷就夠了。

» You'd better bring a copy of your graduation certificate.
你最好帶一份畢業證書的影本。

» Don't be late for your interview.
面試不要遲到。

» Thank you very much for the information.
非常感謝您的通知。

你一定要知道！ *More Tips*

「interview」指的是「面試」，如：「I am going to interview for the position this afternoon.」（我今天下午將要去面試那個職位。）；通知對方面試時間時，則可說：「Could you come over for an interview in this week?」（你這個星期能夠過來面試嗎？）。

02 參加應徵面試

📖 關鍵單字＆片語 Words & Phrases

take a seat	[tek ə sit]	片 坐下
Personnel Manager	[ˌpɝsṇ`l ˈmænɪdʒɚ]	名 人事經理
company	[ˈkʌmpənɪ]	名 公司
recruit	[rɪˋkrut]	動 招募
advertisement	[ˌædvɚˋtaɪzmənt]	名 廣告
impression	[ɪmˋprɛʃən]	名 印象
potential	[pəˋtɛnʃəl]	名 潛力

😊 情境會話 Conversation

A Excuse me.

B Come this way, and please *take a seat*.

B My name is John, the *Personnel Manager* of this company. May I have your name, please?

A My name is Chang Han-Wei.

B How do you know our *company*?

A I read your *recruiting advertisement* in The China Times.

B What's your *impression* of our company?

A I feel that your company has a lot of *potential*.

A：對不起。
B：這邊請坐。
B：我叫約翰，是公司的人事部門經理，請問你貴姓大名？
A：我叫張漢威。
B：你是怎麼知道本公司的？
A：我從中國時報的求職欄上得知的。
B：你對敝公司有什麼印象？
A：我覺得是一個充滿潛力的公司。

超實用精選短句 *Useful Sentences*

» How did you hear of our company?
你怎麼知道我們公司的？

» What kind of working experiences do you have?
你有什麼樣的工作經驗？

» What is the reason to apply for this job?
為什麼想應徵這份工作？

» Let me tell you about the working conditions.
讓我來為你說明一下工作條件。

» How do you like our company?
你覺得我們公司怎麼樣？

» How many languages can you speak?
你會講幾種語言？

» What do you excel in?
你的專長是什麼？

» I am proficient in both written and spoken English.
我精通英語的寫作以及口說。

» How fast can you type?
你打字多快？

» Why did you leave the former company?
你為什麼離開以前的公司？

» The office hours are from 8 to 5.
工作時間是早上九點到下午五點。

» What is your expected salary?
你的期望薪資是多少？

你一定要知道！ *More Tips*

「potential」是「潛力、潛能」的意思，你可以說：「She has a lot of potential in music.」（她在音樂方面有許多的潛能。）；「He has art potential, but he still needs training.」（他在藝術方面有天份，但仍需訓練。）。

03 基本自我介紹

📖 關鍵單字&片語 *Words & Phrases*

briefly	[ˈbrıflı]	副 簡短地
born	[ˈbɔrn]	副 出生的
introduce	[ˌɪntrəˈdjus]	動 介紹
graduate from	[ˈgrædʒæt frɑm]	片 從……畢業
major	[ˈmedʒɚ]	名 主修
single	[ˈsɪŋgl̩]	形 單身的
be good at	[bi gud æt]	片 對……擅長

😊 情境會話 *Conversation*

A Please ***briefly introduce*** yourself!

B OK! I was ***born*** in 1972 in Taipei. I ***graduated from*** National Taiwan University. My ***major*** was Economics. I am still ***single***. I worked for a trading company before.

A Do you have any other certificates or skills?

B I don't have any other skills, but I ***am*** quite ***good at*** computers.

A Do you have any hobbies?

B I have many hobbies, such as fishing, hiking, and playing golf, etc.

A：請你簡單地自我介紹一下。
B：好的！我生於 1972 年，台北市人，畢業於台灣大學經濟系，目前仍未婚，曾在貿易公司任職過。
A：你有沒有什麼證照或特殊技能？
B：沒有什麼其他特別技能，但擅長操作電腦。
A：你有沒有什麼嗜好？
B：我有許多嗜好，像釣魚、登山、打高爾夫球等。

超實用精選短句 *Useful Sentences*

» Please tell me about yourself.
請介紹一下你自己。

» My name is Peter and I live in Shanghai.
我叫彼得，家住在上海。

» What are you good at?
你的強項是什麼？

» I was born in 1984, and majored in Electrical Engineering in university.
我出生於 1984 年，我在大學主修電子工程。

» I have very good communication skills.
我非常善於與人溝通。

» I am very co-operative and well organized.
我能與人合作，且組織能力很好。

» What are your weaknesses and strengths?
你的弱點和優點分別是什麼？

» I'm an optimistic person.
我是個很樂觀的人。

» Do you have any licenses or certificates?
你有執照或資格證書嗎？

» I can work well under pressure.
我能承受工作上的壓力。

» I have an driver's license.
我有駕駛執照。

你一定要知道！ *More Tips*

　　不論是在寫履歷或申請許多證件的時候，總是會看見一欄「martial state」，這就是「婚姻狀態」，若是未婚就要填上「single」（單身），結了婚的話就要填上「married」（已婚）。而在自我介紹的時候你則可以簡單的説：「I am still single.」（我仍未婚。）或是「I am married.」（我已結婚了。）。

04 閒聊話題

📚 關鍵單字&片語 Words & Phrases

kill time	[kɪl taɪm]	片 殺時間、消磨時間
listen to music	[ˈlɪsn̩ tu ˈmjuzɪk]	片 聽音樂
relax	[rɪˈlæks]	動 放鬆
off work	[ɔf wɝk]	片 下班、不在工作時
plant	[plænt]	動 種植
tend	[tɛnd]	動 照顧、照料
garden	[ˈgɑrdn̩]	名 花圃、花園

😊 情境會話 Conversation

A Mr. Smith, What do you do to *kill time*?

B I like to read books or *listen to music* and *relax*.

B When you are *off work*, what do you do, Mr. Wang?

A I enjoy *planting* and *tending* my *garden*.

A Do you drink?

B I do, but not too much.

B How about you?

A Yes! I do, but only before going to bed.

A：史密斯先生，你空閒時作些什麼消遣？
B：我喜歡看看書或聽聽音樂輕鬆一下。
B：王先生，你下班後，都怎麼渡過的呢？
A：我喜歡作園藝或盆栽。
A：你喝酒嗎？
B：我喝，但是不會過量。
B：你呢？
A：是的！我也會，但只在睡前喝。

🐦 超實用精選短句 *Useful Sentences*

» What do you do in your spare time?
你空閒時作些什麼消遣？

» I like to watch TV after dinner.
晚飯後我喜歡看電視。

» I enjoy walking my dog at a cool night.
我喜歡在涼爽的夜晚遛狗。

» Photography is my favorite hobby.
攝影是我最喜愛的嗜好。

» I usually go mountain climbing or fishing on the weekend.
我周末通常會去攀岩或釣魚。

» I play golf on weekends.
我周末會打高爾夫。

» I love to travel abroad with my wife.
我喜歡和我老婆出國去旅行。

» Do you like beer?
你喜歡喝啤酒嗎？

» Do you play poker?
你會打撲克牌嗎？

» I enjoy listening to music, but I can't sing very well.
我喜歡聽音樂，但歌唱得不怎麼樣。

» Why do you like table tennis?
您為什麼喜歡打乒乓球？

» I play basketball very well.
我籃球打得很好。

⚡ 你一定要知道！ ⚡ *More Tips*

　　破除人與人之間的陌生感，最好的話題之一就是「消遣」，你可以問對方：「What do you do to kill time?」（你如何打發時間？）、「What do you do in your leisure / free time?」（你空閒的時候做什麼？），或是直接問「What's your hobby?」（你的興趣是什麼？）。

05 電話錄取通知

📚 關鍵單字&片語 Words & Phrases

inform	[ɪnˋfɔrm]	動 通知
accept	[əkˋsɛpt]	動 接受、承認
beg your pardon	[bɛg juɚ ˋpardn̩]	片 再說一次
determine	[dɪˋtɝmɪn]	動 決定
appoint	[əˋpɔɪnt]	動 任命、指派
assistant	[əˋsɪstənt]	名 助理
employment contract	[ɪmˋplɔɪmənt ˋkɑntrækt]	名 雇用合約

😊 情境會話 Conversation

A This is RM Corporation. I am glad to ***inform*** you that you are ***accepted***!

B What? I ***beg your pardon***?

A We have ***determined*** to ***appoint*** you as the ***assistant*** to our General Manager.

B Oh, I see. Thank you for telling me such good news.

A Could you come to the office tomorrow to sign the ***employment contract***? Just bring a copy of your ID card and two one-inch color photos.

B OK. Thank you very much. See you tomorrow!

A：我是 RM 公司。很高興通知您被錄用了！
B：什麼？可不可以請您再說一遍？
A：我們已經決定任用您為我們總經理的助理。
B：喔，我知道了。謝謝您告訴我這麼好的消息。
A：您明天可以來公司簽雇用合約嗎？你只需要帶身份證影本以及兩張一吋彩色照片就可以了。
B：好的。非常感謝。明天見！

超實用精選短句 *Useful Sentences*

» Please report to the personnel office at half past eight next Monday.
請你下週一早上八點半到人事部報到。

» I want to tell you that you are recruited.
我想告訴你我們錄用你了。

» Could you come to sign the employment contract tomorrow?
請您明天來簽雇用合約好嗎?

» It's our pleasure to have you here.
能聘用你是本公司的榮幸。

» I really appreciate you for giving me this chance.
非常感謝您給我這個機會。

» I am honored to work with you.
我很榮幸能夠與你們一起工作。

» What do I need to bring?
我應該帶什麼東西去呢?

» Would you like to come to work next Monday?
您願意下週一就來工作嗎?

» Congratulations on becoming our colleague!
祝賀你成為我們的同事!

» Welcome to join us!
歡迎加入我們!

» Thank you very much for the exalting news.
非常感謝您告訴我這個令人激動的消息。

你一定要知道! *More Tips*

通知對方錄取,有很多說法,如:「I am pleased to inform you that you are recruited.」(很高興通知您,您被錄用了。),或是:「It's my pleasure to tell you that you have passed the interview.」(非常榮幸通知您,您通過面試了。)。

06 見面招呼

📖 關鍵單字&片語 Words & Phrases

how	[haʊ]	副	如何、怎樣
excuse me	[ɪkˋskjuz mi]	片	不好意思、對不起
anyone	[ˋɛnɪˌwʌn]	代	任何人
there	[ðɛr]	副	在那裡
surname	[ˋsɝˌnem]	名	姓
welcome	[ˋwɛlkəm]	感	歡迎
come in	[kʌm ɪn]	片	進來
help yourself	[hɛlp jʊəˋsɛlf]	片	自己來

😊 情境會話 Conversation

A *How* do you do? My name is Chang Han-Wei.

B How do you do? My name is Tom.

A *Excuse me*, Is *anyone there*?

B Who are you?

A My *surname* is Chen.

A May I come in?

B *Welcome*! *Come in*, please!

B *Help yourself*!

A：幸會，我叫張漢威。
B：幸會，我叫湯姆。
A：對不起，有人在嗎？
B：你是哪一位啊？
A：我姓陳。
A：我可以進來嗎？
B：歡迎，請進。
B：請自便。

超實用精選短句 *Useful Sentences*

» How do you do? I am Lucy.
你好,我叫露西。

» Come on in and make yourself at home.
請進,別客氣。

» May I come in, sir?
先生,我能進來嗎?

» It's very nice to meet you, Mr. Steven.
很高興見到你,史蒂芬先生。

» Excuse me, is anybody there?
打擾了,請問有人嗎?

» Can you tell me who you are?
能告訴我您是誰嗎?

» I'm John from the Marketing Department. Here is my card.
我是市場部的約翰,這是我的名片。

» Grab a seat and suit yourself.
隨便找個地方坐,別客氣。

» I am so glad to see you.
真高興見到你。

» It's so wonderful to have you here!
你能來真是太好了!

» Here's my business card.
這是我的名片。

» You're welcome anytime.
隨時歡迎。

你一定要知道! *More Tips*

在第一次見面的時候,你可以說的問候語有:「How do you do?」(你好嗎?)、「Nice to meet you.」(很高興見到你。),當然此時你也要大方的伸出手與對方握手,來表示友好與禮貌。

07 就職到任

📚 關鍵單字&片語 *Words & Phrases*

department	[dɪˋpɑrtmənt]	名 部門
hesitate	[ˋhɛzəˌtet]	動 猶豫
advice	[ədˋvaɪs]	名 建議、忠告
feel free to	[fil fri tu]	片 隨意
indeed	[ɪnˋdid]	副 確實
pretty well	[ˋprɪtɪ wɛl]	片 非常好
give a hand	[gɪv ə hænd]	片 提供幫助

😊 情境會話 *Conversation*

A Mr. Chang has been assigned to our *department*, and will be working with us from today. Mr. Chang, please say a few words.

B My name is Chang Han-Wei. Please don't *hesitate* to give me *advice*.

A If anything is not clear, please *feel free to* ask.

B Yes, thank you very much *indeed*.

A Mr. Chang is from Taiwan. He can speak English and Japanese *pretty well*. But as a foreigner, there should be lots of things quite confusing for him. Please always *give* him *a hand*.

A：這位是分發到我們部門的張先生，從今天開始會和我們一起工作。張先生，請你說幾句話。
B：我叫張漢威，請多多指教。
A：如果你有任何不懂之處，請直接問不要客氣。
B：是的。真謝謝你們。
A：張先生從台灣來，英語和日語都相當好，但對一個外國人而言，不清楚的地方想必很多，請各位多幫他忙。

🔊 超實用精選短句 *Useful Sentences*

» I am so pleased to be the manager of Marketing Department.
成為行銷部的經理我感到非常高興。

» Thank you so much for your support all these years.
感謝你們這些年來的支持。

» I would love to say some words to you.
我想對你們幾句話。

» I've fought all the way to where I am today.
我一路奮鬥才有了今天。

» Let's stick together and move on!
讓我們攜手前進吧！

» Without you, I would never be who I am today!
沒有你們，我永遠不可能有今天！

» I am going to work with you from now on.
從現在開始我要跟大家一起工作了。

» Please help me out if possible.
請多多幫忙。

» It's been a pleasure working with you.
可以跟你們共事，是我的榮幸。

» He is an outstanding negotiator.
他是個非常出色的談判高手。

» Whatever I am today is because of you.
我能有今天全靠大家。

» I am positive he will succeed.
我相信他會成功。

✏ 你一定要知道！ ✏ *More Tips*

「hesitate」有「質疑、躊躇」的意思，通常的用法是：「She hesitated before she told him the truth.」（她在告訴他實話之前遲疑了。），而「hesitate」在這裡：「Please don't hesitate to give me advice.」（請多多指教。）是更客氣的說法。

08 環境介紹

📖 關鍵單字&片語 *Words & Phrases*

introduction	[ˌɪntrəˋdʌkʃən]	名	介紹
surroundings	[səˋraʊndɪŋz]	名	環境
have a look	[hæv ə lʊk]	片	看一下
gorgeous	[ˋgɔrdʒəs]	形	華麗的、非常好的
considerate	[kənˋsɪdərɪt]	形	體貼的
staff	[stæf]	名	員工、職員
supervisor	[ˌsupəˋvaɪzər]	名	主管

😊 情境會話 *Conversation*

Ⓐ Mr. Robert, let me give you a brief ***introduction*** of the ***surroundings***.

Ⓐ This is your new office. Please come in and ***have a look***.

Ⓑ Wow, it's ***gorgeous***!

Ⓐ Everything you need is well-prepared.

Ⓑ You are very ***considerate***. I like it very much.

Ⓐ And this is the working area for other ***staff***. You are their ***supervisor***.

Ⓑ Oh, I get it.

A：羅伯特先生，讓我給您簡單介紹一下周圍的環境吧。
A：這是您的新辦公室。請進來看看吧。
B：哇，太棒了！
A：您需要的一切東西，我們都已經幫您準備好了。
B：你們真的非常周到。我非常喜歡。
A：這個工作區是其他員工工作的地方。您是他們的頂頭上司。
B：哦，我知道了。

超實用精選短句 *Useful Sentences*

» Let me introduce the surroundings for you.
讓我給您介紹一下周圍環境吧。

» This is the office we prepared for you.
這是我們為您準備的辦公室。

» You'd better familiarize yourself with the facilities here.
你最好熟悉一下這裡的設施。

» It's at the end of the hallway.
在走廊的盡頭。

» There is a restroom in your office.
你的辦公室裡有一間洗手間。

» I can explain things as we move along.
在此過程中，我可以為您解答各種問題。

» These are your table and chair for work.
這是您的辦公桌椅。

» The washroom is over there.
廁所就在那邊。

» Then I will lead you to the meeting room.
接下來我將帶您去會議室。

» Let me show you around this floor.
讓我帶你參觀一下這個樓層。

» Thanks for all your introduction.
謝謝您所有的介紹。

你一定要知道！ *More Tips*

　　為他人介紹環境，可以用「show someone around...」（帶……四處看看）來表示，如：「Let me show you around our office building.」（讓我帶你到我們的辦公大樓四處看看）。大致介紹完環境時，通常會加一句：「Don't hesitate to talk to me if you have any questions.」（如果你有任何問題，請儘管告訴我。）。

工作溝通協調篇

→ Part 2 音檔連結 ←

因各家手機系統不同,若無法直接掃描,
仍可以至以下電腦雲端連結下載收聽。
(https://tinyurl.com/bdheewxw)

01 請同事幫忙

📖 關鍵單字&片語 Words & Phrases

wonder	[ˈwʌndɚ]	動	想知道
kindly	[ˈkaɪndlɪ]	副	好心地
translate	[trænsˈlet]	動	翻譯
letter	[ˈlɛtɚ]	名	信件
German	[ˈdʒɝmən]	名	德文、德國人
need	[nid]	動	需要
complete	[kəmˈplit]	動	完成
no problem	[no ˈprɑbləm]	片	沒問題
bother	[ˈbɑðɚ]	動	打擾

😊 情境會話 Conversation

A Mr. Schmidt, I was **_wondering_** if you could help me with something?

B What can I do for you?

A Could you **_kindly translate_** this **_letter_** into German for me?

B I see, when do you **_need_** it done?

A Could you **_complete_** it by the end of the day?

B **_No problem_**!

A I'm sorry to **_bother_** you with this.

A：史密特先生，有一件事情不知是否可以麻煩您。
B：什麼事呢？
A：希望您幫我把這封信翻譯成德文。
B：知道了，你什麼時候要呢？
A：你能趕在下班之前完成嗎？
B：沒問題！
A：對不起，真是麻煩您了。

🖐 超實用精選短句 *Useful Sentences*

» I think I need your assistance.
我想我需要你的幫助。

» Do you mind if I ask you to do something for me?
你介意我請你為我做點事嗎？

» Would you kindly do me a favor?
你能好心幫我個忙嗎？

» Could you give me a hand?
可以請你幫我個忙嗎？

» Anything I can help?
我能幫什麼忙嗎？

» I am afraid that I can't handle it myself.
我怕我沒辦法自己搞定。

» Can you tell me how to use this printer?
你能不能告訴我怎樣使用這台印表機？

» Is it that urgent as you said?
它有你說的那麼緊急嗎？

» Could you help me type these letters?
可以請你幫我打這些信件嗎？

» I am not available now. Can you wait a minute?
我現在沒時間，你能稍等一會嗎？

» Thank you so much for your help.
非常感謝你的幫助。

⚡ 你一定要知道！⚡ *More Tips*

「kindly」是「親切的、厚道的」的意思，「She kindly gave the poor old man some bread.」（她好心的給了那老人一些麵包。），而「kindly」用在「Could you kindly translate this letter into German for me?」（你能不能幫我把這封信翻成德文？）口氣上更為客氣，「Could you kindly take out the trash?」（你可不可以幫我倒垃圾？）。

02 分派工作

📚 關鍵單字&片語 Words & Phrases

right away	[raɪt əˈwe]	片 立刻、馬上
free	[fri]	形 空閒的
finish off	[ˈfɪnɪʃ ɔf]	片 結束
job	[dʒɑb]	名 工作
on hand	[ɑn hænd]	片 在手邊
fax	[fæks]	動 傳真
document	[ˈdɑkjəmənt]	名 文件

😊 情境會話 Conversation

A Alice, Come here, please!

B Are you calling me?

A Yes.

B I'll be there **right away**.

A Alice, Are you **free** now?

B Give me 5 minutes, I'll **finish off** my work on the computer.

A Please finish your **job on hand**, then **fax** out this **document** for me.

B Yes, I'll do it.

A：愛麗絲，請過來一下！
B：您叫我嗎？
A：是的。
B：我馬上過去。
A：愛麗絲，妳現在有空嗎？
B：再過 5 分鐘，電腦就打完了。
A：那麼，做完後，幫我把這份資料傳真出去。
B：好的。

超實用精選短句 *Useful Sentences*

» Could you book a flight ticket to Hong Kong for me?
請幫我訂一張飛往香港的機票好嗎？

» Please key in these data immediately.
請立刻輸入這些資料。

» Please bring the documents to my office at once.
請馬上把文件送到我的辦公室。

» Please take an inventory before you leave.
下班前查一下庫存。

» You can find someone else to help you.
你可以找其他人來幫你。

» Are we clear with everything?
我交代的你都清楚了嗎？

» You will be out visiting clients with me later.
你等會兒跟我一起出去拜訪客戶。

» If you have any questions, just bring it up.
如果你有任何問題，就提出來。

» You can leave when you finish all these.
把這些做完就可以下班了。

» Please email our clients the price list.
請把價目表寄給客戶們。

» I need you to do something for me right away.
我需要你馬上為我做件事。

» All these should be done by tomorrow morning.
這些事情都要在明天早上以前完成。

⚡ 你一定要知道！⚡ *More Tips*

　　當你想要請同事幫忙，問他有沒有空，你可以說「Are you free now?」（你現在有空嗎？）、「Are you busy now?」（你現在忙嗎？）、「Are you available now?」（你有空嗎？），但是最後這一句話似乎有點雙關語的意思，所以當你想試探對方現在有沒有（男）女朋友，可不可以跟你出去約會時，也可以用這句話。

03 指示叮嚀

📚 關鍵單字 & 片語 Words & Phrases

arrange	[əˋrendʒ]	動 安排
client	[ˋklaɪənt]	名 客戶
hasty	[ˋhestɪ]	形 匆忙的、輕率的
keep in mind	[kip ɪn maɪnd]	片 記住
bottom-line	[ˋbɑtəm laɪn]	名 底線
directly	[dəˋrɛktlɪ]	副 直接地
price	[praɪs]	名 價格
allowance	[əˋlaʊəns]	名 零用金、津貼

😊 情境會話 Conversation

A Alex, we've **_arranged_** for you to visit a **_client_** in Shanghai the day after tomorrow.

A Remember not to be **_hasty_** when talking with the clients.

B I will **_keep_** that **_in mind_**.

A Also, do not give out our **_bottom-line directly_** when talking about the quoted **_price_**.

B OK. I know.

A Now you can apply for **_allowances_** for this business trip from the Finance Department and get prepared for the trip.

A：艾力克斯，你被安排後天去拜訪一位上海的客戶。
A：記住，跟客戶交談時不要急躁。
B：我會記住的。
A：談及報價的問題時，不要直接攤出我們的底線。
B：好的，我知道了。
A：你現在可以去向財務部申請出差費，並準備明天出發。

超實用精選短句 *Useful Sentences*

» There is something that I want you to do.
有件事我想讓你去做。

» I would like you to handle this project.
我想讓你來處理這個項目。

» What else should I pay attention to?
我還應該注意些什麼？

» Do not hurry to answer any substantial questions.
不要急著回答任何實質性問題。

» Can you be kind enough to tell me how to deal with it?
請您告訴我該怎麼處理這件事好嗎？

» Would you like to visit a VIP this weekend?
這週末你願意去拜訪一位 VIP 客戶嗎？

» I will follow your instructions.
我會遵從您的指示的。

» Anything else I should notice?
還有什麼我應該注意的嗎？

» When should I leave for Shanghai?
我應該什麼時候去上海呢？

» Always remember to do everything for our own sake.
請牢記做任何事都要出於我們自己的利益。

» Proper compromises are necessary.
適當的妥協是必要的。

» Pay more attention to your manners.
多多注意你的言行舉止。

你一定要知道！ *More Tips*

「keep in mind」是表示「記住」的片語用法，如：「I want you to keep in mind that don't leak out any confidential information to others.」（我要你記住，不要對其他人洩漏機密資料。），若要強調「切記」，可以用「make sure to keep in mind」或是「bear in mind」來表示。

04 關心工作進度

📚 關鍵單字&片語 Words & Phrases

prepare	[prɪ`pɛr]	動	準備
quote	[kwot]	名	報價
customer	[`kʌstəmɚ]	名	客戶
process	[`prɑsɛs]	動	（用電腦）處理
computer	[kəm`pjutɚ]	名	電腦
May I...?	[me aɪ]	片	我可以……？
the end of	[ðə ɛnd ɑv]	片	……的結尾（結束）
believe	[bɪ`liv]	動	相信
rely on	[rɪ`laɪ ɑn]	片	依賴

😊 情境會話 Conversation

A Ken, What are you doing now?

B I am *preparing* the *quote* for a *customer*.

A Please *process* this document on the *computer*.

B Yes, sir. *May I* know by what time you want it to be done?

A Could you finish it by *the end of* tomorrow?

B It shouldn't be a problem.

A Then, I *believe* I can *rely on* you.

A：肯恩，你現在正在做什麼？
B：正在準備給客戶的報價單。
A：你把這份資料用電腦處理一下。
B：是的，主任，什麼時候要完成呢？
A：明天下班之前可以完成嗎？
B：應該沒有問題。
A：那就靠你了。

超實用精選短句 *Useful Sentences*

» When will I get all the papers?
我什麼時候能拿到所有的資料？

» I hope you could inform me of your progress.
我希望你把你的進度告訴我。

» I am working on it.
我正在努力。

» When do you want me to finish all these?
您希望我什麼時候完成這些呢？

» Can you speed up? You are too slow!
快一點好嗎？你太慢了！

» Could you give it to me by next Thursday?
下週四之前給我可以嗎？

» I am trying to do it faster.
我正試著做快一點呢。

» Why is there a delay?
為什麼會延誤？

» When will it be done?
什麼時候會完成？

» It's almost done. Give me 10 more minutes.
快完成了，再給我 10 分鐘。

» I believe you can finish the task on time.
我相信你能準時完成任務。

» What are you up to these days?
你這些天忙什麼呢？

你一定要知道！ *More Tips*

「process」當名詞的時候有「過程、步驟」的意思「This is the process of learning singing.」（這是學唱歌的步驟。），而它當作動詞的時候就有「處理、沖洗（照片）」的意思：「Please process this film.」（請幫我沖洗這底片。）、「The computer is processing some paper.」（電腦在處理一些文件。）。

05 會議通知

📖 關鍵單字&片語 *Words & Phrases*

back	[bæk]	形	回原處
happen	[`hæpən]	動	發生
away	[ə`we]	副	不在、外出
secretary	[`sɛkrəˌtɛrɪ]	名	祕書
meeting	[`mitɪŋ]	名	會議
reception	[rɪ`sɛpʃən]	名	接待
about	[ə`baʊt]	介	關於
effort	[`ɛfət]	名	努力

😃 情境會話 *Conversation*

Ⓐ Oh, you are ***back***.

Ⓑ Did anything ***happen*** while I was ***away***?

Ⓐ The ***secretary*** of the CEO called us.

Ⓑ What did she say?

Ⓐ At 2 p.m. tomorrow afternoon, there is a ***meeting*** in the ***reception*** room.

Ⓑ Do you know what it's ***about***?

Ⓐ She did not tell me.

Ⓑ That's fine, Thanks for your ***efforts***.

A：喔！您回來了啊！
B：我不在的時候有什麼事嗎？
A：執行長的祕書有打電話來。
B：她說了什麼？
A：明天下午兩點在接待室有個會議。
B：關於什麼的會議？
A：她沒說。
B：好吧！謝了。

🔊 超實用精選短句 *Useful Sentences*

» When shall we have the meeting?
我們什麼時候開會呢？

» Are we going to be late for the meeting?
我們開會會遲到嗎？

» I can't be late for the meeting.
我開會可不能遲到。

» We can have a meeting here if it's okay with you.
如果你們同意我們就在這裡開會。

» Now that everyone is here, let's get started.
既然大家都到了，那就讓我們開會吧。

» Do you want to meet in your office or the conference room?
你想要在你的辦公室還是在會議室開會？

» Please attend the meeting this afternoon.
請參加下午的會議。

» I am just on my way to the meeting room.
我正要去會議室開會呢。

» Would you mind copying the agenda for tomorrow's meeting?
你可以幫我列印明天開會的議程表嗎？

» Our meeting will be at 4 p.m..
我們下午四點開會。

» God! Are we having a meeting again?
天啊！我們又要開會嗎？

» Thank you for telling me that.
謝謝你告訴我這個。

✐ 你一定要知道！ ✐ *More Tips*

「notify」是「通知」的意思；「Please notify everybody that there will be a meeting in five minutes.」（請告訴大家五分鐘後要開會。）

06 指出錯誤

關鍵單字&片語 Words & Phrases

come over	[kʌm ˋovɚ]	片 過來
matter	[ˋmætɚ]	名 問題
a little bit	[ə ˋlɪtḷ bɪt]	片 有一點
strange	[strendʒ]	形 奇怪的
double-check	[ˋdʌbḷ tʃɛk]	動 仔細的檢查
almost	[ˋɔLmost]	副 幾乎
make a mistake	[mek ə mɪˋstek]	片 犯錯
do one's best	[du wʌns bɛst]	片 盡某人最大之力

情境會話 Conversation

A Mr. Shih, could you ***come over*** here?

B Yes, what's the ***matter***?

A This number looks ***a little bit strange***. Could you please check it again?

B Oh, I'll ***double-check*** it.

B Ah! I ***almost made a mistake***.

A It's not an easy job.
A ***Do your best***!

B Thank you very much for your help.

A：施先生，過來一下。
B：是的，有事嗎？
A：這個數字有點怪怪的。可以請你再檢查一次嗎？
B：哦，我再確認一次。
B：啊！我差點弄錯了。
A：不容易啊！
A：多加油了。
B：真謝謝你幫忙。

🔊 超實用精選短句 *Useful Sentences*

» Would you please check on your manuscript again? I found something wrong.
請再檢查一下你的手稿好嗎？我發現一些錯誤。

» I found some mistakes in your article.
我在你的文章中發現了幾處錯誤。

» Please point out my mistake directly.
請直接指出我的錯誤。

» Can you tell me what I did wrong?
你能不能告訴我哪裡錯了？

» The sum is incorrect. Please check it again.
總數錯了，請再確認一次。

» The price list on our website is not right.
網頁上的價目表是錯的。

» There is something wrong with your data. Could you please reconfirm it?
你的數據有些問題。你可以再檢查一次嗎？

» Those numbers seem to be wrong.
這些數字好像錯了。

» Where have we gone wrong?
我們哪裡做錯了？

» It's alright. Be careful next time.
沒關係，下次注意點。

» I am sorry for making the mistake.
很抱歉我犯錯了。

» Thank you very much for reminding me.
非常感謝你提醒我。

✐ 你一定要知道！ ✐ *More Tips*

「I will double-check it again.」（我再檢查一次。），也可以說：「I will reconfirm it.」（我再確認一次。）、「let me look it over again.」（讓我再看一次。）。

07 電話請假

📚 關鍵單字＆片語 Words & Phrases

director	[dəˈrɛktə]	名 主管
moment	[ˈmomənt]	名 片刻
seem	[sim]	動 似乎、看起來好像
catch a cold	[kætʃ ə kold]	片 感冒
see a doctor	[si ə daktə]	片 看醫生
not yet	[nat jɛt]	片 還沒
day off	[de ɔf]	片 休假
rest	[rɛst]	名 休息
today	[təˈde]	副 （在）今天
appreciate	[əˈpriʃɪet]	動詞 感激

😊 情境會話 Conversation

A Hello! May I speak with the **_director_**?

B Hello! Just a **_moment_**.

A Hello! This is John. It **_seems_** that I have **_caught a cold_**.

C Did you go to **_see a doctor_**?

A **_Not yet_**, I would like to have a **_day off_**.

C That's fine. Have a **_rest_** **_today_**.

A I do **_appreciate_** it.

A：喂！請問課長在嗎？
B：喂！他在，請稍待。
A：喂！我是約翰，我好像感冒了。
C：你有沒有去看醫生？
A：還沒有，我想今天請一天假。
C：沒有問題，你好好休息！
A：謝謝您了。

🗣 超實用精選短句 *Useful Sentences*

» Can I take a personal leave today?
我今天可以請事假嗎？

» I have a slight fever.
我有點發燒。

» I need to go to the bank this morning.
我早上必須去一趟銀行。

» I had a car accident on the way to the office.
我上班的途中出了車禍。

» I would like to take a good rest at home.
我想要在家好好休息。

» Is that okay if I take half a day off?
我如果請半天假可以嗎？

» I'd like to visit my sick mother in the hospital.
我想去探望生病住院的母親。

» Can I take funeral leave for the following days?
接下來幾天我可以請喪假嗎？

» I have to look after my injured daughter.
我得照顧受傷的女兒。

» I want to take a break, I need a day off.
我想要休息，我需要一天的假。

» Thanks for your permission.
感謝你的允許。

✍ 你一定要知道！✍ *More Tips*

　　當你要打電話跟老闆請假的時候，你的理由除了「I am not feeling very well this morning.」（我今天早上覺得不是很舒服。），也可說「I have to take care of some personal things today.」（我今天需要處理一些私事。），你甚至可以直接說：「I need a break, I have to take a day off.」（我需要休息，我需要休一天的假。）。

08 午餐會議邀約

📚 關鍵單字&片語 Words & Phrases

lunch meeting	[lʌntʃ `mitɪŋ]	名 午餐會議
purpose	[`pɝpəs]	名 目的
discuss	[dɪ`skʌs]	動 討論
cooperation	[koˌɑpə`reʃən]	名 合作
program	[`progræm]	名 專案、計畫
attend	[ə`tɛnd]	動 參加
on time	[ɑn taɪm]	片 準時

😃 情境會話 Conversation

A Mr. White, we've arranged a *lunch meeting*. Do you have time to join us?

B What time is it?

A 11 a.m. to 1 p.m. today.

B And what's the *purpose* for the meeting?

A To *discuss* the *cooperation program* for next month.

B What do I need to prepare for the meeting?

A Nothing. Just *attend* the meeting *on time*.

B OK. I'll be there.

A：懷特先生，我們安排了一個午餐會議，你有時間參加嗎？
B：什麼時間？
A：今天上午十一點到下午一點。
B：會議的目的是什麼呢？
A：是要討論下個月的合作專案。
B：我需要為會議準備什麼嗎？
A：不必，只要準時出席就可以了。
B：好的，我會出席的。

超實用精選短句 *Useful Sentences*

» We'll arrange a lunch meeting tomorrow.
我們明天將安排一個午餐會議。

» Would you like to take part in the lunch meeting?
您願意來參加這個午餐會議嗎？

» Could you tell me the exact time of the meeting?
請您告訴我會議的確切時間好嗎？

» The meeting will be held during lunch hours.
會議將在午餐時間舉行。

» Do you mind telling me the purpose of the meeting?
您介意告訴我會議的目的嗎？

» We'd better bring some related materials with us.
我們最好帶一些相關的材料。

» Would you like to join us for the lunch meeting today?
願意加入今天的午餐會議嗎？

» We'll talk about the marketing problems.
我們將要探討市場行銷的問題。

» Will you attend our meeting on time?
您會準時參加我們的會議嗎？

» We're going to have a lunch meeting.
我們要進行個午餐會議。

» Why not invite Mr. Black to have a lunch meeting?
為什麼不邀請布萊克先生來參加午餐會議呢？

» Can you explain the proper manners for a lunch meeting?
你能解釋一下午餐會議的禮節嗎？

你一定要知道！ *More Tips*

「join」是「參加」的意思。邀請對方參加午餐會議，可以說：「Are you interested in joining us for the lunch meeting?」（你有興趣和我們一起開午餐會議嗎？），或是「Would you join in the lunch meeting with us?」（你要和我們一起參加午餐會議嗎？）。

09 公司團購

📖 關鍵單字&片語 *Words & Phrases*

promotion	[prə`moʃən]	名	促銷
shopping mall	[`ʃɑpɪŋ mɔl]	名	購物商場
household	[`haʊs‚hold]	形	家用的
appliance	[ə`plaɪəns]	名	用具
discount	[`dɪskaʊnt]	名	折扣
group purchase	[grup `pɝtʃəs]	名	團購

😊 情境會話 *Conversation*

A Judy, have you heard that there will be a *promotion* in the *shopping mall* the day after tomorrow? The *household appliances* are being sold for a 20% *discount*; it could be cheaper for a *group purchase*.

B How many people are needed for a group purchase, and what discount can a group get?

A You will need five or more for a group purchase, and we can get 30% off.

B Wow, let's ask everyone if they want to go together.

A I've asked Sarah and she said yes.

A：茱蒂，你聽說了嗎？後天商場有個促銷活動。家電八折出售，團購的話還可以更便宜。

B：需要多少人才能團購呢？團購能有什麼優惠？

A：組團需要 5 個人以上，折扣能打到七折。

B：哇，那我問問大家是不是想一起去吧。

A：我已經問過莎拉了，她也同意一起去。

🐋 超實用精選短句 *Useful Sentences*

» There is a promotion in the supermarket today.
今天那個超市有促銷活動。

» Would you like to join us?
您願意加入我們嗎？

» The household appliances there are sold with 15% discount.
那裡的家電八五折出售。

» How many people are required for a group purchase?
多少人才能達到「團購」標準啊？

» We must confirm the order by April 28.
我們務必於 4 月 28 日前確認訂單！

» It will be much cheaper for a group purchase.
團購的話要便宜得多。

» Six people will be enough for team buying.
六個人就足夠團購了。

» We need two more people to join us.
我們還需要兩個人的加入。

» Could you try to find one more person?
你能不能試著再找一個人呢？

» What discount can team buyers get?
團購的話有幾折優惠？

» Team buyers can get 25% off.
團購者能拿到七五折。

» We can save a lot of money if we buy together.
如果我們一起買的話，可以省下很多錢。

📐 你一定要知道！ 📐 *More Tips*

　　「group purchase」是指「團購」，也可以用「team buying」來表示；「team buyer」指「團購者」，如：「We will give a special discount of 10 percent for team buyers.」（我們給予團購者九折的特別優惠。）。

10 請託機器維修

📖 關鍵單字&片語 *Words & Phrases*

breakdown	[ˋbrekˏdaʊn]	名 故障、損壞
fix	[fɪks]	動 修理
access	[ˋæksɛs]	動 進入、使用
let	[lɛt]	動 讓、使
detect	[dɪˋtɛkt]	動 察覺、發現
fault	[fɔlt]	名 錯誤
mention	[ˋmɛnʃən]	動 提起

😊 情境會話 *Conversation*

A William, my computer has had a ***breakdown***. Can you help me ***fix*** it?

B Sure! What's the problem with your computer?

A I can not ***access*** the Internet.

B OK, ***let*** me see...

A Have you ***detected*** the ***fault***?

B Well, there is something wrong with the connector. I'll have it fixed in a minute.

A Thanks a lot!

B Don't ***mention*** it.

A：威廉，我電腦好像壞了。請你幫我修修好嗎？
B：當然可以！你的電腦出了什麼問題？
A：我沒辦法上網。
B：好的，我來檢查檢查……
A：你找出毛病了嗎？
B：嗯，連接器有點問題。我馬上就可以把它修好。
A：太謝謝你了！
B：不必客氣。

超實用精選短句 *Useful Sentences*

» There is something wrong with the printer.
這台印表機出問題了。

» The machine seems to have broken down again.
這台機器好像又壞了。

» Can you do me a favor?
你能幫我個忙嗎？

» Could you try to fix it right now?
你能不能試著現在就把它修好呢？

» I am afraid that you forgot to connect the power.
恐怕你忘記連接電源了。

» Do you fit the plug yourself?
是你自己安裝的電源插頭嗎？

» Could you tell me how to deal with it?
可不可以告訴我如何處理這種狀況？

» There is something wrong with the button.
這個按鈕出了點問題。

» You'd better operate the machine according to the procedure next time.
你下次最好按照程序操作機器。

» It's very easy, I am sure you can handle it.
這非常簡單，我相信你能處理好的。

» Would you mind telling me how to operate it?
你能告訴我怎樣操作它嗎？

你一定要知道！ *More Tips*

　　請他人給予協助時，可以用「help... with」這個片語，如：「Could you help me with the operation of this machine?」（你可以幫我看看怎麼操作這個機器嗎？），如果是「請他人幫忙做某事」，則說「Would you mind helping me fix the problem?」（你介意幫我處理這個問題嗎？）。

11 提出建言

📚 關鍵單字＆片語 Words & Phrases

suggestion	[sə'dʒɛstʃən]	名	建議
go ahead	[go 'əhɛd]	片	請説
attach	[ə'tætʃ]	動	附上
coupon	['kupɑn]	名	折價券
doubt	[daʊt]	動	懷疑（沒有）
effectiveness	[ə'fɛktɪvnɪs]	名	有效
lottery ticket	['lɑtərɪ 'tɪkɪt]	名	摸彩券
might	[maɪt]	助	可能
work	[wɝk]	動	起作用

😊 情境會話 Conversation

A Does anyone have any **suggestions** for next month's promotion?

B I have some.

A **Go ahead**.

B How about **attaching** a discount **coupon**?

A I **doubt** the **effectiveness** of that.

B How about attaching a **lottery ticket**? That would be interesting.

A Yes, That **might work**.

A：對於下個月的促銷，各位有什麼建議？
B：我有建議。
A：請説。
B：附上折價券如何？
A：我懷疑這沒什麼效果。
B：那麼附上抽獎摸彩券如何？那會很有趣。
A：嗯，這個辦法也許可行。

超實用精選短句 *Useful Sentences*

» Tell me what is wrong, please.
請告訴我是哪裡出錯了。

» Please feel free to make suggestions.
請盡量提出你們的建議。

» If you have any ideas, please bring it on.
有什麼主意就提出來吧。

» I wish everyone could form a habit of making suggestions.
我希望各位能養成提建議的習慣。

» I am afraid that it will not work.
恐怕它不會起作用。

» Why not use water transport instead?
為什麼不改用水運呢？

» Your suggestion sounds good.
你的建議聽起來不錯。

» Do you have any better ideas?
你還有更好的主意嗎？

» How about offering a discount on some products?
部份產品給予折扣優惠怎麼樣？

» I think I have a better solution.
我認為我有個更好的解決方法。

» Would you like to listen to my opinion?
您願意聽聽我的想法嗎？

» Good. I will take your advice.
很好，我會採納你的建議。

你一定要知道！ *More Tips*

當你想要提出你的建議與想法的時候，你可以說：「I have an idea.」（我有一個主意。）、「I'd like to make a proposal.」（我有一個建議。）、「I think I have come up with something.」（我想我想到了一個主意。）等等。

12 關心新進同仁

📖 關鍵單字 & 片語 Words & Phrases

busy	[ˈbɪzɪ]	形 忙的
be used to	[bi just tu]	片 習慣於
in the beginning	[ɪn ðə bɪˈɡɪnɪŋ]	片 一開始
somehow	[ˈsʌmˌhaʊ]	副 由於某種原因
nervous	[ˈnɝvəs]	形 緊張的
help	[hɛlp]	名 幫忙
anything	[ˈɛnɪˌθɪŋ]	代 什麼東西、什麼事情
kindness	[ˈkaɪndnɪs]	名 善意、仁慈

😊 情境會話 Conversation

A Ms. Wang, are you *busy* now?

B No, I am not.

A *Are* you *used* to working here now?

B *In the beginning*, I felt *somehow* a little bit *nervous*.

A I think you will do well. If you need *help* with *anything*, please feel free to ask me.

B I do appreciate your *kindness*.

A Don't mention it.

A：王小姐，妳正在忙嗎？
B：不，還好。
A：妳在這裡工作習慣了嗎？
B：剛開始難免會比較緊張。
A：我相信妳會做的很好。如果有任何需要我幫助的地方，請不要客氣。
B：真是謝謝您的好心。
A：不客氣。

🖋 超實用精選短句 *Useful Sentences*

» Welcome to our company!
歡迎加入我們公司！

» Please try to relax yourself.
請試著放鬆自己。

» Do you like the working environment here?
你喜歡這裡的工作環境嗎？

» It seems that you are a little nervous.
你似乎有點緊張。

» Our coworkers are all very friendly and nice.
我們的同事都很友好的。

» I am glad that you could be a new member of our team.
我很高興你能成為我們團隊的新成員。

» Are you enjoying your work here?
你喜歡在這裡的工作嗎？

» Thank you for your kindness.
謝謝您的友善。

» I will work hard here in the future.
以後我會在這努力工作的。

» Come to me if you need any help.
如果你需要幫助，請儘管找我。

» I am sure everything will be fine.
我相信一切會沒問題的。

» Don't be shy to ask any questions.
不要害羞，任何問題都可以問。

✏ 你一定要知道！ ✏ *More Tips*

　　每一位剛進公司的新同仁，第一天的心情可以說是最複雜的，此時你可以說一些較溫暖的話使新同事放鬆一下心情：「If you need help, please feel free to ask me.」（若你需要幫忙，請不要客氣。）、「Welcome aboard!」（歡迎加入我們！）。

13 激勵部屬

📚 關鍵單字&片語 Words & Phrases

mind	[maɪnd]	名 心
handle	[`hændl̩]	動 處理
worry	[`wɝɪ]	動 擔心
be responsible for	[bi rɪ`spɑnsəbl̩ fɔr]	片 對……負責
understand	[ˌʌndɚ`stænd]	動 理解
correct	[kə`rɛkt]	動 改正
point	[pɔɪnt]	名 一點、處、地方
perfect	[`pɝfɪkt]	形 完美的

😃 情境會話 Conversation

A Do you have anything on your **_mind_**? You look depressed.

B I feel really sorry that I did not **_handle_** it very well.

A No problem, don't **_worry_**.

B I **_was responsible for_** that mistake.

A I can **_understand_** how you feel.

A Just **_correct_** this **_point_**, then everything is **_perfect_**.

B This time I'll do my best.

A：有什麼心事嗎？你看起來很沮喪
B：對於不當的處理，實在非常抱歉。
A：沒問題，別擔心。
B：那個錯誤是我的責任。
A：你的心情我很能瞭解。
A：只要能改正這一點，其餘就很完美了。
B：這一次我一定全力以赴。

🐦 超實用精選短句 *Useful Sentences*

» You look pale. What is wrong?
  你臉色不好，怎麼了嗎？

» Trust yourself, just do it!
  相信你自己，儘管去做吧！

» After all, to err is human.
  畢竟，犯錯乃人之常情。

» I understand. That is not your fault.
  我了解，那不是你的錯。

» I am really sorry for what I have done.
  對於我做的事我感到非常抱歉。

» What can I do to make it up?
  我能做什麼補償嗎？

» It's alright, don't blame yourself.
  沒關係，不要自責。

» I believe you can do way better next time.
  我相信你下次能做得更好。

» You should be confident of your ability to complete the task.
  你應該相信自己有足夠的能力完成這項任務。

» Thanks for your understanding and support.
  謝謝您的理解和支持。

» Take it easy, and try your best.
  別緊張，盡力而為。

✐ 你一定要知道！ ✐ *More Tips*

　　做一個好主管除了要公私分明之外，也要關心下屬的工作情緒：
「Is everything ok?」（一切都好吧？）、「Is everything under
control?」（一切都在掌握之中吧？）、「I believe in you! You can do
it.」（我相信你，你可以做到的。）、「I know you have been working
real hard.」（我知道你工作很勤奮。）等等。

14 請示加薪

📖 關鍵單字&片語 Words & Phrases

discuss	[dɪˋskʌs]	動	討論
quite	[kwaɪt]	副	相當、頗
embarrassed	[ɪmˋbærəst]	形	羞愧的
suddenly	[ˋsʌdn̩lɪ]	副	突然地
request	[rɪˋkwɛst]	名	要求
raise	[rez]	名	加薪
inform	[ɪnˋfɔrm]	動	告知
boss	[bɔs]	名	老闆
deserve	[dɪˋzɝv]	動	應受、該得

😊 情境會話 Conversation

A Sir, I would like to *discuss* something with you.

B What's the matter?

A I feel *quite* *embarrassed* for *suddenly* having to make this kind of *request*.

B That's fine, please tell me!

A Could you give me a *raise*?

B Well, I will *inform* the *boss* about this. You *deserve* it.

A I appreciate your help.

A：經理，有事想和您商量一下。
B：什麼事？
A：突然提出這樣的請求，實在不好意思。
B：沒有關係，請說！
A：能不能給我加薪？
B：嗯，我會向上面轉達。你也該加薪了。
A：那就拜託了。

超實用精選短句 *Useful Sentences*

» I would like to ask for a raise.
我想要要求加薪。

» This is the wrong time to ask for it.
現在並不適合要求這個。

» Why do you deserve a raise?
為什麼你認為你應該加薪？

» Give me a good reason to give you a raise.
給我一個幫你加薪的好理由。

» I need a pay raise.
我需要加薪。

» It's impossible to ask for a raise after working for only a month.
才工作一個月就要求加薪是不可能的。

» I am walking if you say no!
如果你不答應我就走人！

» I am wondering if you could increase my salary.
我想知道您可不可以給我加薪。

» Don't even think about it.
想都別想。

» I will think about it.
我會考慮考慮的。

» It's about time to give you a raise.
是時候幫你加薪了。

» You truly deserve higher pay.
你的確值得更高的薪水。

你一定要知道！ *More Tips*

「raise」當名詞是「加薪」的意思，如：「I got a raise today.」（我今天加薪了。）；當動詞的時候就有「舉起、撫養」的意思，如：「The father raised the child with care.」（那個爸爸很細心的撫養小孩。）、「I raised my hand.」（我舉起我的手。）。

15 提辭呈

📖 關鍵單字 & 片語 Words & Phrases

resign	[rɪˋzaɪn]	動 辭職
complaint	[kəmˋplent]	名 抱怨
such	[sʌtʃ]	代 這樣的事
reconsider	[ˏrikənˋsɪdɚ]	動 重新考慮
disapprove of	[ˏdɪsəˋpruv ɑv]	片 不贊成
true	[tru]	形 真的
alternative	[ɔlˋtɝnətɪv]	名 選擇的餘地
pity	[ˋpɪtɪ]	名 可惜的事

😊 情境會話 Conversation

Ⓐ Sir, I feel very sorry, could you let me ***resign***?

Ⓑ Why? Do you have any ***complaints*** about our company?

Ⓐ No, not as ***such***.

Ⓑ Please ***reconsider***!

Ⓐ My wife ***disapproves of*** it.

Ⓑ Is that ***true***? So there is no ***alternative***?

Ⓐ I am really sorry about this.

Ⓑ What a pity!

A：經理，很抱歉，能不能請你讓我辭職？
B：咦！怎麼了，對公司有不滿嗎？
A：不，不是的。
B：請再好好考慮一下吧！
A：我的太太反對。
B：是嗎？那麼，一點辦法都沒有嗎？
A：實在很對不起。
B：真可惜。

超實用精選短句 *Useful Sentences*

» Can I have a word with you, boss?
老闆，我能跟您談談嗎？

» I am afraid I have to resign.
恐怕我得辭職了。

» I would like to quit this job.
我想要辭職。

» Please accept my resignation.
請接受我的辭呈。

» Is it possible to change your mind?
你可不可以改變主意呢？

» Tell me what you don't like here.
告訴我你對這裡有什麼不滿意。

» Why do you want to switch job?
你為什麼要換工作？

» I was offered $150,000 a month to work in Vietnam. It really attracts me.
有公司提供我駐越南的工作，月薪 15 萬。這真的很吸引我。

» I've turned in my resignation.
我已經遞辭呈了。

» Please consider it carefully.
請慎重考慮。

» Have you been offered a better job by another company?
是不是有其他公司給你更好的工作？

» Please do not forget us.
請別忘了我們。

你一定要知道！ *More Tips*

「not as such」是「沒這樣的事」的意思；「Are you mad at me?」「No, not as such.」（你在生我的氣嗎？）（不，沒這回事。）。

16 申請轉調部門

📖 關鍵單字&片語 Words & Phrases

consult	[kənˋsʌlt]	動 商量
another	[əˋnʌðɚ]	代 另一個
transfer	[trænsˋfɝ]	名 調職
know	[no]	動 知道
find out	[faɪnd aʊt]	片 找出
latent	[ˋletn̩t]	形 潛在的
capacity	[kəˋpæsətɪ]	名 能力

😊 情境會話 Conversation

A Mr. Lawrence, I have something to **_consult_** with you about.

B Oh, what's the matter?

A Well, I wish I could work in **_another_** department.

B Why do you want a **_transfer_**?

A I want to **_know_** more about our company and **_find out_** more of my **_latent_** **_capacity_**.

B Is that all?

A I am afraid so.

B Fine. I will think about it.

A：勞倫斯先生，我有事情跟您商量。
B：喔，有什麼問題嗎？
A：是這樣，我希望能在另外一個部門工作。
B：你為什麼想調換部門呢？
A：我想更多地瞭解我們的公司，並且發堀自己更多潛力。
B：僅此而已？
A：恐怕是這樣的。
B：好。我會考慮一下的。

🔊 超實用精選短句 *Useful Sentences*

» I am Steven from Marketing Department.
我是來自市場部的史蒂芬。

» I am looking forward to entering another department.
我希望進入另一個部門。

» I have worked in the department for more than 3 years.
我已經在這個部門工作三年多了。

» I think I am a diligent and creative person.
我認為我是個勤奮並且有創造力的人。

» Could you give me an opportunity to know more about our company?
能給我個機會更好地瞭解我們公司嗎？

» Finance Department is what I dream of.
財務部正是我嚮往的部門。

» I really hope that you could fulfill my expectations.
我真的希望您能滿足我的願望。

» I will work harder in the new department.
我會在新部門更加努力工作。

» Why do you want to go to that department?
你為什麼想去那個部門呢？

» Anything that you are dissatisfied with the current department?
當前的部門你有什麼不滿意的嗎？

» I want to know more about other departments.
我想更多地瞭解其他部門。

» Let me think it over.
讓我考慮一下吧。

✍ 你一定要知道！ ✍ *More Tips*

「transfer」指的是「轉換、調動」，如：「Jenny is not working in this department anymore. She has been transferred to the Planning Department.」（珍妮已經不在這個部門工作了，她被調到企劃部去了。）。

17 申請留職停薪

📖 關鍵單字&片語 Words & Phrases

urgent	[ˈɝdʒənt]	形 緊急的
important	[ɪmˈpɔrtn̩t]	形 重要的
since	[sɪns]	連 因為
abroad	[əˈbrɔd]	副 在國外
resume	[rɪˈzjum]	動 重新開始
post	[post]	名 職位
opinion	[əˈpɪnjən]	名 意見

😊 情境會話 Conversation

A Do you have anything **_urgent_**?

B Not very urgent, but I think it's **_important_** to me.

A OK. Go ahead. What's up?

B **_Since_** I'm planning to study **_abroad_**, I am wondering if it is possible for me to be on leave without pay.

A How long will you be abroad?

B For one year. I hope I can **_resume_** my **_post_** when I come back. What's your **_opinion_**?

A Well, I'll have to think about it.

A：你有緊急的事情嗎？
B：不是很緊急，但是我認為對我很重要。
A：好的。你說吧。什麼事？
B：因為我計畫出國讀書，所以想知道我可否申請留職停薪。
A：你要在國外待多久？
B：一年。我希望到時候我還可以回來為公司工作。您意下如何呢？
A：喔，我得考慮一下。

🔊 超實用精選短句 *Useful Sentences*

» Could I speak to you for a moment?
我能佔用您幾分鐘的時間嗎？

» I am going to study abroad for one year.
我想出國留學一年。

» Can we talk a moment later if it is not so urgent?
如果不是非常緊急我們稍後再談好嗎？

» What do you want me to do?
你找我幹什麼呢？

» I am afraid that I am rather busy now.
恐怕我現在非常忙。

» It has always been my dream to study in that college.
去那個大學念書一直是我的夢想。

» How long will you stay there?
你要在那裡待多久呢？

» I want to know if I could be on leave without pay.
我想知道我是否可以停薪留職？

» I wish I could still work here when I get back.
我希望我回來的時候仍然可以在這工作。

» Could you tell me the reason?
能告訴我是什麼原因嗎？

» I want to improve my professional skill.
我想提升我的專業技能。

» I'll have to think about this.
這事我得考慮一下。

✐ 你一定要知道！ ✐ *More Tips*

「be on leave without pay」是表示「留職停薪」的意思，如：「Steven Lin is currently on leave without pay.」（史帝文李目前人留職停薪中。）；如果是因工作疏失而遭留職停薪處分的，則要用「be suspended without pay」（被罰以留職停薪）來表示。

18 申請外派

📚 關鍵單字 & 片語 *Words & Phrases*

take charge of	[tek tʃɑrdʒ ɑv]	片 負責管理
project	[`prɑjɛkt]	名 企劃
recommend	[ˌrɛkəˋmɛnd]	動 推薦
task	[tæsk]	名 任務
later on	[ˋletə ɑn]	片 稍後
set off	[sɛt ɔf]	片 出發、動身

😊 情境會話 *Conversation*

Ⓐ Boss, I heard that you are finding someone to *take charge of* the *project* in Australia.

Ⓐ I'd like to *recommend* myself for the *task*.

Ⓑ Fine. I believe you are the most suitable person for the job.

Ⓐ So how is the project progressing at present?

Ⓑ Ms. Wang will give you the related documents *later on*.

Ⓐ OK. When shall I *set off*?

Ⓑ You will be leaving next Friday, which means you have one week to make arrangements for the work in your own department.

A：老闆，我聽説您正在找人負責在澳洲的那個案子。
A：我想毛遂自薦，接下這個任務。
B：好啊。我相信你是最適合這件工作的人選。
A：請問該專案現在的進度如何？
B：王祕書一會兒會把相關資料給你。
A：好的。請問我什麼時候出發呢？
B：下週五出發，這表示你有一週的時間安排部門裡的工作。

🖋 超實用精選短句 *Useful Sentences*

» We have to send somebody to Congo.
我們得派一個人去剛果。

» Is there anyone want to take charge of this project?
有人想負責這個專案嗎？

» Are you interested in that project in Canada?
你對加拿大的那個專案感興趣嗎？

» Which one do you think is the best for that project?
你覺得負責那個專案的最佳人選是誰？

» I want to take charge of that project in person.
我想親自負責那個專案。

» How long shall I work there?
我要在那裡工作多長時間？

» It has always been my dream to work there.
去那裡工作一直是我的夢想。

» What do you think if I take it over?
如果我接手這項工作你覺得怎麼樣？

» I wish I could be in charge of the engineering project.
我希望我可以負責這項工程專案。

» Could I recommend myself for the project?
我能毛遂自薦接手這個項目嗎？

» I am sure you can do it well.
我相信您一定能做好。

» You will leave next Monday. Just make some preparations.
你下週一就離開。做些準備吧。

⚡ 你一定要知道！⚡ *More Tips*

　　「to recommend oneself」是指「毛遂自薦」的意思，也可以用「volunteer for...」來表示。如：「Would anyone recommend himself for this task?」=「Would anyone volunteer for the task?」（有沒有人要毛遂自薦，接下這份任務？）。

電話禮儀

篇

→ Part 3 音檔連結 ←

因各家手機系統不同，若無法直接掃描，
仍可以至以下電腦雲端連結下載收聽。
（https://tinyurl.com/mrxbnyuw）

01 電話禮儀（總機、櫃檯）

📚 關鍵單字&片語 Words & Phrases

hotel	[ho`tɛl]	名 旅館
his	[hɪz]	代 他的
her	[hɝ]	代 她的
well	[wɛl]	感嘆 好吧、嗯
try	[traɪ]	動 嘗試
again	[ə`gɛn]	副 再一次
minute	[`mɪnɪt]	名 分鐘

😃 情境會話 Conversation

Ⓐ Four seasons _Hotel_, may I help you?

Ⓑ Could you kindly connect me to room 217?

Ⓐ Yes, do you know _his_ or _her_ name?

Ⓑ Mark Lee.

Ⓐ Please wait a moment.

Ⓑ OK. Thank you very much!

Ⓐ It seems that no one is in now. What do you want me to do now?

Ⓑ _Well_, I'll _try again_ in 10 _minutes_.

Ⓐ OK, I understand.

A：四季飯店您好，我能為您服務嗎？
B：可不可以請你幫我接 217 號房間。
A：好，你知道對方的名字嗎？
B：李馬克先生。
A：請稍待。
B：好！很謝謝你！
A：對方好像不在。要怎麼辦呢？
B：那麼，我十分鐘以後再打來好了。
A：好，知道了。

🐦 超實用精選短句 *Useful Sentences*

» I am so sorry to have kept you waiting.
很抱歉讓您久等了。

» He is in conference and cannot come to the telephone. Could you call again later?
他在開會，不能接電話。你可以等會兒再打嗎？

» I'd like to speak to your manager.
我想和你們經理說話。

» I am afraid that Mr. Green is not available now.
恐怕格林先生現在沒有空。

» Are you sure he will be free after eleven o'clock?
你確定他十一點後會有空嗎？

» Please call again later. Mr. White is quite busy now.
請晚點再打過來。懷特先生現在很忙。

» Would you mind waiting for a moment, Mr. Brown? He's not available right now.
布朗先生，您介意稍等一會兒嗎？他現在沒空。

» Sorry, he is out.
不好意思，他外出了。

» Sorry, he is on the phone.
不好意思，他在電話中。

» Who's calling, please?
請問你是哪位？

» May I know who this is?
請問你是哪位？

» May I have your name?
請問您尊姓大名？

🖊 你一定要知道！ 🖊 *More Tips*

　　當你請「operator」（電話接線生）幫你轉接電話的時候，你就可以用「connect」這個字。

02 電話轉接

📚 關鍵單字&片語 Words & Phrases

lose	[luz]	動 遺失
hear	[hɪr]	動 聽
repeat	[rɪ`pit]	動 重覆
stolen	[`stolən]	動（steal 的過去分詞）偷
immediately	[ɪ`midɪtlɪ]	副 立刻
transfer	[træns`fɝ]	動 轉接
patience	[`peʃəns]	名 耐心

😊 情境會話 Conversation

A American Express, may I help you?

B Yes, I *lost* my credit card, I need your help.

A I couldn't *hear* you very well, could you *repeat* that?

B My wallet was *stolen* somehow, I need your help *immediately*!

A I see, I will *transfer* your phone call to Customer Service.

A Please wait a moment.

C This is Mary Chen of Customer Service. Thank you for your *patience*.

A：這裡是美國運通，您好！
B：是的！我遺失了我的信用卡，我需要你的協助！
A：電話有點聽不清楚，能不能請你再說一次？
B：我的皮夾被偷了，我需要你們立刻的協助！
A：知道了，我替你轉接客服部。
A：請稍候。
C：我是客戶部陳瑪麗，讓您久等了。

超實用精選短句 *Useful Sentences*

» I will connect you to his new extension right away.
  我馬上為您轉接到他的新分機。

» I am afraid that you have to wait for several minutes.
  我想你恐怕得等幾分鐘。

» Can I speak to your General Manager directly?
  我可以直接和你們的總經理說話嗎？

» Hold on, please. I will put you through to the president's office.
  請稍後。我將為您轉接總裁辦公室。

» I'll switch you over to Mr. Wu.
  我將您的電話轉給吳先生。

» How can I help you?
  我能幫你什麼嗎？

» I am transferring your call.
  我現在就幫你轉接。

» I'll put you through.
  我幫您轉接。

» Could you connect me to extension 206?
  你能幫我轉接分機號碼 206 嗎？

» Hold on, please.
  請稍等。

» Please hold on a second.
  請稍等。

» Mandy is on line 2.
  曼蒂在 2 線。

你一定要知道！ *More Tips*

當你聽不清楚對方在電話那一頭所說的話的時候，你就可以說「Please repeat that.」（請重複你剛說的話。）、「Please speak up.」（請說話大聲一點。）、「I didn't get a thing you just said.」（你剛剛說的我都沒聽到。）。

03 國際電話

📖 關鍵單字＆片語 Words & Phrases

Hamburg	[ˈhæmbɝg]	名 漢堡（德國一個城市）
reach	[ritʃ]	動 與……取得聯繫
what for	[whɑt fɔr]	片 為什麼
on a business trip	[ɑn ə ˈbɪznɪs trɪp]	片 出差
mobile phone	[ˈmobɪl fon]	名 手機
um	[ʌm]	感嘆（表示遲疑）嗯
alright	[ˈɔlˈraɪt]	副 沒問題

😊 情境會話 Conversation

Ⓐ Hello, This is Alice calling from **Hamburg**.

Ⓑ Hello, You have **reached** the General Manager's office. May I help you?

Ⓐ Is Mr. Wang there?

Ⓑ Excuse me. May I know **what for**?

Ⓑ I am sorry, but he is **on a business trip**.

Ⓐ I have something very urgent, please!

Ⓐ Could you kindly let me know his **mobile phone** number?

Ⓑ **Um... alright**. The number is 0912-345-678.

A：喂，我是愛麗絲，從漢堡打來的。
B：喂，總經理辦公室，您好！
A：請問王先生在嗎？
B：對不起，有什麼事情？
B：對不起，他去出差了。
A：我有很緊急的事，拜託！
A：可不可以告訴我他的手機號碼？
B：嗯……好吧。電話是 0912-345-678。

🔊 超實用精選短句 *Useful Sentences*

» By the way, how can I make an overseas call?
順便問一下，我怎麼樣才能打越洋電話？

» How do I place an international call to Taiwan?
我要怎麼打國際電話到台灣。

» I want to make a collect call.
我要打一個對方付費的電話。

» Would you please be quick?
您可以快一點嗎？

» Please charge the call from the other party.
這通電話請向對方收費。

» I would like to make an international call to San Francisco.
我想打一通國際電話到舊金山。

» My phone has been cut off. Please connect me again.
我斷線了，請再幫我接通一次。

» I can hear you well. Speak louder, please.
我聽不清楚你說的，請大聲點。

» Please cancel the call.
請幫我掛斷電話。

» Hello. Overseas operator. May I help you?
你好，國際電話總機。需要我為您服務嗎？

» I've never made an overseas call for over one hour.
我從來沒有打過超過一小時的越洋電話。

» You have an overseas collect call from Ms. Wang in Tokyo.
你有一通王小姐從東京打來的國際電話，指定要您付費。

✏ 你一定要知道！ ✏ *More Tips*

「mobile phone」、「mobile」、「cell phone」、「cellular phone」等都是「行動電話、手機」的說法。

04 記下來電留言

📚 關鍵單字&片語 *Words & Phrases*

southern	[ˈsʌðən]	形 南方的
Pacific	[pəˈsɪfɪk]	名 太平洋
at the moment	[æt ðe ˈmoment]	片 這個時候
leave	[liv]	動 留
message	[ˈmɛsɪdʒ]	名 訊息
regarding	[rɪˈɡɑrdɪŋ]	介 關於
ring	[rɪŋ]	動 打電話

😊 情境會話 *Conversation*

Ⓐ This is Alan Chao calling from *Southern Pacific* Trading Company. Could I speak to Mr. Peter?

Ⓑ Unfortunately, Mr. Peter is out *at the moment*.

Ⓐ Excuse me, when will he be back?

Ⓑ He said he would be back by three o'clock.

Ⓐ Could I *leave* a *message* for him?

Ⓑ Yes, please do.

Ⓐ It's *regarding* the new order. Could you kindly ask him to *ring* me?

Ⓑ Yes, I will.

A：我是南太平洋貿易公司的趙亞倫，請接彼得先生。
B：彼得不巧正好外出了。
A：對不起，他幾點會回來？
B：他說 3 點會到。
A：可以留個話給他嗎？
B：是的，請說。
A：是有關於新的訂單，可否請你轉告他打電話給我？
B：好，我會的。

超實用精選短句 *Useful Sentences*

» Can I take a message?
您需要留言嗎？

» Would you kindly give a message to him?
你可以幫我傳達留言給他嗎？

» I would like to leave a message for her.
我想要留言給她。

» Could you tell him to call me back tomorrow?
請您告訴他明天回我的電話好嗎？

» Please tell him that his order has been shipped.
請轉告他，他訂的貨已經裝運了。

» Could you leave your cell phone number?
您能留下您的手機號碼嗎？

» What do you want me to tell her?
您有什麼要讓我轉告她的？

» Sorry, could you please repeat that?
不好意思，可以請你再說一次嗎？

» I need her to call me back as soon as possible.
我需要她儘快回電給我。

» I'll be glad to give him the message.
我會很樂意轉告他的。

» I will give her the message as soon as she gets back.
她一回來我就會轉達她。

» Does she have you telephone number?
她有您的電話號碼嗎？

你一定要知道！ *More Tips*

　　當你打電話給對方，而對方恰巧不在的時候，你除了請接電話的人幫你留言之外，還可以請對方回電話給你，這時候你就可以說：「Please tell him / her to call me back.」，或是「Please tell him / her give me a ring.」（請叫他 / 她回我電話。）。

05 在語音信箱留言

📚 關鍵單字&片語 *Words & Phrases*

off	[ɔf]	副 不在工作、休息
quantum	[ˋkwɑntəm]	名 量子
fund	[fʌnd]	名 基金
application	[ˏæpləˋkeʃən]	名 申請
handsome	[ˋhænsəm]	形 英俊的
announce	[əˋnaʊns]	動 發佈

😊 情境會話 *Conversation*

A This is Mary Lin of First Trust Customer Service, I'm **_off_** now, please leave your message.

B This is Lin, I would like to buy a **_Quantum Fund_**.

B Could you fax me a copy of the **_application_** form? My fax number is 02-2777-3817.

A This is **_Handsome_**, this is Sweetie, we are not in now, please leave your message!

B This is Starr speaking, I have got a report, could you double-check it for me before I **_announce_** it?

A：這裡是第一信託客服部林瑪莉，現在是下班時間，請留言！
B：我姓林啦！我想買量子基金。
B：可不可以傳真一份申請表給我，我的傳真號碼是 02-2777-3817。

A：我是帥哥，我是甜心，我們都不在家，請留話！
B：我是史塔爾，我有一份報告，想在發表前請你們過目一下內容。

超實用精選短句 *Useful Sentences*

» Please leave a message after the beep.
請在聽到嗶聲後，留下你要說的話。

» I want to check on my answering machine.
我要來檢查答錄機裡的留言。

» This is Cathy, I am not home now, leave your message!
我是凱茜，我現在不在家，請留言！

» I am so worried about you. Call me back!
我很擔心你，回電話給我！

» This is Jane. Don't forget to bring me the document tomorrow!
我是珍。別忘了明天給我帶那份文件喔！

» Hello, this is David. There is a party tomorrow. Would you like to come?
嗨，我是大衛。明天有個聚會你想參加嗎？

» You left your bag in my house. Call me.
你把包包忘在我家了，打給我。

» I know you are there, pick up the phone right now!
我知道你在，馬上給我接電話！

» Nothing special. I'm just calling to say hi.
沒什麼特別的事，我打來只是想說聲嗨。

» I am not available now. Please leave your number and I will call you back. Thank you!
我現在不方便接聽電話。請留下您的號碼我會打給您。謝謝！

你一定要知道！ *More Tips*

「This is the Henderson's. We are not available right now, please leave your name and phone number after the beep, we will get back to you as soon as possible. Thank you!」（我們是韓得森家，我們現在不方便接聽電話，請在嗶聲後留下你的姓名與電話，我們會盡快與你聯絡。）這是一句許多人都會錄在答錄機裡的話。

06 婉拒推銷電話

📚 關鍵單字＆片語 *Words & Phrases*

summit	[ˋsʌmɪt]	名 尖峰
information	[͵ɪnfəˋmeʃən]	名 資訊
survey	[səˋve]	名（調查）報告
necessary	[ˋnɛsə͵sɛrɪ]	形 必需的
copy machine	[ˋkɑpɪ məˋʃin]	名 影印機
in case	[ɪn kes]	名 假使、免得
future	[ˋfjutʃə]	名 未來

😊 情境會話 *Conversation*

A **Summit** International, this is Jenny. How may I help you?

A Thank you for the **information**, but we are not interested in participating in the **survey**.

A You can send us an email and I will pass the information to related departments. They will contact you if it is **necessary**.

A We don't need new **copy machines** at the moment, but I will take your contact info **in case** we need new machines in the **future**.

A I am really sorry again that I can't help you.

A：頂尖國際您好，我是珍妮。很高興為您服務。
A：謝謝您提供的資訊，不過我們對參加這項調查沒有興趣。
A：您可以寄電子郵件給我們，我會將資料交給相關部門。如果有需要，他們就會跟您聯絡。
A：目前我們不需要新的影印機，但是我會留下您的聯絡資料，以便未來我們需要新機器的時候，可以與您聯絡。
A：無法幫上忙，真的很抱歉。

🔊 超實用精選短句 *Useful Sentences*

» Is there anyone who likes to receive telemarketing calls?
會有人喜歡接到推銷電話嗎？

» I think you called the wrong person.
我想您打錯電話了。

» Sorry, I am not interested in your product.
很抱歉，我對您的產品不感興趣。

» Many people don't like to take calls from telemarketers.
許多人不喜歡接到電話推銷員的來電。

» The one you want is not here.
您要找的人不在這裡。

» We'll get in touch. Bye.
我們再聯絡，再見。

» We don't need what you supply.
您提供的產品我們不需要。

» I am afraid I am rather busy now.
恐怕我現在非常地忙。

» If necessary, we will call you some day.
如果必要的話，我們改天會聯絡你的。

» I am sorry that I never talk to strangers.
很抱歉我從來不跟陌生人講話。

» I can't pass the CEO's contact info to you.
我無法將執行長的聯絡資料給你。

» Thanks for your information, but we don't need it actually.
謝謝您的資訊，但是事實上我們不需要。

✐ 你一定要知道！ ✐ *More Tips*

　　應付推銷電話時，務必明確讓對方知道自己無意購買產品，如：「Thank you very much, but I am not interested in investing in foreign currencies.」（謝謝你，不過我對投資外幣沒興趣。）。

07 請對方回電

📖 關鍵單字&片語 *Words & Phrases*

phone	[fon]	動 打電話
representative	[ˌrɛprɪˈzɛntətɪv]	名 代表
sales person	[selz ˈpɝsn]	名 業務人員
finally	[ˈfaɪnḷɪ]	副 終於
each other	[itʃ ˈʌðɚ]	片 對方、彼此

😊 情境會話 *Conversation*

A Hi, my name is Jenny Spencer. I need some information on your service plan. Please ***phone*** me back at 04-555-555.

A Hi, this is Jenny Spencer again. I left a message for your sales department yesterday requesting some information.

A One of your customer service ***representatives*** returned my call and said a ***sales person*** called Mike would give me a call back today.

A Hi Mike, I just missed your call. I will be in my office until 5 today. I hope that we will ***finally*** talk to ***each other*** by the end of today.

A：嗨，我的名字是珍妮史賓瑟。我需要一些有關你們服務方案的資料。請撥 04-555-555 回我電話。

A：嗨，我是珍妮史賓瑟，又是我。我昨天已經留言給你們的業務部要求資料了。

A：你們其中一位客服代表回電跟我說一個叫做麥可的業務會在今天給我電話。

A：嗨，麥可，我錯過你打來的電話了。我今天五點前都會在辦公室。希望我們今天結束之前能夠和對方講到話。

超實用精選短句 *Useful Sentences*

» Could you please ask her to call me back?
可否麻煩你轉告她回電給我？

» I'll call you back soon.
我會很快給你回電話的。

» Can you call me as soon as you get the message?
你收到訊息後馬上回電好嗎？

» Please call me back as soon as you can.
請你儘快回電話給我。

» I'll have her return you call as soon as she comes back.
等她一回來，我就請她馬上回電。

» I am busy now, can I call you back later on?
我現在很忙，我稍後給你回電話行嗎？

» Did you get that telephone message down?
你把電話留言記下來了嗎？

» Would you like to leave a message for her?
你要留話給她嗎？

» Is there any messages for me?
有我的留言嗎？

» I have something urgent to tell him.
我有緊急的事情找他。

» Tell him to call me back when he gets back.
他回來的時候請他給我打電話。

» Would you please call me back before Thursday?
請在週四之前回電給我好嗎？

你一定要知道！ *More Tips*

「leave a message for someone」是表示「留話給某人」，如：「Would you like to leave a message for Mr. Lin?」（你要留話給林先生嗎？）；「receive a message from someone」是指「收到某人的留言」，如：「I didn't receive any messages from your company.」（我沒有收到任何你們公司的留言。）。

08 緊急專線

📚 關鍵單字&片語 *Words & Phrases*

mainline	[`menˌlaɪn]	名詞	專線
office hour	[`ɔfɪs aʊr]	名詞	辦公時間
security	[sɪ`kjʊrətɪ]	名詞	保安
record	[`rɛkəd]	名詞	紀錄
robbery	[`rɑbərɪ]	名詞	搶案

😊 情境會話 *Conversation*

A As you all know, our company has a 24h support number that our customers can call in case there is a system emergency.

A This number is for emergency service only. If it is not an emergency, please call our *mainline* during *office hours*.

A For *security* and safety reasons, our employees also need to provide an emergency contact person and numbers for our *records*.

A Speaking of emergency contact, if there is an emergency or *robbery* in the office, please call 911.

A：誠如各位所知，我們公司設有廿四小時專線，讓我們的客戶萬一在系統上出現緊急狀況時可以撥打的支援專線。

A：這支號碼僅供緊急服務。如果不是緊急事件，在上班時間請撥打我們公司的主要號碼。

A：基於保安及安全理由，我們的同仁也必須提供緊急連絡人和電話讓我們作紀錄。

A：說到緊急連絡，若是辦公室發生緊急事件或是搶案，請打 911。

超實用精選短句 *Useful Sentences*

» This is an emergency call! Get an ambulance here right away!
這是緊急電話！請馬上派一部救護車來這裡！

» There is an urgent call for you.
有你的緊急電話。

» Please call me back as soon as possible.
請你儘快回電話給我。

» This is a matter of the utmost gravity.
這件事情十萬火急。

» Please verify that the phone line is available.
請驗證電話線是否可用。

» Remember that the number is for emergency only.
記得此號碼僅供緊急事故之用。

» There is an emergency button under front desk.
櫃台下方有一個緊急按鈕。

» If it's not an emergency, please don't call this number.
如果不是緊急事件，請不要打這個號碼。

» I tried to call Mr. Smith, but the line was busy.
我想打電話給史密斯先生，但電話佔線。

» If you are in an emergency situation, please dial this number.
如果你發生緊急狀況，請撥打這支號碼。

» If there is something urgent, call this number.
如果有緊急事件，請打這個電話。

你一定要知道！ *More Tips*

「emergency」指的是「緊急事故」，而「emergency contact person」就是「緊急連絡人」，一般公司人事表格都會要求填入這項，如：「Please fill in the name of your emergency contact person as well as the emergency contact number in the blanks.」（請在空格處填入你的緊急連絡人姓名及緊急連絡電話。）。

會議討論

篇

→ **Part 4 音檔連結** ←

因各家手機系統不同，若無法直接掃描，
仍可以至以下電腦雲端連結下載收聽。
（https://tinyurl.com/3vkpw38r）

01 開場致辭

📚 關鍵單字&片語 Words & Phrases

fellow	[ˋfɛlo]	名 同事、同伴
employee	[ˌɛmplɔɪˋi]	名 員工
smoothly	[smuðlɪ]	副 流暢地
intention	[ɪnˋtɛnʃən]	名 意圖
review	[rɪˋvju]	動 預習
agenda	[əˋdʒɛndə]	名 議程
query	[ˋkwɪrɪ]	名 問題
internal	[ɪnˋtɝnl̩]	形 內部的

😊 情境會話 Conversation

A Good morning, my ***fellow employees***. I hope our meeting today will go ***smoothly***.

B That's our ***intention***, too.

A First of all, let's ***review*** today's ***agenda***, which is on the yellow sheet on your table. If you have any ***queries***, please put them forth immediately.

A The meeting is presided over by myself as usual. I won't give a long speech as in formal conferences, because it's just an ***internal*** meeting. Okay. Back to the agenda. Any questions?

A：早安，各位員工。希望今天的會議進行順利。

B：我們也衷心希望如此。

A：首先，讓我們看看今天的議程，就是放在你們桌上的那張黃色的紙。如果有什麼問題，請立刻提出。

A：會議和往常一樣由我主持。我不打算像正式會議一樣做冗長的演講，因為這只是個內部會議。好吧，回到議程，有任何問題嗎？

超實用精選短句 *Useful Sentences*

» First of all, thanks for attending the meeting on time.
首先，感謝各位準時參加此次會議。

» Let's start the meeting.
會議開始吧。

» We have to wait for our CEO to get here.
我們必須先等執行長過來。

» The first thing we'll discuss is advertising.
首先我們要討論的是廣告。

» We'll discuss personnel allocation today.
我們今天將會討論的是人員配置問題。

» The purpose of this meeting is to discuss the distribution channel.
這個會議的目的是討論經銷通路的問題。

» Please look at the first page.
請看第一頁。

» Make sure everyone is here.
確定全部人都到了。

» Stop chatting. We need to begin now.
不要聊天了，我們要開始了。

» Let's go over the main points of the discussion.Turn to page 2.
我們先看一下主要討論的項目。請翻到第二頁。

» I would love to listen to your bright ideas.
我非常願意聽聽各位的高見。

» Please fill out the forms first.
請先填一下這些表格。

你一定要知道！ *More Tips*

「smoothly」是表示「順利、順暢」的意思，如：「The interview went smoothly.」（那個面試很順利。）。「give a speech」是表示「演講」的意思，也可以說「deliver a speech」或者是「make a speech」。

02 報告討論內容

📚 關鍵單字&片語 Words & Phrases

estimate	[ˈɛstəˌmet]	動 估計
research	[rɪˈsɝtʃ]	名 研究
item	[ˈaɪtəm]	名 物品
consideration	[kənsɪdəˈreʃən]	名 考慮
street survey	[strit sɚˈve]	名 街頭訪問
reduce	[rɪˈdjus]	動 減少
error	[ˈɛrɚ]	名 誤差

😊 情境會話 Conversation

A Our team has worked on a special project to *__estimate__* the market size of our new product. According to our *__research__*, many of the young people find it an attractive *__item__* that they would like to purchase.

A If the price is under 800 dollars, they will buy it without any *__considerations__*. If the price is between 800 dollars to 2000 dollars, they may give it a second thought.

A We have used both telephone sampling and *__street surveys__* to *__reduce__* possible *__errors__*.

A：我們這一組所做的特別企劃是估計公司新產品的市場大小。根據我們的研究，許多年輕人覺得這是個會引起他們購買衝動的魅力商品。

A：如果價格在八百元以下，他們二話不說就買了。如果價格在八百到二千元，他們可能會再考慮一下。

A：我們利用電話抽樣和街頭訪問兩種方式，以減少可能的誤差。

超實用精選短句 *Useful Sentences*

» Does everybody have a copy of our work plan?
大家手邊是不是都有一份工作計畫的資料了？

» We've got too many complaints about our PDA recently.
我們最近收到太多抱怨 PDA 的客訴了。

» Are things going on as planned?
工作進展和計畫一致嗎？

» I'm not getting on fast with this job.
我這份工作進行得不太快。

» I've made a financial analysis.
我做了份財務分析報告。

» I am working on the preliminary evaluation.
我正在做初步的評估。

» I think it's necessary to think about it.
我認為我們有必要考慮這點。

» What about making a questionnaire survey?
做個問卷調查怎麼樣？

» Did you come up with any ideas to solve the problem?
您有想到方法來解決這個問題了嗎？

» I don't think it will lead to a good result.
我認為這事不會有什麼好成果。

» We mainly focus on female market.
我們主要鎖定女性市場。

» I have been working on a marketing plan.
我最近在做一份行銷計畫。

你一定要知道！ *More Tips*

「thought」是「think」（想）的過去式，但「second thought」是一個片語，表示「再想一下」：「I am having second thoughts as to if I should buy that expensive dress.」（我得再考慮一下要不要買那一件昂貴的裙子。）。

03 檢討業務

📖 關鍵單字&片語 *Words & Phrases*

report	[rɪˋport]	名 報告
volume	[ˋvɑljəm]	名 數量
period	[ˋpɪrɪəd]	名 期間
crisis	[ˋkraɪsɪs]	名 危機
influence	[ˋɪnfluəns]	動 影響
would rather	[wud ˋræðɚ]	片 寧願

😊 情境會話 *Conversation*

A According to the ***report***, your team did not do well last month, John. The sales ***volumes*** were down by 26% in comparison with the same ***period*** last year. Can you explain this?

B First of all, the economic ***crisis*** worldwide has ***influenced*** consumer's purchase habits. They are hesitating to buy anything. Secondly, the products we are responsible for have been on the market for over three years.

B People nowadays ***would rather*** buy newly designed ones than an old-fashioned product, no matter how durable the old one may be.

A：約翰，根據報表，你們的小組上個月業績不怎麼好。跟去年同期比起來，業績下滑百分之二十六。這怎麼解釋？

B：首先，全球經濟危機對消費者的消費習慣有影響。他們買東西時更猶豫了。第二，我們負責的產品已經上市三年了。

B：今天大家寧願買新設計的東西，也不想拿老式產品，不管老產品如何耐用。

超實用精選短句 *Useful Sentences*

» Sales dropped 30% last month.
上個月的銷售下降 30%。

» Sales are down this month.
這個月的銷售額下降了。

» Can you tell me the reason of this failure?
能告訴我此次失敗的原因嗎？

» Do you have any recommendations for improvement?
你有任何改進建議嗎？

» According to the report, our sales this season were very good.
報告顯示，我們這個季度的銷售業績非常好。

» We are losing our customers.
我們的客戶正在流失。

» How do you explain it this time?
這次你又作何解釋呢？

» You must emphasize the high quality of our products.
你們必須強調我們產品的高品質。

» Didn't you notice that point?
你沒有注意到這一點嗎？

» I think after-sales service is more important than low prices.
我認為售後服務比低價更重要。

» Maybe we should conduct a survey to see whether high prices are affecting our sales.
或許我們應該進行市調，看是否高價位真的影響我們的銷售。

你一定要知道！ *More Tips*

「feasible」的意思是「可行的、可能的」：「This is a feasible plan.」（這是一個可行的計劃。），「It is not feasible that the company will fire him.」（公司不可能開除他。）。

04 提案資料

📚 關鍵單字&片語 Words & Phrases

redo	[ri`du]	動 改裝
dated	[`detɪd]	形 陳舊的
energy-efficient	[`ɛnɚdʒɪ ɪ`fɪʃənt]	形 節能的
worthwhile	[`wɝθ`hwaɪl]	形 值得的
investment	[ɪn`vɛstmənt]	名 投資
environmentally	[`ɛnˌvaɪrən`mɛntl̩ɪ]	副 有關環境方面
sustainable	[sə`stenəbl̩]	形 能保持的

😊 情境會話 Conversation

A I can see why you would like to *redo* this kitchen. The space is very attractive, but the features are *dated*.

A I think you would agree that there is a need to purchase new appliances which are more *energy-efficient*.

A I also think that new cabinets will be a *worthwhile investment*.

A I know that *environmentally sustainable* items are important to you, and for that reason, I would like you to consider wooden counter tops.

A：我能明白為什麼您會想要改裝這個廚房。這個空間非常吸引人，但是東西都過時了。

A：我想您會同意有採購較節能的新設備之必要。

A：同時我也認為新的廚櫃會是個值得花費的投資。

A：我知道環保產品對你們而言很重要，因此，我希望你們能考慮木製的檯面。

🕊 超實用精選短句 *Useful Sentences*

» Thank you for listening to my proposal.
謝謝你們聽我的提案。

» How do you think of this motion?
你認為這個提案怎樣？

» I hope this proposal will be passed.
我希望這提案能通過。

» I think your proposal is not quite in place.
我認為你的提案不太妥當。

» This proposal sounds very interesting.
這項提案聽起來很有趣。

» I don't think the proposal is practical.
我覺得這個提案不實際。

» There's a controversy over this proposal.
這個提案存有爭議。

» I am very confident of my proposal.
我對我的提案非常有信心。

» I hope you could put that in your pipe and smoke it.
我希望您能好好考慮一下。

» What is your opinion of the motion?
你認為這項提議如何？

» It would be absolutely a promising project.
這絕對是個有前途的項目。

» There's a need to purchase new machine.
有必要採購新機器。

✒ 你一定要知道！ ✒ *More Tips*

「show signs of...」是表示「顯示出……的跡象」的常用片語。如：「The cabinet can last for a couple of years but it is showing signs of wear.」（這個廚櫃還可以用個幾年，不過已經開始顯得破舊了。）。

05 說明反對意見

📚 關鍵單字&片語 *Words & Phrases*

assumption	[ə`sʌmpʃən]	名	假設
development	[dɪ`vɛləpmənt]	名	發展
timeline	[taɪm͵laɪn]	名	時間進程
unrealistic	[͵ʌnrɪə`lɪstɪk]	形	不實際的
generation	[͵dʒɛnə`reʃən]	名	世代
catch up	[kætʃ ʌp]	片	趕上

😊 情境會話 *Conversation*

A While I think that your idea is an interesting one, I have a couple of things to say.

A You have made too many ***assumptions*** in coming to the conclusions you have.

A Experiences show that the ***development timeline*** you have shown us today is ***unrealistic***.

A We are still 6 months from production.

A By the time we get to production, there is a good chance our competitors will be on their next ***generation*** of this device and we will be playing ***catch up*** again.

A：雖然我認為你的想法很有趣，不過我有幾點意見。

A：你的結論裡有太多假設了。

A：過去的經驗告訴我們，你今天給我們看的研發時間進程不太實際。

A：我們離生產還有六個月。

A：當我們做出產品的時候，我們的競爭對手很可能生產同款設備的第二代，而我們就只能再度想辦法迎頭趕上。

超實用精選短句 *Useful Sentences*

» You need to think about what our competitors are doing.
你必須思考我們的競爭對手在做什麼。

» I don't think it is a good idea.
我覺得這不是個好主意。

» I disagree with you on this point.
關於這一點我不同意你的意見。

» The proposal sounds interesting but unpractical.
這項提案聽起來很有趣但是不實際。

» There are too many uncertain factors in your plan.
在你的計畫中有太多的不確定因素。

» About your proposal, I still have several questions.
關於你的提議，我還有些疑問。

» I'm afraid I can't approve of your point.
我恐怕不能認同你的觀點。

» I disagree. I think they look good together.
我不同意，我覺得它們配起來很好看。

» I don't think the proposal is feasible.
我覺得這個提案不具有可行性。

» Why are you opposed to my proposal?
你為什麼反對我的提議？

» I am afraid I can't agree with you.
恐怕我無法同意你。

» Our time is better used finding a unique solution to this problem.
我們的時間最好用來找出一個獨特的辦法來解決這個問題。

你一定要知道！ *More Tips*

　　通常，在提出反對意見之前，會禮貌性的先對對方的提議表示嘉許，如：「That was indeed a very innovative proposal, but I'm afraid that it is not very practical.」（那的確是個很創新的提案，不過恐怕並不實際。）。

06 拉回主題

📖 關鍵單字＆片語 *Words & Phrases*

valuable	[ˋvæljuəbl]	形	有價值的
quickly	[ˋkwɪklɪ]	副	快速地
suit	[sut]	動	適合
further	[ˋfɝðɚ]	副	進一步地
back on track	[bæk ɑn træk]	片	重新步入正常軌道
sidetrack	[ˋsaɪdˌtræk]	動	轉變話題

😊 情境會話 *Conversation*

A I would just like to stop everyone for a moment. I know time is *valuable,* so I suggest that we get back to the topic at hand.

A Before we do, we can *quickly* look at a time that *suits* the three of us to take this side discussion *further*.

A If we can sit down at 4 to go through this then, we can let this meeting get *back on track*.

A Now that we are back on track, could someone please remind us where we were before we got *sidetracked*?

A：我想打斷各位一下。我知道每個人的時間都很寶貴，所以我建議我們回到手邊的主題。

A：在那之前，我們可以很快地找一個我們三個人都可以的時間來繼續這個額外的議題。

A：如果我們能在四點時坐下來，到那時候再討論這個議題，我們就可以讓這個會議回到正軌上來。

A：既然我們言歸正傳了，有沒有人可以提醒我們一下，在偏離主題之前我們討論到哪裡了？

超實用精選短句 *Useful Sentences*

» May I have your attention, please?
請大家注意，好嗎？

» I am sorry to interrupt you.
很抱歉打斷你了。

» Could you please listen to me for a moment?
請各位聽我說幾句行嗎？

» This suggestion is good but out of focus a little bit.
這個建議很好，但有點離題了。

» We can discuss that later on, but now we should focus on today's subject.
那個我們待會兒在討論，現在我們必須先討論今天的主題。

» Most people in the room are not affected by it.
在場的大多數人都與這件事無關。

» The discussion wanders too far from the subject.
談得離題太遠了。

» What you just said is irrelevant to the subject.
你剛剛說的跟主題無關。

» Let's not mention any side issues.
我們不要提及週邊議題。

» Don't cut me off while I'm talking.
我在講話時你別插話。

» Your response is obviously beside the question.
你的回答很顯然地離題了。

» Let's get back to the subject, OK?
讓我們回到主題好嗎？

你一定要知道！ *More Tips*

　　通常開會很常遇到的問題之一，就是偏離主題。因此可以在會議開始之前，就提醒與會人士：「I wish we confine our discussion to the main issue during this meeting.」（我希望這次會議期間，我們只討論主題。）。

07 臨時動議

📚 關鍵單字&片語 Words & Phrases

propose	[prə`poz]	動 提議、提案
revamp	[ri`væmp]	動 修補、改造
out of date	[aut ɑv det]	片 過時的
communicate	[kə`mjunəˌket]	動 溝通、通訊
provide	[prə`vaɪd]	動 提供
rapid	[`ræpɪd]	形 快速的
thorough	[`θɝo]	形 徹頭徹尾的

😊 情境會話 Conversation

Ⓐ I'd like to ***propose revamping*** our computer system.

Ⓐ The computer system we are using is ***out of date***. It's hard for our sales people to ***communicate*** with our clients directly to ***provide rapid*** service.

Ⓑ I think it's a general problem in our company. Not only the computers in the sales department need revamping. How about assigning a special team to do some ***thorough*** research and put forth a proposal?

A：我要提議，更新我們的電腦系統。
A：我們現在用的電腦系統已經過時了。我們的業務員很難和客戶直接連線，提供迅速的服務。
B：我想這是我們公司內普遍的問題，不只業務部的電腦需要更新。何不指派一個特別小組，做一番徹底的檢查，再提出方案？

超實用精選短句 *Useful Sentences*

» Can you explain?
可否說明得再清楚一點？

» The annual conference will be held next week.
年度會議將在下禮拜舉行。

» I would like to make a new plan.
我想制定一個新計畫。

» Our computer system needs to be upgraded.
我們的電腦系統需要升級。

» We'd better try our best to reduce the risks.
我們最好盡力去降低風險。

» Do you have any better suggestions?
你還有更好的建議嗎？

» I think we need more staffs in the office.
我覺得我們辦公室需要增加人手。

» Could anyone think of a better idea?
有人能想到更好的主意嗎？

» We have to improve our working efficiency from now on.
從今以後，我們必須提高我們的工作效率。

» I'd like to introduce new technology and equipment.
我想引進新的技術和設備。

» It's time to arrange a staff trip!
是時候安排員工旅遊了！

» I suggest we go to Hong Kong for our staff trip.
我建議員工旅遊可以去香港。

你一定要知道！ *More Tips*

在開會的時候當你聽不懂對方的說法時，你就可以說：「Could you explain it for me?」（你可不可以幫我解釋一下？）、「Could you clarify what you just said?」（你可不可以把剛剛說的說清楚一點？）、「I am sorry, I didn't understand what you just said.」（對不起，我沒聽懂你剛剛說的話。）。

08 談論市場動態

📚 關鍵單字&片語 *Words & Phrases*

commodity	[kə'mɑdətɪ]	名	商品
recovery	[rɪ'kʌvərɪ]	名	復甦
infrastructure	['ɪnfrəˌstrʌktʃə]	名	公共建設、基礎建設
scale back	[skel bæk]	片	按比例縮小
alternnatively	[ɔl'tɜnətɪvlɪ]	副	二者擇一地
albeit	[ɔl'biːt]	介	儘管
offshore	['ɔfʃor]	形	國外的

😊 情境會話 *Conversation*

> **A** *Commodity* markets are starting to show signs of *recovery*.
>
> **A** However, major projects that might use our *infrastructure* still seem some way off.
>
> **A** I would recommend one of two actions with this present economy.Either we *scale back* our development plans, which allow us to produce a much cheaper product, *albeit* with limited function. *Alternatively* we look to *offshore* markets which are showing stronger signs of recovery.

A：商品市場開始顯示復甦的跡象。

A：不過可能會用到我們的基礎建設的大案子看起來情況似乎仍然有點不好。

A：針對目前的經濟情況，我想建議兩種作法擇一。要不我們縮小研發計畫，讓我們得以生產儘管功能有限，卻便宜得多的產品。要不我們就寄望目前顯示較強復甦跡象的國外市場。

超實用精選短句 *Useful Sentences*

» We suffered huge losses in the financial crisis.
我們在金融危機中損失慘重。

» China economy remains in good shape overall.
整體來說,中國經濟情況仍然良好。

» In recent years, the global economic situation is very good.
近年來全球的經濟形勢都非常樂觀。

» Economic disparities can be quite marked even within a single region.
經濟的差異即使在單一區域也非常顯著。

» The economic outlook is very bright.
經濟前景非常光明。

» If future economy picks up, the company is expected to resume growth.
如果未來經濟回暖,公司仍有望恢復增長態勢。

» It's wrong to assume that economy cannot recover until America rebounds.
認為經濟必須在美國經濟回暖之後才會復甦是不正確的。

» The economy is on the mend.
經濟情況正在好轉。

» The economic position of the country is disastrous.
國家的經濟形勢非常糟糕。

» Bad economic condition may be responsible for social unrest.
經濟狀況不佳可能是造成社會動亂的根源。

你一定要知道! *More Tips*

「some way」是表示「有一點」的副詞用法。如:「The economy seems to be some way off.」(經濟情況似乎有點不好。),也可以說成:「The economy seems to show signs of recession.」(經濟情況有顯示衰退的跡象。)。

09 討論未來展望

📖 關鍵單字&片語 *Words & Phrases*

map out	[mæp aʊt]	片 安排
focus on	[ˈfokəs ɑn]	片 專注於
penetration	[ˌpɛnəˈtreʃən]	名 滲透、侵入
improvement	[ɪmˈpruvmənt]	名 改進
struggle	[ˈstrʌgl̩]	動 掙扎

😃 情境會話 *Conversation*

A I would like to take a few minutes to ***map out*** the plan for the next year.

A I believe that we need to ***focus on*** two areas, namely market ***penetration*** and new product development.

A There is much room for ***improvement*** in our market penetration. We need to find out why our product is ***struggling*** in some areas and change our marketing if necessary.

A Secondly, I think we need to have something vastly better in the market place, but I don't see that product in our pipeline yet.

A：我想花幾分鐘的時間，安排一下明年的計畫。

A：我認為我們必須將重心放在兩個地方，也就是市場滲透以及新產品的研發。

A：我們的市場滲透有很大的改進空間。我們必須找出我們的產品何以在某些地區很難賣的原因，並視需要改變我們的行銷方式。

A：第二，我認為我們的市場上需要有一些更好的東西，不過目前我們的生產線上還沒有這樣的產品。

超實用精選短句 *Useful Sentences*

» I wish we could do better in the coming year.
希望來年我們能做得更好。

» We try to plan wisely.
我們設法計畫周到。

» It is time for some fresh blood and new ideas.
現在是時候加入一些新血和新點子了。

» We should pay more attention to the elder market.
我們應該更關注老年市場。

» We should start to roadmap out the details of this strategy.
我們應該開始規劃這項策略的細節。

» I believe that we could get more achievements next year.
我相信我們明年能取得更大的成就。

» Let's think about what we should do next.
讓我們想想接下來該做什麼。

» Currently I am at work on future plans.
目前我正為未來做規劃。

» Any particular plan to open up new markets?
有沒有特別的計畫打開新的市場？

» To expand the market is one of the key links in developing the economy.
開拓市場是發展經濟的一個重要環節。

» We should seriously learn the tradition and courageously develop the future.
我們要認真地學習傳統又要大膽地開拓未來。

你一定要知道！ *More Tips*

公司進入下一年度時，經常就是「除舊佈新」的好時機。主管通常會趁此時勉勵員工有新的展望，如：「I want you to do away with old-fashioned values, and think and act creatively.」（我希望大家能破除老舊的價值觀，創新地思考與行動。）。

10 總結

📖 關鍵單字&片語 Words & Phrases

several	[ˈsɛvərəl]	形 幾個的
reach	[ritʃ]	動 達到
conclusion	[kənˈkluʒən]	名 結論
result	[rɪˈzʌlt]	名 結果
that's all	[ðæts ɔl]	片 就這樣

😊 情境會話 Conversation

A We've completed our discussion for today. But there are still **several** points that need further discussion. When shall we have our next meeting?

B How about Tuesday afternoon?

A That'll be all right for me.

B It seems to be no problem.

A Fine. I hope everyone will give some thought to the points we have discussed today.

A We have **reached conclusions** today for the projects, and I hope we'll see some **results** on Wednesday afternoon at 2 o'clock. **That's all** for today. Thank you, everybody.

A：我們已經完成今天的討論。但還有幾點需要再額外討論的。下一次要何時開會？
B：星期二下午怎麼樣？
A：我可以。
B：好像沒問題。
A：好。我希望每個人都想想今天討論的重點。
A：今天已經得出結論的案子，就去進行。希望星期三下午兩點時，已能看到一點成果。今天到此為止。謝謝大家。

超實用精選短句 *Useful Sentences*

» Is there anyone else who wants to say something?
有沒有其他的人想發言？

» Let me sum up the main points.
讓我把重點做個總結。

» This is a fruitful meeting.
這是一次富有成果的會議。

» Let's draw the meeting to a close.
會議就到此結束吧。

» We will discuss this topic next time.
我們將在下次會議上討論這個議題。

» We will end the meeting in a minute.
我們將馬上結束會議。

» Thanks for your participation.
感謝你們的參與。

» We will continue our discussion tomorrow.
我們明天會繼續討論。

» We must try our best to achieve this goal.
我們一定要盡力達成這個目標。

» I will give you a preliminary report in our next meeting.
下次開會我會提出初步的報告。

» I wish our company would be better in the future.
希望我們的公司將來會更好。

» Thank you for suggestions.
感謝各位建言獻策。

你一定要知道！ *More Tips*

在結束一個會議之後，可以說一些較輕鬆的話，或是謝謝大家的參與：「Thank you for your time and participation.」（謝謝你們投入的時間與參與。）、「That's all for today.」、「Let's call it a day.」（今天就到此為止。）。

Part

5

簡報技巧

篇

→ Part 5 音檔連結 ←

因各家手機系統不同，若無法直接掃描，
仍可以至以下電腦雲端連結下載收聽。
（https://tinyurl.com/36ssw424）

01 精簡開場白

📚 關鍵單字＆片語 *Words & Phrases*

folk	[fok]	名	各位
first of all	[fɜst ɑv ɔl]	片	首先
monitor	[ˈmɑnətə]	名	螢幕
opportunity	[ˌɑpəˈtjunəti]	名	機會
present	[prɪˈzɛnt]	動	報告
opinion	[əˈpɪnjən]	名	意見
let's	[lɛts]	片	（=let us）讓我們……

😊 情境會話 *Conversation*

A Good day, ***Folks***!

A ***First of all***, I would like to thank each one of you for making time to come to this meeting.

A I'll briefly introduce myself.

A My name is Kevin. I'm in charge of the computer ***monitor***'s marketing plan in Europe.

A I am very glad that I can take this ***opportunity*** to ***present*** our marketing plan for the coming year.

A I would also like to listen to your ***opinions***.

A OK. ***Let's*** start the meeting now.

A：各位伙伴，大家好。
A：首先非常感謝各位能在百忙之中撥冗，大家共聚一堂。
A：我簡單地自我介紹一下。
A：我叫凱文，負責公司電腦監視器在歐洲市場的行銷企劃。
A：我很高興能藉這個機會，報告下個年度的行銷企劃。
A：我也很願意聽聽各位的意見。
A：那麼現在會議就開始吧！

🦜 超實用精選短句 *Useful Sentences*

» First of all, I appreciate everyone's coming!
首先,感謝各位的到來!

» I've prepared a short PowerPoint presentation for you.
我為大家準備了一段簡短的投影片報告。

» Let me introduce myself first.
首先我來介紹一下我自己。

» OK. Let's begin our meeting now.
好,我們現在開始開會吧。

» Today's meeting is about exploring new market.
今天的會議是關於新市場的開發。

» I am very to share my experiences with you.
非常高興與各位分享我的經驗。

» Thanks very much for your participation.
非常感謝各位的參與。

» Compare with their advanced equipment, we still have a long way to go.
與他們的先進設備相比,我們還有很長一段路要走。

» We will discuss the after-sales service today.
我們今天將要討論的是售後服務問題。

» Please take a look at the copy of the manual.
請各位看一下說明書的影印本。

» I would love to listen to your bright ideas.
我非常願意聽聽各位的高見。

» Please don't hesitate to make any comments.
請大家不吝指教。

✒ 你一定要知道! ✒ *More Tips*

　　通常在開會之前,會議的召集人總是會先寒喧一下,並告知大家這場會議的主題是什麼:「We will be discussing the new products in this meeting.」(我們將在這個會議中討論我們的新產品。)。

02 達成目標說明

📚 關鍵單字&片語 *Words & Phrases*

increase	[ɪn`kris]	動 提升
brand	[brænd]	名 品牌
ratio	[`reʃo]	名 比率
maintain	[men`ten]	動 保持
environmentally	[ɛnˌvaɪrən`mɛntlɪ]	副 有關環境方面
friendly	[`frɛndlɪ]	副 友善的
image	[`ɪmɪdʒ]	名 印象、形象

😊 情境會話 *Conversation*

A I hope to achieve the following goals this year!

A One, To ***increase*** our market share in Europe to 15%.

A Two, To bring our own ***brand ratio*** up to 40%.

A Three, To set up a distribution warehouse in Amsterdam, Holland.

A Four, To add three new OEM orders.

A Five, To become the No.5 brand in the European Market.

A Six, To ***maintain*** an ***environmentally friendly*** "Green Quality" company ***image***.

A：今年本公司希望達成的目標如下：
A：一、提昇在歐洲市場佔有率至 15%。
A：二、提昇自有品牌的比率達到 40%。
A：三、在荷蘭的阿姆斯特丹建立發貨倉庫。
A：四、爭取新的 3 家 OEM 客戶訂單。
A：五、成為歐洲市場第五大品牌。
A：六、保持環保「綠色品質」企業形象。

🔊 超實用精選短句 *Useful Sentences*

» To become the preeminent consultant company in the 21st century.
成為二十一世紀最卓越的顧問公司。

» To be the best partner for customers.
做客戶最佳合作夥伴。

» Our first priority of this year is to expand international market.
今年的首要目標就是打入國際市場。

» We aim to raise market share to 20% this year.
我們今年的目標是提高 20% 的市場佔有率。

» To increase our profitability by expanding new market.
藉由開拓新市場來提高我們的獲利率。

» To increase our market share in Asia to 10%.
增加在亞洲 10 % 的市場佔有率。

» We are planning to set up a new branch in Beijing.
我們計劃在北京開設一家新的分公司。

» To become the top-2 TFT-LCD vendor in Taiwan.
成為台灣 TFT-LCD 的第二大廠商。

» To become one of the most competitive enterprises.
成為最具競爭力的企業之一。

» To maintain the dominance in the electron industry.
在電子業繼續保持優勢地位。

» We need to branch out into a new line of business.
我們需要擴充新的事業路線。

✎ 你一定要知道！ ✎ *More Tips*

　　「achieve a goal」是「達到一個目標」的意思。「I would like to achieve my goal as being a writer.」（我想要達成當一個作家的目標。）、「In order to achieve my goal I have to work hard.」（想要達成目標我得努力一點。）。

03 提案說明

📖 關鍵單字＆片語 *Words & Phrases*

rapid	[ˋræpɪd]	形	快速地
growth	[groθ]	名	成長
fascinating	[ˋfæsṇˌetɪŋ]	形	迷人的、極好的
attain	[əˋten]	動	達成
profitability	[ˌprɑfɪtəˋbɪlətɪ]	名	獲利
strengthen	[ˋstrɛŋθən]	動	強化、加強
distribution	[ˌdɪstrəˋbjuʃən]	名	分配、分發

😊 情境會話 *Conversation*

A Due to the ***rapid growth*** of the Internet, there has been a ***fascinating*** increase of personal computer purchasing in Europe.

A I hope we can ***attain*** a 15% market share.

A For long-term ***profitability***, we hope as well to achieve the goal of adding three new OEM customers, and to increase the ratio of our own brand up to 40%.

A In order to ***strengthen*** our competitiveness and to provide better service, We should set up a ***distribution*** warehouse in Amsterdam, Holland.

A：因為網際網路的迅速普及，造成歐洲個人電腦市場的快速增長。
A：我希望我們能達成至 15% 的市場佔有率。
A：為了長期的獲利性，我們希望除了新增 3 家的 OEM 客戶，更將自有品牌的比率提昇至 40%。
A：為了加強競爭力，及提供更好的服務，我們應在荷蘭的阿姆斯特丹設置發貨倉庫。

超實用精選短句 *Useful Sentences*

» I think it's necessary for me to explain it.
我認為我有必要對這一點作出解釋。

» The economy is showing signs of recovery.
經濟有開始復甦的跡象。

» We should pay more attention to the children's market.
我們應該更關注兒童市場。

» We should make an adjustment in order to react to the change in global economy.
我們需要做些調整以因應全球經濟情勢的變化。

» We need to replace our old machinery.
我們必須換掉舊的機器設備了。

» We can boost our market share by offering this service.
提供這項服務會提高我們的市佔率。

» To increase the profit margin, we have to reduce the production cost.
為了增加利潤，我們必須降低生產成本。

» Sales are down. We will need more advertising.
銷售下降了，所以我們需要做更多廣告。

» We should always make change to meet market needs.
我們應該隨著市場需求的變化而變化。

» Due to the decrease in oil price, we can ask our cooperation manufacturer for a lower price.
因應油價下跌，我們可以跟合作廠商要求降價。

» We should hold a sale to minimize inventory level.
我們應該舉辦特賣會，可以把庫存量降到最低。

你一定要知道！ *More Tips*

「attain」是「達成、得到」的意思：「We hope to attain a 20% market share.」（我希望得到 20% 的市場佔有率。），「He attained the position of our class leader.」（他晉身成為我們的班長。）

04 市場分析

📖 關鍵單字&片語 *Words & Phrases*

majority	[mə`dʒɔrətɪ]	名	多數
potential	[pə`tɛnʃəl]	形	潛在的
try out	[traɪ aʊt]	片	試驗
mean	[min]	動	意謂著
budgeting	[`bʌdʒətɪŋ]	名	編預算
involved	[ɪn`vɑlvd]	形	牽扯在內的

😊 情境會話 *Conversation*

A Customer service definitely will be an important part for us to continue to focus on this year.

A As I know many of our competitors have set up 24h customer service lines. This will be something that we have to work on, too.

A The survey shows that the *majority* of our *potential* customers prefer to get samples of our product to *try out*.

A To send out samples *means* that sales costs will increase. Thus, I will have to redo our yearly *budgeting* and get other related departments *involved*.

A：客戶服務絕對會是我們今年要繼續集中努力的重點。

A：就我所知，我們許多競爭對手已經設立了 24 小時的客服專線。這將是我們也必須做到的事情。

A：調查顯示，我們大部分的潛在顧客都想要拿到我們產品的樣品做試用。

A：送出樣品意味著行銷成本將會增加。因此我必須重新編年度預算，並讓其他相關部門也一起參與其中。

🔊 超實用精選短句 *Useful Sentences*

» Could you tell me the result of the market survey?
你能告訴我市場調查的結果嗎？

» Successful marketing strategies create a desire for a product.
成功的行銷策略會創造對產品的需求。

» I think a smart marketing strategy is necessary.
我認為一個聰明的行銷策略是必要的。

» When shall we carry out a market survey?
我們什麼時候進行一個市場調查？

» Will the price affect the sales in the future?
將來價格會影響到銷售情況嗎？

» What do you think the customers really want?
你覺得顧客真正需要的是什麼呢？

» Have you read the market research report?
你看過市場調查報告了嗎？

» Does price really count in the market?
價格在市場上真的很重要嗎？

» I think service is way important than price.
我認為服務遠比價格重要。

» What are the advantages of their product?
他們產品的優勢是什麼？

» We must pay close attention to our rival's movements.
我們必須密切關注競爭對手的動態。

» We should never lower our guard at any time.
任何時候我們都不應該掉以輕心。

⚡ 你一定要知道！⚡ *More Tips*

公司常會以市場分析作為修正營運方針的參考，如：「Our investigation reveals that there has not been much competition so far in the China market in regard to this product.」（調查顯示，這項產品目前在中國市場尚未有太多競爭。）。

05 主題討論

📚 關鍵單字&片語 Words & Phrases

voice	[vɔɪs]	動 發聲
above	[ə'bʌv]	形 前述的
specifically	[spɪ'sɪfɪklɪ]	副 特別地
recycle	[ˌri'saɪkl̩ɪŋ]	名 可回收物
consumption	[kən'sʌmpʃən]	名 消耗
radiation	[ˌredɪ'eʃən]	名 輻射
etc.	[ɛt'sɛtərə]	副 （=et cetera）其他等等

😊 情境會話 Conversation

A Everyone, please **_voice_** your opinions regarding the **_above_** issues.

B I have a question, do we have a suitable person who can speak Dutch to be in charge of that distribution warehouse?

A In Holland, more than 95% of Dutch people can speak English. Language won't be a problem.

C The "Green Quality" you mentioned includes what **_specifically_**?

A The "Green Quality" includes using **_recycled_** packing material, low energy **_consumption_**, low **_radiation, etc_**.

A：針對以上敘述，請各位踴躍發言，表達意見。
B：我有一個疑問，我們是否已有適當的通曉荷語人才負責倉儲事宜？
A：在荷蘭 95% 以上的人都通曉英語，所以語文不是問題。
C：你所指的「綠色品質」包括那些內容？
A：包含使用回收包裝材料、低能源消耗量、低幅射線等。

超實用精選短句 *Useful Sentences*

» Does anyone have anything to add?
有任何人想要附加説明的嗎？

» I am afraid that it's a little difficult to achieve.
恐怕它有點難以達成。

» Do you have any comments?
你有任何意見嗎？

» How much will your advertising budget be?
你的廣告預算會是多少？

» May I say something?
我可以説一些話嗎？

» We will discuss the new ideas at tomorrow's meeting.
我們將在明天的會議上討論這些新的構想。

» Does the way really work in reality?
現實中這個方法真的奏效嗎？

» How to put these ideas into practice?
如何把這些構想付諸實踐呢？

» Do you have any specific idea to the big plan?
您對這個大計畫有什麼高見？

» I am willing to listen to your advice.
我非常樂意聽取你的建議。

» If you are in favor, raise your hand.
如果你贊成，請舉手。

» I am against this proposal.
我反對這個提案。

✔ 你一定要知道！✔ *More Tips*

「budget」可以當「預算」的意思：「What is our budget?」（我們有多少預算？）；也可以當成「特價」的意思：「Come and enjoy our budget prices.」（來享受我們的特價吧。）。

06 提案表決

📖 關鍵單字&片語 Words & Phrases

waterproof	[ˈwɔtəˌpruf]	形 防水的
microfiber	[ˈmaɪkroˈfaɪbə]	名 超細纖維
narrow down	[ˈnæro daʊn]	片 縮減
display	[dɪˈsple]	名 展示
mass	[mæs]	形 大量的
response	[rɪˈspɑns]	名 反應
vote	[vot]	動 投票

😊 情境會話 Conversation

A As you all have been aware, the company has been working on developing the new **_waterproof_** jacket with the lightweight **_microfiber_** material.

A We have **_narrowed down_** to three designs as you can see on the **_display_** here.

A In order to reduce the risks, we decided to **_mass_** produce one of the designs first. If the market **_response_** is good, we can then go ahead and produce other designs.

A I need you all to **_vote_** for the design that you think we should go for first.

A：各位都知道公司一直在努力以輕量超細纖維材質開發新的防水夾克。

A：我們已經減少至你們所看到展示在這裡的三款設計。

A：為了減少風險，我們決定先大量生產其中一款設計。如果市場反應不錯，屆時我們可以再繼續生產其他款式。

A：我需要所有人投票，給你們認為應該率先生產的款式。

超實用精選短句 *Useful Sentences*

» Just tell me which one you like the best.
只要告訴我你們最喜歡哪個。

» Listen to me carefully and fill out these forms.
仔細聽我說，並且填寫這些表格。

» We'd better decide it by vote.
我們最好表決一下吧。

» What do you think of choice 3?
你覺得選項3怎麼樣？

» Let's decide the matter by voice vote.
我們口頭表決這件事情吧。

» There are 5 votes in favor of my proposal.
5 票贊成我的提案。

» There are 6 votes against my suggestion.
6 票反對我的提議。

» Why not decide the matter by vote?
我們為什麼不表決一下這件事呢？

» As we can't all agree on this matter, let's vote on it.
既然大家意見不一，我們表決好了。

» Asterisk (*) indicates required fields.
帶星號者為必填項目。

» I suggested putting the matter to a vote.
我建議對此事投票表決。

» If we can't reach a consensus by the end of the meeting, a vote will be necessary.
會議結束前我們若還不能取得一致意見，那就必須投票表決了。

你一定要知道！ *More Tips*

「final decision」表示「最後的決議」，也可以用「conclusion」（結論）來表示。如：「As soon as we have reached a conclusion, we will inform the related departments of the result.」（一旦我們得到結論，就會將結果通知相關部門。）。

07 簡報總結

📚 關鍵單字&片語 Words & Phrases

invite	[ɪnˋvaɪt]	動 邀請
conclude	[kənˋklud]	動 作結論
participate	[parˋtɪsəˌpet]	動 參與
bright	[braɪt]	形 聰明的
within	[wɪˋðɪn]	介 在……範圍內
together	[təˋgɛðɚ]	副 一起
participation	[parˌtɪsəˋpeʃən]	名 參與

😊 情境會話 Conversation

A Thanks for all your suggestions.

A Is there anyone else with other opinions to mention?

A If not, I would like to **_invite_** the general manager to **_conclude_**.

B Hi, everybody, I am glad to have **_participated_** in the meeting today. I have heard many **_bright_** ideas.

B I believe we can achieve our goals **_within_** the next year.

B Let's work it out **_together_**! Thank you for your **_participation_**!

A：感謝各位的建議。
A：各位是否還有什麼意見要提的？
A：沒有的話，我現在請總經理作總結。
B：各位好，很高興今天自己能與會，各位所提意見都很好。
B：我相信明年我們一定能達成目標。
B：讓我們一同努力吧！謝謝你們的參與！

超實用精選短句 *Useful Sentences*

» I would like to summarize the main points now.
現在我要來歸納重點。

» I appreciate your bright ideas.
感謝各位的高見。

» Let's add up the pros and cons.
我們把正反兩方的意見總結一下吧。

» The vote was a unanimous 15 out of 15.
全部 15 人一致贊成。

» When is our next meeting?
下個會議是什麼時候？

» We will cover the rest next time.
剩下的我們下次再討論。

» There is no need to discuss it further.
不需要再討論下去了。

» Is that OK for every one of you?
你們每個人對這樣的安排都可以接受嗎？

» I wish our company will be more prosperous in the future.
希望將來我們的公司會更加繁榮。

» Taken as a whole, the meeting today is fruitful.
就整體而言，今天的會議是富有成果的。

» That's all for you.
那麼今天就這樣吧！

» Thank you for your participation.
非常感謝各位的參與。

你一定要知道！ *More Tips*

會議的結束總是會有結語，通常是一些振奮人心的話，如：「I hope our firm keeps on growing stronger with the help of everyone of you.」（我希望我們公司因為大家的幫忙越來越強大。）。

Part

6

客戶來訪

篇

→ **Part 6 音檔連結** ←

因各家手機系統不同，若無法直接掃描，
仍可以至以下電腦雲端連結下載收聽。
（https://tinyurl.com/233ph5cd）

01 名片交換

📖 關鍵單字&片語 *Words & Phrases*

last name	[læst nem]	名 姓
surname	[ˋsɝˌnem]	名 姓
this	[ðɪs]	代 這個
business card	[ˋbɪznɪs kɑrd]	名 名片
thank you	[θæŋk ju]	片 謝謝你
mine	[maɪn]	代 我的
nice	[naɪs]	形 好的
too	[tu]	副 也

😊 情境會話 *Conversation*

A How do you do? My *__last name__* is Fang.

B How do you do? My *__surname__* is Wang.

A *__This__* is my *__business card__*.

B *__Thank you__*, this is *__mine__*.

B Let me introduce you, this is Mr. Lin.

C *__Nice__* to meet you!

C My name is Tom Lin.

A Nice to meet you, *__too__*!

A：幸會！敝姓方，請多指教。
B：幸會！敝姓王，請多指教。
A：這是我的名片。
B：謝謝，這是我的名片。
B：我替你介紹，這位是林先生。
C：幸會！
C：我是林湯姆，很高興認識你。
A：幸會！我也很高興認識你！

超實用精選短句 *Useful Sentences*

» Nice to meet you.
見到您很高興。

» Here's my business card.
這是我的名片。

» My surname is Jones.
敝姓鐘斯。

» I would appreciate your comments.
請你多多指教。

» I am so pleased to meet you.
我很高興能見到你。

» I have heard so much about you.
久仰大名。

» I am delighted to make your acquaintance.
很高興認識你。

» It's nice to finally meet you.
很高興終於見到你了。

» There's my phone number on it.
上面有我的電話號碼。

» Our company's address is printed on my card.
我的名片上有公司地址。

» Here is my business card.
這是我的名片。

» Could I have your card?
可以給我你的名片嗎？

你一定要知道！ *More Tips*

　　名片可以說「name card」、「business card」或是直接用「card」來表示。「last name」、「surname」都是「姓」的意思，「first name」、「given name」則是「名」的意思。

02 公司產品介紹

📚 關鍵單字 & 片語 Words & Phrases

product line	[ˈprɑdəkt laɪn]	名 產品線
in total	[ɪn ˈtotl̩]	片 總共
type	[taɪp]	名 類型
keyboard	[ˈkiˌbord]	名 鍵盤
producer	[prəˈdjusɚ]	名 製造商
market share	[ˈmɑrkɪt ʃɛr]	名 市場佔有率
expand	[ɪkˈspænd]	動 拓展

😊 情境會話 Conversation

A Now I would like to briefly introduce our ***product line*** to you.

A We have ***in total*** three ***types*** of ***keyboards***.

A Now we are the third largest keyboard ***producer*** in the world.

B How much ***market share*** does your company have?

A Our Market share is around 15%.

B Have you ever thought of ***expanding*** your line to other computer products?

A So far we don't have any plans.

A：現在由我向各位介紹一下本公司的產品概要。
A：我們全部有三種類型的鍵盤。
A：現在是全球第三大鍵盤製造廠。
B：你們的市場佔有率有多少？
A：市場佔有率大約在 15% 左右。
B：想要拓展其他的電腦產品嗎？
A：目前無此計劃。

超實用精選短句 *Useful Sentences*

» Can you provide some information about your products?
能提供我一些關於貴公司產品的資訊嗎？

» Could you introduce your products in detail?
能詳細介紹一下您的產品嗎？

» We have a computer system that helps our sales.
我們有支援銷售的電腦系統。

» Our product's technology is more advanced than what's on the market now.
我們的產品技術比目前市場上的產品還要先進。

» I am sure this product would meet the needs of the target market.
我相信這個產品會符合目標市場的需求。

» Here are some of our best selling products.
這是一些我們最暢銷的產品。

» Our market share is more than 12%.
我們的市場佔有率超過 12%。

» This cell-phone is pretty user-friendly.
這支手機是很容易使用的。

» Our products are sold worldwide.
我們的產品行銷世界各地。

» Carpet is our main product.
地毯是我們的主打產品。

» Our product has an advantage of low price.
我們的產品優勢在於價格低廉。

你一定要知道！ *More Tips*

「share」原本當動詞是「分享」的意思：「Can you share the pie with me?」（你可不可以跟我分享你的派？），但在這裡「market share」的解釋是「市場佔有率」；「shareholder」則表示「股東」。

03 介紹主管

TRACK* 054

關鍵單字 & 片語 Words & Phrases

trading	[`tredɪŋ]	名 貿易
CEO	[si i o]	名 執行長
look forward to	[luk `fɔrwəd tu]	片 期待
hope	[hop]	動 希望
pleasant	[`plɛznt]	形 愉悅的
very much	[`vɛrɪ mʌtʃ]	片 非常

情境會話 Conversation

A Sir, these are Mr. Paul and Mr. Ken from the DF **Trading** Company.

A Mr. Paul and Mr. Ken, this is our **CEO**, Mr. Lee.

B Mr. Lee, How do you do?

C Mr. Lee, How do you do? We've been **looking forward to** meeting you.

D Mr. Paul and Mr. Ken, how do you do? I **hope** you two will have a **pleasant** time in our company.

B Thank you **very much**.

C Thank you very much.

A：執行長，這是 DF 貿易公司的保羅先生和肯恩先生。
A：保羅先生，肯恩先生，這是我們的執行長李先生。
B：李先生，您好！
C：李先生，您好！我們一直很期待跟您見面。
D：保羅先生和肯恩先生，你們好，希望兩位在本公司停留時能夠很愉快。
B：真謝謝您。
C：真謝謝您。

超實用精選短句 *Useful Sentences*

» This is our CEO, Mr. White.
  這是我們的執行長懷特先生。

» It's an honor to meet you.
  很榮幸與您見面。

» She is our new creative director.
  她是我們新的創意總監。

» She is the best marketing manager I have ever seen.
  她是我見過最棒的行銷經理。

» Let me introduce our manager to you.
  讓我來為您介紹我們的經理。

» He set up a good example for us.
  他為我們樹立了好榜樣。

» I'd like you to meet my boss.
  我要向你介紹我的老闆。

» I have long been looking forward to meeting you.
  我一直盼望能有機會與您見面。

» She is the one who cuts my checks.
  我是領她薪水的。

» I have never met your CEO before.
  我沒見過你們的執行長。

» It's certainly a pleasure to meet you.
  認識您真是我的榮幸。

» Thank you for offering the opportunity.
  感謝您提供這個機會。

你一定要知道！ *More Tips*

「Nice to meet you.」（很高興見到你。）這句話與「How do you do?」（你好嗎？）都是初次見面時說的話。「look forward to」是「期待」的意思，後接動名詞或名詞，如「I'm looking forward to hearing from you.」（期待你的消息。）。

04 介紹同事

📖 關鍵單字&片語 *Words & Phrases*

colleague	[ˋkɑlig]	名 同事
university	[͵junəˋvɝsətɪ]	名 大學
then	[ðɛn]	副 然後
must	[mʌst]	助 一定
speak	[spik]	動 説
still	[stɪl]	副 仍然
bad	[bæd]	形 差的、不好的

😊 情境會話 *Conversation*

A Mr. Paul, Mr. Ken, this is my ***colleague*** Mr. Wang.

D Mr. Paul, Mr. Ken, How do you do?

B C Mr. Wang, How do you do?

A Mr. Wang graduated from Tokyo ***University*** in Japan.

B Really? ***Then*** you ***must speak*** Japanese very well!

D On, my Japanese is ***still*** very ***bad***. It's very nice to meet you.

B I am also very glad to meet you.

A：保羅先生、肯恩先生，這是我的同事王先生。
D：保羅先生、肯恩先生，初次見面，請多指教。
B&C：王先生，初次見面，請多指教。
A：王先生是日本東京大學畢業的。
B：真的嗎？日本話一定説得很好了！
D：不，還差得很遠呢！很高興見到你們。
B：我也很高興見到你。

超實用精選短句 *Useful Sentences*

» I would like to introduce you one of my colleagues.
我要為您介紹我的一位同事。

» He is our general manager's assistant.
他是我們總經理的助理。

» This is our new colleague, Betty.
這是我們的新同事貝蒂。

» This is David, an outstanding engineer.
這是大衛，他是個非常厲害的工程師。

» This is Mary, the accountant of our company.
這位是瑪麗，我們公司的會計。

» You look familiar to me.
你好面熟。

» David and I are in the same team.
大衛和我是同一組的。

» Have you met before?
你們見過嗎？

» This is John, the personnel officer.
這位是約翰，人事部主管。

» Catherine can speak four different languages.
凱薩琳能講四種不同的語言。

» Please introduce us.
請幫我們介紹一下。

» I feel honored to be invited here.
被邀請到這裡來我感到很榮幸。

你一定要知道！ *More Tips*

「同事」的英文可以用「colleague」或是「coworker」。若要說某種語言講得很流利，可說：「You speak good English.」、「You speak English well.」（你的英語說得很好。）。

05 介紹公司環境

📖 關鍵單字&片語 Words & Phrases

washroom	[ˈwɑʃ͵rum]	名 洗手間
opposite	[ˈɑpəzɪt]	形 相反的
vending machine	[ˈvɛndɪŋ məˈʃin]	名 自動販賣機
sink	[sɪŋk]	名 水槽
division	[dəˈvɪʒən]	名 部門
warehouse	[ˈwɛr͵haʊs]	名 倉庫

😊 情境會話 Conversation

A The ___washrooms___ are at the end of this hallway. The men's washroom is on the right hand side and the lady's is on the ___opposite___ side of it.

A Here is the kitchen. As you can see, there is a ___vending machine___ there if you need any snack food or drinks. The coffee machine is right beside the ___sink___ on the kitchen counter, please help yourself.

A The south side of the building is the production ___division___ and the north side is the sales division. The ___warehouse___ and shipping department is located on the lower level.

A：洗手間位於這條走廊的盡頭。男士洗手間在右手邊，女士洗手間則在另一邊。

A：這裡是廚房。如您所見，如果您需要任何點心或飲料，這兒就有一台自動販賣機。咖啡機就在廚房洗水槽的右邊，您可以隨意使用。

A：這棟大樓的後面是生產部，前面是行銷部。倉庫和運務部位在下方樓層。

🔊 超實用精選短句 *Useful Sentences*

» There are three emergency exits.
這兒有三個緊急出口。

» This is the new desk for you.
這是你的新辦公桌。

» I will show you around.
我帶你去參觀一下吧。

» Please feel free to ask me if you have any questions.
如果你有什麼問題儘管問我。

» I hope I didn't miss anything here.
希望我沒有漏掉什麼地方。

» The third floor of the building is the Marketing Department.
大樓的三層是市場部。

» The shipping department is on the lower level.
運務部在下方樓層。

» The employee restaurant is on the first basement level.
員工餐廳在地下一層。

» The washroom is at the end of the corridor.
盥洗室就在走廊的盡頭。

» Now I'm leading you to the Personnel Department.
現在我就帶你去人事部。

» Next to the meeting room is the washroom.
會議室隔壁就是洗手間。

✏ 你一定要知道！✏ *More Tips*

　　為訪客或來賓大致介紹公司環境時，通常只要介紹幾個跟對方較有關的地方即可，如：「Let me introduce to you our newly built plant and research center.」（讓我為您介紹我們新建的工廠和研究中心。），或是「Let me show you around the headquarter building.」（容我帶您到總部大樓四處看看。）。

06 會客室接待

📚 關鍵單字&片語 Words & Phrases

brochure	[broˋʃʊr]	名 小冊子
relate to	[rɪˋlet tu]	片 相關
look for	[lʊk fɔr]	片 尋找
grab	[græb]	動 抓取
explain	[ɪkˋsplen]	動 解釋
feature	[ˋfitʃɚ]	名 特色
demonstrate	[ˋdɛmənˏstret]	動 示範
procedure	[prəˋsɪdʒɚ]	名 步驟

😊 情境會話 Conversation

Ⓐ Thanks for coming. Have a seat, please.

Ⓐ Here are the **brochures related to** the product that you are **looking for**.

Ⓐ Do you need a minute to browse through these brochures?

Ⓐ While you are browsing through them, I will go **grab** a couple of samples.

Ⓐ Here are the samples, and I will **explain** the **features** of this product to you and **demonstrate** the basic **procedure** on how to use it later.

A：謝謝您過來。您請坐。
A：這裡是與您所要找的產品有關的冊子。
A：您需要時間翻閱一下這些冊子嗎？
A：您翻閱這些冊子的同時，我會去幫您拿一些樣品過來。
A：這些是樣品。我會為您解釋這項產品的特色，稍後並會為您示範使用這項產品的基本步驟。

超實用精選短句 *Useful Sentences*

» Could you wait here for a moment?
您能在這稍待一會嗎?

» Here is the colored-sheet that you want.
這是您想要的彩頁。

» Wait a minute. I will get you a brochure.
請稍等。我拿份宣傳冊子給您。

» Do you want some more samples?
您還想要一些樣品嗎?

» Perhaps you can browse through these brochures.
或許您可以翻閱一下這些冊子。

» Would you like a cup of tea?
你想米杯茶嗎?

» How do you think of our new product?
您覺得我們的新產品如何?

» I hope you could give some valuable advice.
希望您能夠提出寶貴的建議。

» Would you please go to the reception room?
請到接待室好嗎?

» Our manager is coming soon!
我們經理馬上就到!

» You have to fill out these forms first.
您必須先填寫這些表格。

» Thanks for your coming.
感謝您的到來。

你一定要知道! *More Tips*

「browse through」表示「瀏覽、隨意翻閱」的意思。如:「Would you like to browse through our catalogue?」(您想翻閱一下我們的目錄嗎?);也可以用在表示「瀏覽網站」,如:「I saw your advertisement while I was browsing the Internet.」(我在網路上瀏覽時看到了貴公司的廣告。)。

07 送客道別

📖 關鍵單字&片語 *Words & Phrases*

leave	[liv]	動 離開
enjoy	[ɪnˈdʒɔɪ]	動 享受
stay	[ste]	動 停留
gift	[gɪft]	名 禮物
compliment	[ˈkɑmpləmənt]	名 敬意
be kind of sb.	[bi kaɪnd ɑv ˈsʌmˌbɑdɪ]	片 ……人真好
visit	[ˈvɪzɪt]	動 拜訪
again	[əˈgɛn]	副 再一次

😊 情境會話 *Conversation*

A I have to *leave* now.

B Did you *enjoy* your *stay* in Taiwan?

A We had a very pleasant time.

B This is a small *gift* for you with our *compliments*.

A That*'s* very *kind of* you.

B I hope you can *visit* Taiwan *again*.

A I'll definitely come again.

A See you.

A：那麼我就要告辭了。
B：停留台灣的期間愉快嗎？
A：很愉快。
B：這是表達我們謝意的小禮物。
A：你們真好。
B：希望你以後可以再來台灣。
A：我一定會再來。
A：再見。

超實用精選短句 *Useful Sentences*

» I am sorry, but I have to go.
很抱歉，我必須告辭了。

» Why not stay longer?
為什麼不多待一會呢？

» Goodbye, and take care.
再見，保重了。

» I have to say goodbye now.
我現在必須告辭了。

» Please accept this as a souvenir for our friendship.
請接受這個作為我們友誼的紀念品。

» That is very kind of you to drive me to the station.
承蒙送到車站，您真是太客氣了。

» I am afraid that I must be going now.
恐怕我得走了。

» Have a nice trip.
祝您一路順風。

» Thanks for the gift.
謝謝你的禮物。

» It's very nice of you to see me off.
您來給我送行真是太好了。

» I hope to see you again.
希望能再次見到您。

» Thank you very much for your warm hospitality.
非常感謝你們熱情的款待。

你一定要知道！ *More Tips*

當送客戶的時候可以說「It was a pleasure meeting you.」（見到你是我的榮幸。），「It was a pleasure doing business with you.」（和你做生意是我們的榮幸。），若客戶是由外地來的，要搭飛機回國，那你就可以說「Have a nice flight.」（祝你旅途愉快。）。

Part

7

招呼訪客篇

→ **Part 7 音檔連結** ←

因各家手機系統不同，若無法直接掃描，
仍可以至以下電腦雲端連結下載收聽。
（https://tinyurl.com/3eaah4d6）

01 接待訪客

📚 關鍵單字&片語 Words & Phrases

sir	[sɝ]	名	先生
first	[fˋst]	形	第一的
from	[frɑm]	介	從……來
General Manager	[ˋdʒɛnərəl ˋmænɪdʒɚ]	名	總經理
new	[nju]	形	新的
product	[ˋprɑdəkt]	名	產品
I see	[ai si]	片	我懂了
wait a moment	[wet ə ˋmomənt]	片	等一下

😊 情境會話 Conversation

A Good Afternoon!

B Good Afternoon, **_sir_**! May I have your name, please?

A This is my **_first_** time here. I am John **_from_** the ABC Company.

B Is there anything I can help you with?

A I would like to see your **_General Manager_** to introduce our **_new products_**.

B Oh, **_I see_**.

B Please **_wait a moment_**.

A：午安！
B：午安！先生，請問您是？
A：第一次來拜訪，我是 ABC 公司的約翰。
B：請問您有何貴事？
A：我想要見你們的總經理，介紹新產品。
B：哦，我知道了。
B：請稍待。

超實用精選短句 *Useful Sentences*

» Is there anything I can do for you?
我能為您做什麼嗎？

» I have an appointment at 4 with your manager.
我與你們經理下午四點有約。

» Please wait in here.
請在這稍等一下。

» Our manager is waiting for you in his office. Please come this way.
我們經理正在辦公室等您呢。請這邊走。

» What would you like?
有什麼事嗎？

» Is she expecting you?
你跟她有約好嗎？

» Would you like a cup of coffee?
你想來杯咖啡嗎？

» Please wait a minute, she is coming.
請稍等，她馬上就來。

» Wait a second. I'll tell her you're here.
請等一下，我會轉告她你已經來了。

» How do I get to the marketing department? Could you show me the way?
我要怎麼去行銷部？你能跟我說怎麼走嗎？

» This way, please. Our president is expecting you.
請往這邊走，我們董事長正在等您。

» Take the elevator to the eighth floor.
搭電梯到八樓。

你一定要知道！ *More Tips*

　　當你去飯店吃飯或店裡買衣服的時候，侍者、店員會說：「May I help you?」，或是「Is there anything I can help you with?」（我可以幫你嗎？）。

02 受訪者不在時

📖 關鍵單字＆片語 Words & Phrases

unfortunately	[ʌnˈfɔrtʃənɪtlɪ]	副	不幸、不巧
tied up	[taɪd ʌp]	片	脫不了身
return	[rɪˈtɜn]	動	返回
until	[ənˈtɪl]	介	直到
possible	[ˈpɑsəbl̩]	形	可能的
soon	[sun]	副	不久地、很快
while	[hwaɪl]	名	一會兒
make an appointment	[mek æn əˈpɔɪntmənt]	片	預約

😊 情境會話 Conversation

A I'm sorry, **_unfortunately_**, the General Manager is **_tied up_** with something urgent. He has not yet **_returned_**.

B Excuse me, when do you think he will be back?

A I am afraid he won't be back **_until_** 3 o'clock.

A If it is **_possible_**, you may tell me first.

A I think he will be back very **_soon_**.

A Could you wait here for a **_while_**?

A Did you **_make an appointment_** with him?

A：對不起，很不巧，總經理有急事，還沒有回到公司來。
B：對不起，他幾點會回到公司呢？
A：我想可能會過了三點以後。
A：如果可以的話，有事可以先告訴我。
A：我想過一會兒他就會回來了。
A：能請你稍待一下嗎？
A：你和他有約嗎？

🔖 超實用精選短句 *Useful Sentences*

» What can I do for you, miss?
小姐，能為您效勞嗎？

» He hasn't shown up yet.
他還沒來。

» Mr. Brown isn't here yet.
伯朗先生還沒來。

» When will he return to the company?
他什麼時候會回公司呢？

» Our manager is visiting a client.
我們的經理去拜訪客戶了。

» Can you tell me when your manager will get back?
能告訴我你們經理什麼時候回來嗎？

» I think he might be back before 5 p.m..
我想他可能會在下午五點之前回來。

» Maybe you could come again the other day.
或許您可以改天再來。

» I am not sure when he will get back.
我不確定他什麼時候會回來。

» She won't be back till 5 o'clock.
她五點前不會回來。

» He is on vacation this week.
他這禮拜休假。

» She has left already.
她已經離開了。

⚡ 你一定要知道！⚡ *More Tips*

「tie up」原本是「綁起來」的意思：「The zoo keeper tied up the lion.」（動物園的管理員把獅子綁起來。），但當「tie up」用來形容一個人的時候就表示那個人「正忙著……」或「受困於……」，如：「I got tied up with the house work. That is why I am late.」（我被家事纏身，所以遲到了。）。

03 帶領訪客

📚 關鍵單字＆片語 Words & Phrases

ask	[æsk]	動 要求、請求
right	[raɪt]	副 直接地、逕直地
find	[faɪnd]	動 找到
office	[ˋɔfɪs]	名 辦公室
keep	[kip]	動 繼續不斷
turn right	[tɜn raɪt]	片 右轉
seat	[sit]	名 座位
Would you like...?	[wʊd ju laɪk]	片 你想要……？
thanks	[θæŋks]	名 感謝

😊 情境會話 Conversation

A Our General Manager **_asks_** you to go **_right_** in.

B Where can I **_find_** his **_office_**?

A Just **_keep_** walking to the end, then **_turn right_**, you will see it.

B I see, Thank you!

C Please have a **_seat_**, he will be here very soon.

B Thank you!

C **_Would you like_** tea or coffee?

B No, **_thanks_**.

A：我們總經理請你進去。
B：我怎樣可以找到他的辦公室呢？
A：你向前走到底，再右轉，就會看見他的辦公室。
B：知道了。謝謝！
C：你稍坐一下，他馬上就出來。
B：謝謝！
C：你要喝杯茶或咖啡嗎？
B：謝謝，不必了。

🔊 超實用精選短句 *Useful Sentences*

» This way, please. Mr. White.
懷特先生，請這邊走

» How can I get to his office?
我怎樣找到他的辦公室呢？

» His office is at the end of the corridor.
他的辦公室就在走廊的盡頭。

» Follow me, please. I'll lead you there.
請跟我來，我帶您去那裡。

» You can go upstairs to find him.
您可以上樓去找他。

» Would you like to wait here for a moment?
您願意在這裡等一下嗎？

» Come this way, please.
這邊請。

» The manager's office is just next door.
經理辦公室就在隔壁。

» Please be seated. He is going downstairs.
請坐。他正下樓。

» The president's office is on the top floor.
董事長的辦公室在頂樓。

» It's very nice of you to show me the way.
您給我帶路真是太感謝了。

» It's easy to find.
很容易找。

⚡ 你一定要知道！⚡ *More Tips*

　　一般人通常把「seat」與「sit」搞混，「seat」是「座位、使就坐」的意思：「Please have a seat.」；「sit」是「坐」的意思：「Please sit down.」，兩句的解釋都是「請坐下」，但用法不同，請特別注意。

04 請訪客稍等

📚 關鍵單字＆片語 Words & Phrases

probably	[ˋprɑbəblɪ]	副	可能地
wait	[wet]	動	等待
here	[hɪr]	副	這裡
magazine	[ˌmægəˋzin]	名	雜誌
on the phone	[ɑn ðə fon]	片	電話中
fine	[faɪn]	形	好的
room	[rum]	名	房間

😊 情境會話 Conversation

A I am really sorry, the General Manager is still in the meeting. You will *probably* need to *wait* for quite a while.

B It doesn't matter, I'll wait for him.

A *Here* are some *magazines*. If you would like, you may read them while you are waiting.

B Thank you very much indeed.

A He is talking *on the phone* now, please wait a moment.

B That's *fine*.

A Mr. Wang, please take a seat and wait for him in this *room*.

A：很抱歉，總經理正在開會當中，你可能要稍微等一下。
B：沒關係。我等他。
A：這裡有雜誌，如果你喜歡的話，可以邊看邊等他。
B：真謝謝你。
A：他目前正在電話上，請稍候。
B：沒有問題。
A：王先生，請坐在這個房間等候。

超實用精選短句 *Useful Sentences*

» Please have a seat.
請坐。

» He is holding a meeting now.
他現在主持一個會議。

» Mr. Smith is on his way to the company.
史密斯先生正在回公司的路上。

» Would you like to read some newspaper or magazines while waiting?
要不要邊等邊看報紙或雜誌呢？

» Please be seated. He will be here in two minutes.
請坐，他兩分鐘後就來。

» I am afraid that you have to wait a moment. He's not available now.
恐怕您不得不等一會了。他現在沒空。

» Please have a cup of tea.
請喝杯茶。

» I'll let you know if he is available.
他一有空我就會告訴您的。

» Where should I sit?
我該坐哪裡？

» That's OK. I can wait.
沒關係，我可以等。

» Would you like a cup of coffee?
要喝杯咖啡嗎？

» Thank you for waiting.
讓您久等了。

你一定要知道！ *More Tips*

「沒關係」可用「It doesn't matter.」來表達，也可以說「It's ok.」或是「That's fine.」來表示。

05 臨時訪客應對

📚 關鍵單字&片語 Words & Phrases

photo	[ˋfoto]	名 照片
visitor	[ˋvɪzɪtɚ]	名 訪客
tag	[tæg]	名 標籤
finish	[ˋfɪnɪʃ]	動 完成
available	[əˋveləb!]	形 有空的
follow me	[ˋfɑlo mi]	片 跟我來
take	[tek]	動 帶
meeting room	[ˋmitɪŋ rum]	名 會議室

😊 情境會話 Conversation

Ⓐ Hi, how may I help you?

Ⓐ Who are you going to meet today? And what time is the meeting?

Ⓐ We will need a *photo* ID. And can you please sign your name here?

Ⓐ Here is your *visitor*'s name *tag*.

Ⓐ Mr. Gail is in a meeting now. The meeting should be *finished* in 10 minutes.

Ⓐ Mr. Chen, Mr. Gail is *available*, please *follow me*, I will *take* you to the *meeting room*.

A：嗨，有什麼需要協助的地方嗎？
A：您今天要見哪一位呢？會面的時間是幾點呢？
A：我們需要一張有您相片的證件，還有麻煩您在這簽名。
A：這是您的訪客証。
A：蓋爾先生目前人在會議中。應該再十分鐘內就會結束了。
A：陳先生，蓋爾先生現在可以見您了。請您跟我來，我帶您到會議室去。

超實用精選短句 *Useful Sentences*

» Our director is in the meeting and not available to see you.
我們主管現在開會，不能見您。

» Anything I can do for you?
我能為您做什麼嗎？

» May I ask when the manager will be free?
請問經理何時會有空？

» Can I bring you some water or tea?.
要不要我為您準備一些茶水呢？

» Mr. Brown, the general manager is expecting you.
布朗先生，我們總經理在等您了。

» Can you tell me when your manager is available?
可以告訴我你們經理什麼時候有空呢？

» Mr. Black will be free around eleven. Would you like to wait a moment?
布萊克先生十一點左右會有空。您願意等一會嗎？

» This way, please. Our president is waiting for you in his office.
請這邊走，我們總裁正在辦公室等您。

» Is it possible for me to see your manager now?
我可以現在見你們經理嗎？

» Our boss is having a meeting now.
我們的老闆現在正在開會。

» You can't see him if you didn't make an appointment.
如果你沒預約就無法見他。

∕ 你一定要知道！∕ *More Tips*

「be available」是指「有空的、可以與之聯繫的」。如：「Our manager is available to see you now.」（我們經理現在可以見您了。）或是：「Our manager is not available for the meeting right now.」（我們經理現在沒空去開那個會議。）。

06 接待VIP貴賓

📚 關鍵單字&片語 *Words & Phrases*

input	[ˈɪnˌput]	名 投入
definitely	[ˈdɛfənɪtlɪ]	副 肯定地、當然
resolve	[rɪˈzɑlv]	動 解決
documentation	[ˌdɑkjəˈmɛntərɪ]	名 文件
presentation	[ˌprizɛnˈteʃən]	名 報告、說明
session	[ˈsɛʃən]	名 會議
interrupt	[ˌɪntəˈrʌpt]	動 打斷

😊 情境會話 *Conversation*

A Hi, Mr. Smith. Welcome! How are you doing today?

A We are so glad that you could come today. With your ***input***, we ***definitely*** will get the problem ***resolved*** for this project.

A Please have a look at the ***documentation*** that we prepared for you here.

A I will have a power point ***presentation*** shortly followed by a discussion ***session***. I hope that we can get this meeting finished in 1 hour.

A Please ***interrupt*** me anytime you have any questions.

A：嗨，史密斯先生。歡迎！您今天可好？

A：很高興您今天可以過來。有您的投入，我們這個案子的問題一定可以解決。

A：這是我們為您準備的文件，請您過目。

A：我會簡短地作一個 power point 說明，隨後就會展開討論會。希望我們能夠在一小時內結束這個會議。

A：如果您有任何問題，請您隨時打斷我。

🔈 超實用精選短句 *Useful Sentences*

» Mr. Robertson, welcome to our company.
羅伯遜先生，歡迎您到訪我們公司。

» Please let me know if there is anything I can do for you.
如果有什麼能為您效勞的請讓我知道。

» Thank you for your time, Miss Yang.
謝謝您抽空前來，楊小姐。

» Please don't hesitate to ask any question at any time.
如果您有任何問題，請隨時提出。

» Your coming means a lot to us.
您的蒞臨對我們來說意義重大。

» You've been very helpful in this matter.
您在這件事上真是幫了個大忙。

» Thank you for your participation.
非常感謝您的參與。

» Thanks to you help, so that we could successfully complete this project.
多虧您的幫助，我們才成功完成了這個計畫。

» Thank you for the input.
感謝您的投入。

» I will send you an Email to follow up with today's meeting.
我會將今天會議的後續行動以電子郵件寄送給您。

⚡ 你一定要知道！⚡ *More Tips*

　　接待貴賓時，必先感謝對方的到來，如：「We would like to thank you for coming to our company.」（感謝您蒞臨敝公司。）正式一點的致歡迎謝詞，可說：「It is a great honor and privilege to receive a visit to our company from you.」（承蒙您造訪本公司，實屬榮幸之至。）。

07 不速之客的應對

📚 關鍵單字＆片語 *Words & Phrases*

send	[sɛnd]	動 寄送
E-mail	[ˋimel]	名 電子郵件
a phone call	[ə fon kɔl]	名 一通電話
schedule	[ˋskɛʤul]	名 行程
fully	[ˋfulɪ]	副 完全地
pass on	[pæs ɑn]	片 傳遞
info	[ˋɪnfo]	名 資訊

😊 情境會話 *Conversation*

A Do you have an appointment with Mr. Daniel? You will have to make an appointment with him by **_sending_** him an **_E-mail_** or making **_a phone call_**.

A Let me check his **_schedule_** and see when Mr. Daniel will be available. It looks like he is **_fully_** booked today.

A Here is Mr. Daniel's business card. His contact **_info_** is on it.

A Can I also have your contact information so that I can **_pass_** it **_on_** to Mr. Daniel as well?

A Thanks for your understanding.

A：您與丹尼爾先生有約嗎？您必須透過電子郵件或電話和他約時間喔。

A：我查一下丹尼爾先生的行程表，看看他是否有時間。看來他今天好像行程全滿了呢。

A：這是丹尼爾先生的名片。他的聯絡資訊都在上面。

A：可否將您的聯絡資訊也留給我，好讓我交給丹尼爾先生？

A：謝謝您的諒解。

超實用精選短句 *Useful Sentences*

» What can I do for you, sir?
先生，能為您效勞嗎？

» Is there anything I can do for you?
我能為您做什麼嗎？

» He is with a customer right now.
他目前正在招呼客戶。

» Do you have an appointment with our boss?
您與我們老闆有約嗎？

» Our manager is attending a meeting now.
我們經理現在正在開會。

» When is your manager available?
你們經理什麼時候有時間呢？

» His schedule for today is full.
他今天的行程都排滿了。

» Mr. Smith is very busy now.
史密斯先生現在非常忙。

» Is it possible for me to have a word with him?
我可以現在跟他談談嗎？

» May I have you name and work unit?
可以告訴我您的名字和工作單位嗎？

» Maybe you could come again some other day.
或許你可以改天再來。

» I am sorry. Our general manager is meeting visitors.
很抱歉，我們總經理現在正接待訪客呢。

⚡ 你一定要知道！⚡ *More Tips*

「schedule」有「安排、預定」及「行程表」之意。表示某人行程全滿時，可以說：「Mr. Smith has a very tight schedule today.」（史密斯先生今天的行程非常緊湊。），或是：「Mr. Smith is fully scheduled this entire week.」（史密斯先生這整週的行程都滿了。）。

Part

8

接待國外客戶

篇

→ **Part 8 音檔連結** ←

因各家手機系統不同，若無法直接掃描，
仍可以至以下電腦雲端連結下載收聽。
（https://tinyurl.com/bdfnedfa）

01 重點介紹公司

📚 關鍵單字&片語 *Words & Phrases*

brief	[brif]	動 簡報、作……的提要
set up	[`sɛt ʌp]	片 建立、創立
turnover	[`tɜ˞ˏ͵ovə˞]	名 營業額
million	[`mɪljən]	名 百萬元
headquarter	[`hɛd`kwɔrtə˞]	名 總部
branch	[bræntʃ]	名 分公司
be located in	[bi `loketɪd ɪn]	片 位於
accessory	[æk`sɛsərɪ]	名 附件

😊 情境會話 *Conversation*

A Let me *brief* you on our company. Our company was *set up* in 1976.

A At present we have a *turnover* of about $250 *million*.

B Where is your *headquarters*? Do you have any *branches*?

A The headquarters is in Taipei. One branch *is located in* New York, U.S.A., the other one is in Tokyo, Japan.

B What is your major product?

A Computer *accessories*.

A：讓我來對公司作個簡介，敝公司設立於 1976 年。
A：目前我們年營業額大約台幣 2.5 億。
B：你們的總公司在那裡？有分公司嗎？
A：總公司在台北，分公司在美國紐約及日本東京。
B：你們的主力產品是什麼？
A：電腦零組件。

🐬 超實用精選短句 *Useful Sentences*

» Let me show you around our sales department.
我帶你參觀一下我們的業務部。

» Our company was established in 1984.
我們的公司於 1984 年成立。

» Would you like to have a visit?
您願意參觀一下嗎?

» Our turnover is up to $12 million.
我們的營業額高達一千二百萬美元。

» We have 23 branches all over the world.
全世界我們設有二十三家分公司。

» What type of business is the company in?
公司從事什麼業務?

» It's my pleasure to show you around.
帶您參觀是我的榮幸。

» We mainly deal in office equipments.
我們主要的營業項目是辦公室設備。

» We are a new company, only two years.
我們是家新的公司,剛剛成立兩年。

» Our firm has 200 employees in total.
我們公司總共有兩百名員工。

» Here we have the marketing department.
這裡是我們的行銷部。

» We do business with more than twenty countries.
我們與二十多個國家有生意往來。

⚡ 你一定要知道! ⚡ *More Tips*

「brief」當動詞是「對……作簡報」的意思,或當形容詞是「簡單、簡短」的意思,如:「Let me make a brief introduction of myself.」(讓我來做個簡單的自我介紹。)、「Please make it brief, I don't have much time.」(請簡潔一點,我沒有太多的時間。)。

02 參觀工廠

📖 關鍵單字&片語 *Words & Phrases*

building	[ˈbɪldɪŋ]	名 建築物
shift	[ʃɪft]	名 輪班
QC management	[kju si ˈmænɪdʒmənt]	名 品質控管
strictest	[ˈstrɪktəst]	形 （strict 的最高級）嚴格
standard	[ˈstændəd]	名 標準
meanwhile	[ˈminˌhwaɪl]	名 同時
certified	[ˈsɝtəˌfaɪd]	形 認證的
industry	[ˈɪndəstrɪ]	名 行業

😊 情境會話 *Conversation*

A Ladies and gentlemen, the ***building*** right behind me is our factory.

B Could you take us to have a look?

A OK! Just follow me!

B How many ***shifts*** are there in this factory?

A In total, there are three shifts.

B How is your company's ***QC management***?

A We follow the ***strictest*** QC ***standards***. ***Meanwhile***, we are the first company ***certified*** with ISO9001 in the ***industry***.

A：各位，在我身後的這幢建築，就是敝公司的工廠。
B：能請你帶我們去參觀一下嗎？
A：好啊！我來帶路吧！
B：你們的工廠總共幾班制？
A：總共三班制。
B：貴公司在品質管理上如何？
A：我們有非常嚴格的品質管理要求，而且是同業之中最先獲得 ISO9001 認證的工廠。

超實用精選短句 *Useful Sentences*

» This is our new factory.
這個是我們的新工廠。

» Would you like to see our factory where we make most of our products?
您想不想看看我們生產大部分產品的工廠呢？

» Would you mind showing us around your factory?
能否請您帶我們參觀一下你們的工廠？

» Would you come this way?
請跟我來好嗎？

» That would be great.
好啊。

» We have employed 300 workers.
我們雇用了 300 名工人。

» The room is the monitoring center.
這個房間是監控室。

» Employee dormitory is on the third floor.
員工宿舍在三樓。

» We have a new factory covering 10,000 square meters.
我們有佔地一萬平方米的新廠房。

» How many people are working in the factory?
多少人在這間工廠工作啊？

» Now I'm leading you to the factory.
現在我帶您去工廠看看。

» The factory looks very large and clean.
這間工廠看起來非常乾淨寬敞。

你一定要知道！ *More Tips*

「shift」在這裡是「輪班」的意思：「I work on the night shift at the factory.」（我在工廠做晚班。），而它當動詞的時候還可以當作「轉換、改變、移動」的意思：「I shifted in my chair impatiently.」（我很不耐煩的在椅子上移動。）。

03 用餐接待

📚 關鍵單字＆片語 Words & Phrases

be my guest	[bi maɪ gɛst]	片 我請客
cuisine	[kwɪˋzin]	名 菜餚、食物
prefer	[prɪˋfɝ]	動 較喜歡
menu	[ˋmɛnju]	名 菜單
cheers	[tʃɪrz]	感 大家乾杯
bottoms up	[ˋbɑtəms ʌp]	片 乾杯
full	[fʊl]	形 飽的

😊 情境會話 Conversation

A Would you **_be my guest_**, tonight?

B That's very kind of you!

A What kind of **_cuisine_** do you **_prefer_**?

B Any kind of food is fine with me.

C Please have a look at the **_menu_**!

A **_Cheers_**!

B **_Bottoms up_**!

A Do you want to order anything else?

B I am **_full_**.

A：今天晚上我請客如何？
B：真的不好意思。
A：想吃什麼樣的食物呢？
B：我什麼都喜歡。
C：請您看一下菜單吧！
A：乾杯吧！
B：乾了哦！
A：還要叫些什麼？
B：我已經飽了。

🐦 超實用精選短句 *Useful Sentences*

» What would you like to have tonight?
您今晚想吃什麼呢？

» Could I have the menu, please?
請給我菜單好嗎？

» It's kind of cold outside. Why don't we have hot pot?
外面有些冷。不如我們去吃火鍋？

» Help yourself with whatever you like.
您想吃什麼就吃什麼。

» It's on me.
我請客。

» Would you like some more bread?
您要不要再來點麵包呢？

» I'll take care of this.
我來付帳。

» Would you like to try spaghetti?
您要不要試試義大利麵？

» The dinner is very delicious.
晚餐非常的美味。

» Would you like some ice cream or cheese cake for dessert?
你要不要來點冰淇淋或乳酪蛋糕做飯後甜點？

» Would you prefer white or red wine?
要喝白酒還是紅酒呢？

» Did you enjoy the meal?
餐點還滿意嗎？

⚡ 你一定要知道！⚡ *More Tips*

想要說自己已經吃飽了，可以用「I am full.」、「I am stuffed.」、「I have enough.」（我夠了。）、「I can't eat anymore.」（我吃不下了。）等等來表達。

04 招待旅遊

📖 關鍵單字&片語 *Words & Phrases*

depressed	[dɪˈprɛst]	形 鬱悶的
idea	[aɪˈdɪə]	名 主意
fun	[fʌn]	形 有趣的
scenery	[ˈsinərɪ]	名 風景
by the way	[baɪ ðə we]	片 順帶一提
nudist beach	[ˈnjudɪst bitʃ]	名 天體海灘

😊 情境會話 *Conversation*

A I'm bored and *__depressed__*. Do you have any good *__ideas__*?

B This weekend we are going on a group tour, would you like to join us?

A Where do you plan to go?

B Kenting National Park.

A Do you think that's a *__fun__* place?

B There's really gorgeous *__scenery__* with pleasant weather. *__By the way__*, I heard that they have got the only *__nudist beach__* in Taiwan.

A Really? What are we waiting for? Let's go!

A：我很煩也很鬱悶，你有沒有什麼好點子？
B：這個週末，我們公司舉辦郊遊，你要不要也一起去？
A：你們打算去哪裡呢？
B：墾丁國家公園。
A：你認為那裡好玩嗎？
B：那裡風景優美、氣候怡人，對了，聽說還有台灣唯一的天體海灘。
A：真的嗎？那還等什麼？趕快走吧！

🔊 超實用精選短句 *Useful Sentences*

» Do you want to visit some famous places?
你想去參觀一些有名的景點嗎？

» Here is the most popular spot for wedding photo in Taipei.
這裡是台北最受歡迎的拍婚紗照的地方。

» The scenery here is really beautiful.
這裡的風景真的太美了。

» The Jade Mountain is rather spectacular.
玉山真是壯觀。

» This is the only one five-star hotel in here.
這是這裡唯一的五星級飯店。

» I'll pull back the curtains so that you can enjoy the view.
我去把窗簾拉開，您就可以好好欣賞風景了。

» Would you like to soak in a hot spring in Beitou?
你想去北投泡溫泉嗎？

» How about going to the beach?
去海邊怎麼樣？

» If you come here in summer, you'll see more beautiful scenery.
如果您夏天來的話，您會欣賞到更美的景色。

» Do you want to visit somewhere?
您想去什麼地方參觀嗎？

» Is there any place you want to go?
您有沒有想去的地方呢？

» Thank you very much for your company.
非常感謝您的陪伴。

✔ 你一定要知道！✔ *More Tips*

　　墾丁不僅我們自己國人很愛去，外國人也為它深深的著迷。因此我們若要向外國人介紹墾丁，不妨用「The beach is beautiful.」（那裡的海灘很漂亮。）、「The weather is great!」（天氣很棒。）等等。

05 特色美食招待

📚 關鍵單字&片語 Words & Phrases

try	[traɪ]	動 嘗試
taste	[test]	動 品嚐
make from	[mek frɑm]	片 以……做成
fudge	[fʌdʒ]	名 軟糖
dream of	[drim ɑv]	片 渴望
sweet tooth	[swit tuθ]	片 嗜吃甜食的人
keep	[kip]	動 持有、留著
flattered	[ˋflætəd]	形 受寵若驚的

😊 情境會話 Conversation

A Please _try_ one!

B What's this? I've never _tasted_ this before.

A This is Taiwan's Ma-Shu, _made from_ rice and sugar.

B It reminds me of British _fudge_.

A Do you like it?

B It's really the best thing I could _dream of_ for people like me with a _sweet tooth_.

A Oh, really? Then _keep_ it as a gift.

B I am _flattered_, thank you very much indeed.

A：請嚐嚐看！
B：這是什麼東西？我從未吃過。
A：這個是台灣的麻糬，用米和砂糖作成的。
B：它使我想起英國的軟糖。
A：你喜歡吃嗎？
B：對於我這個愛好甜食的人，真是太好了！
A：啊！真的嗎？那就給你作禮物吧！
B：我真是受寵若驚，真是太謝謝你了。

超實用精選短句 *Useful Sentences*

» Why not try the snack?
為什麼不嚐嚐這個小吃呢？

» Do you like its flavor?
你喜歡它的味道嗎？

» How do you think of the refreshments?
您覺得這些茶點怎麼樣？

» It's the greatest biscuit I have ever had.
這是我吃過的最好吃的餅乾。

» I am glad that you like it.
您能喜歡我很高興。

» Refreshments will be served at the meeting room.
會議室裡有準備茶點。

» How about having some tea and pastries?
享用一些茶點如何啊？

» Refreshments are ready. Please help yourself.
茶點已經準備好了，請慢用。

» This is my first time to try pearl milk tea.
這是我第一次喝珍珠奶茶。

» Do you like chips, Miss Lee?
李小姐，你喜歡吃薯片嗎？

» It's really yummy. I love it!
真好吃。我非常喜歡！

» It's made from sugar, sesame and flour.
它是用糖、芝麻和麵粉做的。

你一定要知道！ *More Tips*

　　當有人稱讚你如：「You are the prettiest girl I have ever seen.」（你是我見過最美麗的女生。）、「This painting of yours is great!」（你畫的這張圖真棒！）等等，你都可以說：「I am flattered.」（真是不好意思、我受寵若驚。）。

06 工作同仁介紹

📚 關鍵單字 & 片語 *Words & Phrases*

administration	[ədˌmɪnəˈstreʃən]	名 行政
assistance	[əˈsɪstəns]	名 援助
supply	[səˈplaɪ]	名 生活用品、補給品
head	[hɛd]	名 首領、頂頭上司
committee	[kəˈmɪtɪ]	名 委員會
accounting	[əˈkaʊntɪŋ]	名 會計

😊 情境會話 *Conversation*

Ⓐ Mr. Johnson, we would like to introduce some of the staff here to you.

Ⓐ Mr. Black is in charge of the office ***administration***. You can get ***assistance*** regarding office ***supplies***, customer contact info, or filing from him.

Ⓐ Mrs. Stevenson is the ***head*** of the inventory department. She also is in charge of the company's safety ***committee***.

Ⓐ And this is Mr. Roberts, who has been with the company for 12 years. He is in charge of the ***accounting*** department.

A：強森先生，我們想為您引見一些這裡的職員。
A：布萊克先生負責辦公室行政。與辦公室用品、客戶聯絡資訊或是檔案方面有關的事情，都可以找他協助您。
A：史蒂文森女士是庫存部的經理。她同時也負責公司的安全委員會。
A：再來這位是羅勃茲先生，他已經在本公司服務十二年了。他管理會計部。

🔊 超實用精選短句 *Useful Sentences*

» I would like to introduce our colleagues to you.
我要為你介紹我們的同事。

» Mr. Green is in charge of the administrative work.
格林先生主要負責行政工作。

» This is Miss Lynn, our sales supervisor.
這位是林恩小姐，我們的銷售總監。

» Tom is also in charge of the logistics work.
湯姆同時也管理物流工作。

» Miss Young is the personal assistant of our manager.
楊小姐是我們經理的私人助理。

» This is our new colleague Barbara.
這是我們的新同事芭芭拉。

» Mr. boyd is the director of IT department, which will have your computer set up shortly.
鮑伊德先生是資訊技術部的主任，該部門會馬上設置您的電腦。

» If I can be of service, do not hesitate to tell me.
有用得著我的地方儘管來找我。

» Welcome to join our company!
歡迎加入我們公司！

» He is responsible for the personnel allocation.
他負責人員配置的工作。

» Ms. Cann will be your personal assistant.
坎恩小姐將會是您的個人助理。

» You can ask him about the financial problems.
你可以問他有關財務的問題。

✗ 你一定要知道！ ✗ *More Tips*

請對方「不用客氣，有疑問儘管問」時，通常會說：「Please feel free to talk to anyone here.」（請儘管問這裡任何一個人。），或是：「Please do not hesitate to ask me for help.」（別客氣，儘管找我幫你。）。

07 產品簡介

📖 關鍵單字&片語 *Words & Phrases*

cellular phone	[ˈsɛljulɚ fon]	名 手機
due to	[dju tu]	片 由於
current	[ˈkɝənt]	形 現在的
throw in	[θro ɪn]	片 投入、增添
touch screen	[tʌtʃ skrin]	名 觸控式螢幕
function	[ˈfʌŋkʃən]	名 功能
demonstrate	[ˈdɛmənˌstret]	動 示範

😊 情境會話 *Conversation*

A We have been working on this new ***cellular phone*** model for two years.

A When we first came up with the production plan, there was no touch screen. ***Due to*** the needs of the ***current*** market, we decided to ***throw in*** the ***touch screen function***.

A I believe E-230 is one of the most powerful cellular phones on the market today.

A We are going to ***demonstrate*** this cellular phone, so that you will have more detailed ideas of this new model.

A：我們已經為這款新手機努力了長達兩年的時間。
A：當我們第一次提出生產計畫時，那時並還沒有觸控式螢幕。由於目前市場的需要，我們決定增加觸控式螢幕這項功能。
A：我相信 E-230 會是現今市場上功能最強大的手機之一。
A：我們將會為您示範使用這支手機，如此一來您就對這款新商品有更詳盡的概念。

🔊 超實用精選短句 *Useful Sentences*

» Can you give me this month's marketing plan?
可以把本月行銷計畫給我嗎？

» I would like to introduce the first point, market demands.
我想先介紹第一點：市場需求。

» The technician will have the projector fixed soon.
技術人員會儘快把這部投影機修好。

» I've prepared a short PowerPoint for you.
我為大家準備了一段簡短的投影片報告。

» Please pay attention to the screen behind me.
請大家注意我後面的螢幕。

» Current economic state is pretty good.
目前的經濟形勢是挺好的。

» We still need to do a lot of things to cultivate the market.
我們還要做許多事情去開拓市場。

» As you can see, profits rose 11% last year.
正如你們看到的，去年的利潤提高了百分之十一。

» I believe that it will be popular in near future.
我相信不久的將來它會流行的。

» Please open the brochure on the desk.
請打開桌子上的宣傳冊。

» I'll demonstrate this camera for you.
我將為您示範使用這款相機。

» Well, do you have any questions?
那麼，你們有任何問題要問嗎？

🖊 你一定要知道！ *More Tips*

做新產品簡報時，首要的就是要宣傳新產品的優點，如：「Our new cellular phone is the best in the market with its lightweight and a low price.」（我們的新手機輕巧價廉，是市場上最佳的產品。）。

08 迎賓接機

📚 關鍵單字&片語 Words & Phrases

communication	[kəˌmjunəˈkeʃən]	名 通訊
parking lot	[ˈpɑrkɪŋ lɑt]	名 停車場
bag	[bæg]	名 包包、袋子
give	[gɪv]	動 給
hotel	[hoˈtɛl]	名 旅館
straight	[stret]	副 直接地
stop by	[stɑp baɪ]	片 短暫的停留或拜訪

😊 情境會話 Conversation

A Hi, Mr. Adams. My name is Jeff from Motion **Communications**. Nice to meet you.

A It's a short walk to the **parking lot**. Do you need me to carry your **bags**?

A The office is expecting you in at 11 a.m.. That **gives** you two hours.

A Do you want me to take you to the **hotel** first, or **straight** to the office?

A Also we can **stop by** somewhere to eat, if you missed your breakfast.

A Is there anything else you want me to help you with or should we be on our way?

A：嗨，亞當斯先生。我是傳動通訊的傑夫。很高興認識您。
A：到停車場要走一小段路。您需要我幫您拿行李嗎？
A：公司的人會等您上午 11 點時過去。所以您還有兩小時。
A：您是要我先帶您到飯店去，還是要直接去公司呢？
A：如果您沒吃早餐的話，我們也可以中途停下來吃東西。
A：還有沒有其他事需要幫忙的，或者我們就直接上路了？

超實用精選短句 *Useful Sentences*

» You must be tired after such a long trip.
飛這麼久你一定累了。

» Mr. Adams, I came to pick you up to the hotel.
亞當斯先生，我來接您去您的飯店。

» How was your flight?
您的旅途還好嗎？

» I feel very tired, because it's a very long trip.
我感覺很累，因為飛行時間很長。

» Let's go and check in the hotel.
我們到飯店登記吧。

» Let me help you with your luggage.
讓我幫你拿行李吧。

» I am taking my car at the parking lot.
我去停車場開車。

» This way please. My car is waiting outside.
這邊請，我的車在外面等。

» Let's go to the parking space directly.
讓我們直接到停車場去吧。

» We can have a quick meal in the restaurant near your hotel.
我們可以在您飯店附近的餐廳用個便餐。

» Would you like to sit down and have a rest?
要坐下來休息一會兒嗎？

» Let us go to the company directly.
我們直接去公司吧。

你一定要知道！ *More Tips*

通常接機時，第一句話就是問候對方旅程是否舒適，如：「How was your flight?」（這趟飛行如何？），這時可以回答：「It was fine-smooth all the way.」（很好，一點搖晃感也沒有。），或是：「I felt airsick all the way through the flight.」（整段航程我都在暈機。）。

09 確認住宿

📖 關鍵單字&片語 *Words & Phrases*

luxury	[ˈlʌkʃərɪ]	形 豪華的
suite	[swit]	名 套房
upgrade	[ˈʌpˈɡred]	名 升級
reward	[rɪˈwɔrd]	名 獎勵
for free	[fɔr fri]	片 免費
bellboy	[ˈbɛlˌbɔɪ]	名 旅館大廳的服務生

😊 情境會話 *Conversation*

A Mr. Adams, how are you doing? Do you have the reservation number?

A Yes, we do have the *luxury suite* available. Do you want an *upgrade*?

A If you are a member of our *reward* program, we will be able to upgrade from the economy room to luxury *for free*.

A You can just leave your luggage in the baggage area. The *bellboy* will bring it to your room shortly.

A Enjoy your stay and let us know if there is anything else we can do for you.

A：亞當斯先生，您好嗎？您有預約號碼嗎？
A：是的，我們的豪華套房的確還是空的。您想要升等嗎？
A：如果您是我們獎勵計畫的會員，我們就能免費將您的房間從經濟客房升等為豪華客房。
A：您只要將行李放在行李區就可以了。服務生不久就會把它們送到您的房間。
A：祝您住得愉快。如果有任何需要服務的，請告訴我們。

🔊 超實用精選短句 *Useful Sentences*

» I'd like a suite with an ocean view.
我想要一間海景套房。

» I need a room for tomorrow night.
我要一個房間，明晚住。

» Do you serve lunch for deluxe room?
您們為豪華客房提供午餐嗎？

» Could you tell me the current price?
您能告訴我現在房價是多少嗎？

» Can I book a room for next week?
我能預訂下周的房間嗎？

» Is it possible for me to reserve a double room now?
我現在可以預定一間雙人房嗎？

» I am planning to go to Tokyo for two days.
我計畫到東京兩天。

» I'd like to book a single room for tomorrow.
我明天想訂一個單人房。

» We offer a 20% discount for group reservation.
我們給團體訂房打八折。

» Can you provide accommodation for twenty people?
你有足夠 20 人住的房間嗎？

» Have a joyful stay here. Good night!
祝您住得愉快！晚安！

» We will provide place to stay if necessary.
如果有需要，我們會提供住宿。

⚡ 你一定要知道！ ⚡ *More Tips*

「available」表示「可用的」，如：「We do have a double room available on that day.」（我們那天的確還有雙人房可供住宿。），表示「有空房」的方式還有：「We have a vacancy for those dates.」（我們那幾天還有空房。）及「There is still a twin room unlet.」（還有空的雙床房。）。

10 送機

📖 關鍵單字 & 片語 Words & Phrases

airline	[ˈɛrˌlaɪn]	名 航線
drop off	[drɑp ɔf]	片 下車
departure area	[dɪˈpɑrtʃɚ ˈɛrɪə]	名 離境區
park	[pɑrk]	動 停車
board	[bord]	動 登機
boarding pass	[ˈbordɪŋ pæs]	名 登機證
passport	[ˈpæsˌport]	名 護照
security	[sɪˈkjʊrətɪ]	名 安全

😊 情境會話 Conversation

🅐 Mr. Adams, which ___airline___ are you with to Austin, and what time is your flight?

🅐 I will ___drop___ you ___off___ at ___departures___ at the First Terminal and I will go ___park___ the car and meet you at the check-in counter.

🅐 It's time for ___boarding___. Make sure you have your ___boarding pass___ and ___passport___ ready.

🅐 It takes quite a long time to go through the ___security___ in this airport.

🅐 See you soon and fly safely.

A：亞當斯先生，您是搭哪一家航空公司的班機到奧斯汀，還有班機時間是幾點？

A：我會讓您在第一航廈的離境處下車，然後我會把車停好後，與您在辦理手續的櫃檯碰面。

A：登機時間到了。請確認一下是不是帶好登機證和護照。

A：在這機場，安全檢查要花相當長的時間。

A：希望能很快再見面，祝您旅途平安。

超實用精選短句 *Useful Sentences*

» I hope you could come again soon.
  希望您很快能再來。

» When is the next flight to New York?
  下一班去紐約的飛機是幾點呢？

» See you soon!
  再見。

» It's time for me to check in.
  我該去辦理登機手續了。

» There is two hours more before boarding.
  離登機還有兩個多小時呢。

» Let me see you off at the airport.
  讓我送您到機場吧。

» Could you kindly arrange somebody to take me to the airport?
  請你派人把我送到機場好嗎？

» That's very nice of you both to drive us to the airport.
  謝謝你們二位把我們送到機場來。

» It's time for you to go through the security.
  您該去接受安全檢查了。

» You'd better check in earlier at the airport.
  你最好早點到機場辦登機手續。

» Have a safe fligth.
  祝你旅途平安。

» Have a nice flight!
  祝您一路順風。

你一定要知道！ *More Tips*

　　送機時，會說些祝福對方的話語，如：「Fly safely.」（祝你飛航平安。），或是「Have a save trip.」（祝一路順風。），另外，也可以說：「Bon voyage.」（祝旅途愉快。）。

Part

9

商務互動

篇

→ **Part 9 音檔連結** ←

因各家手機系統不同，若無法直接掃描，
仍可以至以下電腦雲端連結下載收聽。
（https://tinyurl.com/yc4a37xe）

01 電話詢問

📖 關鍵單字＆片語 *Words & Phrases*

be interested in	[bɪ ˈɪntərɪstɪd ɪn]	片 對……感興趣
catalog	[ˈkætəlɔg]	名 目錄
quotation	[kwoˈteʃən]	名 報價
would love to	[wʊd lʌv tu]	片 想要
international	[ˌɪntɚˈnæʃənl]	形 國際化的
carry	[ˈkærɪ]	動 出售
mostly	[ˈmostlɪ]	副 大部分地

😊 情境會話 *Conversation*

A We have seen your advertisement and ***are interested in*** your products. Can I have your ***catalogs*** and ***quotation***?

B Thank you very much for calling, we'***d love to*** mail you our detailed information. Who's calling, please?

A This is Mr. Brown from the ABC Company. We are an ***international*** trading company.

B OK, so, the main products you ***carry*** are sporting goods?

A ***Mostly***!

A：我們看過貴公司的廣告且甚感興趣，可以要一份你們的目錄及報價嗎？
B：非常感謝您打電話來，我們很樂意寄上我們詳盡的資料。請問貴寶號？
A：我是 ABC 公司的布朗，我們是一家國際貿易公司。
B：好，所以貴公司主要是代理運動用品囉？
A：大部份是！

🖐 超實用精選短句 *Useful Sentences*

» We'd like to get exclusive distribution rights for the television.
我們想要取得貴公司電視的獨家代理權。

» Could you introduce your products in detail?
能詳細介紹一下您的產品嗎？

» I'd like to know the price including tax of your product.
我想要知道產品含稅的價格。

» I want to know the lowest quotation of the refrigerator.
我想要知道貴公司冰箱的最低報價。

» We're one of leading cosmetics companies in Asia.
我們是亞洲化妝品的領導廠商之一。

» We are planning to grant exclusive distribution rights in Asia.
我們正計劃在亞洲授予獨家代理權。

» We are agent as you.
我們跟你們一樣都是代埋商。

» What else do you produce?
你們還生產其他東西嗎？

» Are you a manufacturer or an agent?
您是製造商還是代理商呢？

» I am very interested in your products.
我對貴公司產品非常感興趣。

» Could you give me a brief introduction to your product?
您能簡要介紹一下您的產品嗎？

» Thank you for providing information!
感謝提供資料。

✏ 你一定要知道！✏ *More Tips*

　　「top」是「上面」的意思：「The sugar jar is on the top of the shelf.」（糖罐子在櫃子上面。）；也可以當作是「頂尖」的意思：「She is at the top of her class.」（她是她們班上最頂尖的。）。

02 推銷商品

📚 關鍵單字&片語 *Words & Phrases*

latest	[ˋletɪst]	形	最新的
notebook	[ˋnot͵bʊk]	名	筆記型電腦
compact	[kəmˋpækt]	形	小巧的
weight	[wet]	動	重
deal	[dil]	名	特價
honest	[ˋɑnɪst]	形	誠實的

😊 情境會話 *Conversation*

A This is our **_latest_** model of our mini **_notebook_** we've been discussing.

B Oh, it's so **_compact_**!

A Yes, its **_weight_** is only 1.5 kg, and it's small enough to carry everywhere easily.

B Um, it looks pretty. How much is it?

A The market price is around NT$45,000. I'll give you a super **_deal_**.

B It's hard for me to know for sure cause I'm not familiar with the market.

A Don't worry about it, give me your **_honest_** opinion about our product and price.

A：這是我們討論過的最新型迷你電腦。
B：噢，好小巧！
A：是啊，它只有 1.5 公斤重，而且小到隨身攜帶也不麻煩。
B：嗯，看起來不錯，多少錢一台？
A：市價大約新台幣 4 萬 5 仟，不過我會給你一個特別價。
B：我很難確定價格對不對，因為這個市場我不是很熟悉。
A：不必擔心。告訴我你對我們產品及價格的意見吧！

超實用精選短句 *Useful Sentences*

» The digital camera is really light.
這台數位相機真的很輕。

» The monitor of this cell phone is big enough.
手機的螢幕夠大。

» It looks very novel and unique.
它看起來非常地新穎別致。

» No, Thanks. I am just looking.
不用了，謝謝。我只是看一下。

» What makes your products so special?
你們的產品有何特別之處？

» We'd like to inquire whether you are interested in these lines.
不知貴公司對這一系列的產品是否有興趣。

» What are the merits of your product?
您的產品有什麼優點？

» Can you show me how to use it?
你可以教我怎麼使用嗎？

» Our products are well-received by our customers.
顧客對我們的產品評價非常高。

» This is our best selling digital camera.
這是我們最暢銷的數位相機。

» That sounds great. Is it that good as you said?
聽起來還不錯，它真有你說的那麼好嗎？

» Will you give me a special discount?
您會給我一個特別折扣嗎？

你一定要知道！ *More Tips*

「deal」在這裡是當作「特價」的意思：「Could you give me a good deal?」（你可以給我特價嗎？），但它當動詞的時候就有「處理」的意思：「Let me deal with this problem.」（讓我來處理這一件事。）。

03 強調商品賣點

📖 關鍵單字&片語 Words & Phrases

superior	[sə`pɪrɪə]	形 更好的
selling point	[`sɛlɪŋ pɔɪnt]	名 賣點
design	[dɪ`zaɪn]	名 設計
impressive	[ɪm`prɛsɪv]	形 令人印象深刻的
colorful	[`kʌləfəl]	形 鮮豔的
quality	[`kwɑlətɪ]	名 品質
guarantee	[ˌgærən`ti]	動 保證

😊 情境會話 Conversation

A How's your product better than other competitor's?

B We can offer a ***superior*** product at the same price as our competitor's product.

A What are other ***selling points***?

B The ***design*** is cute and ***colorful***. Teenagers would like it.

A Sounds ***impressive***. How about its ***quality***?

B We ***guarantee*** its quality. We strongly recommend this product. I'm sure you'll be pleased with it.

B We always sell the best!

A：你們的產品優於其它競爭者的地方在哪？
B：在同樣的價格下，我們可以提供更好的產品品質。
A：還有沒有其它賣點？
B：它的外觀可愛、顏色鮮豔，青少年最喜歡了。
A：聽起來很令人心動，品質方面呢？
B：我們保證其品質。我們真的是強力推薦這項產品，我相信你一定會滿意的。
B：我們總是賣最好的東西！

超實用精選短句 *Useful Sentences*

» What's the key selling point?
它的關鍵賣點是什麼？

» What makes it better than others?
它有什麼比其他產品好呢？

» Why do you think your product is competitive?
你為什麼認為你的產品具有競爭力呢？

» What about its after-sales service?
它的售後服務如何啊？

» What's its main selling point?
它主要的賣點是什麼呢？

» Our products are very popular in Europe.
我們的產品在歐洲市場上非常暢銷。

» What is so special about this product?
這個產品有什麼特別之處？

» It is very light and portable.
它非常輕巧，便於攜帶。

» We provide a 12-month warranty.
我們提供十二個月的保固。

» I am sure you will be satisfied with it.
我相信您會對它滿意的。

» The advantages of it are high quality and mini size.
這種產品的優點之一就是高品質和小尺寸。

» The quality is superior to everything.
品質高於一切。

你一定要知道！ *More Tips*

　　我們最常分不清楚的兩個單字，一個是「quality」（品質），另一個則是「quantity」（量），而英文裡的:「Quality is more important than the quantity.」就是我們中文的「重質不重量。」。

04 報價及議價

📖 關鍵單字 & 片語 Words & Phrases

depend on	[dɪˋpɛnd ɑn]	片	依靠、信賴
quantity	[ˋkwɑntətɪ]	名	數量
best offer	[bɛst ˋɔfɚ]	片	最好的價格
unit	[ˋjunɪt]	片	單位
special offer	[ˋspɛʃəl ˋɔfɚ]	片	特惠價
extra	[ˋɛkstrə]	形	額外的
competitive	[kəmˋpɛtətɪv]	形	競爭性的

😊 情境會話 Conversation

A Please quote a price for this product.

B It *depends on quantity*, but this time I'll give my *best offer*.

A If we order 1,000 *units* or more, how much will you bring the price down?

B After the *special offer*, I'll make an *extra* ten percent discount.

A Another manufacturer has offered me a price lower than yours.

B I believe this price is quite reasonable.

A However, this price is not *competitive*.

A：關於這個產品，請報個價給我吧。
B：價格要依數量決定。不過這次我一定給你最好的價錢。
A：如果我們訂購 1000 台以上。可以降價到怎樣的價格？
B：特別優惠價之外，再打 9 折。
A：有另一家提供給我的價格比你們低。
B：我相信這個價格是合理的。
A：但是，這個價格不具競爭力。

超實用精選短句 *Useful Sentences*

» I'd like to discuss the price.
我想討論一下價格問題。

» I am afraid it is the lowest price we can offer.
恐怕這是我們能提供的最低價格。

» Isn't it possible to give us even a little more discount?
難道不能多打點折扣嗎？

» Is there a big difference of price between them?
它們的價錢有很大的差別嗎？

» It is too much higher than I expected.
比我預期的高太多了。

» I am glad we have reached an agreement on price.
很高興我們在價格問題上取得了一致意見。

» What is the best price you can offer?
您能提供最佳的價格是多少呢？

» Is it possible to give me a lower price?
能不能給我一個更低的價格呢？

» How much is it?
它賣多少錢啊？

» If I order more, will you give me a discount?
如果我訂貨更多的話，您會給我折扣嗎？

» I am sure this price is very reasonable.
我確信這個價格是非常合理的。

» Since the price is so high, I have to think about it.
既然價格這麼高，我必須再考慮一下。

你一定要知道！ *More Tips*

在討價還價的時候通常會用到以下的一些句子：「Could you lower the price?」（你可不可以降低價錢？）、「Could you give me a better price?」（你可不可以給我更好的價錢？）、「Is this the special offer?」（這是特價嗎？）、「Is there any discount?」（有沒有折扣？）等等。

05 推進對方下決定

📖 關鍵單字&片語 Words & Phrases

expect	[ɪksˋpɛkt]	動	預計
answer	[ˋænsɚ]	名	答案
proposal	[prəˋpozl]	名	提案
make a decision	[mek ə dɪˋsɪʒən]	片	做決定
expiration date	[ɪkˋspaɪrɪ det]	名	到期日

😊 情境會話 Conversation

A How soon can we *expect* your *answer* to our *proposal*?

B I'm not sure. Before I *make a decision*, I have to check many other things.

B Could you get me another sample before I leave?

A I'll bring it to you tomorrow morning.

B Thanks! After I go back, I'll discuss it with my boss as soon as I can.

A Well, you know, special offers always have an *expiration date*.

B I understand that. I'll give you my decision by next Friday.

A：關於我們的提議，多久能得到你的答覆？
B：不確定，下決定之前，我還必須查閱一些其它的事情。
B：你能不能在明天我離開之前再給我一個樣品？
A：我明天早上就帶來給你。
B：謝啦！我一回去，會儘快跟老闆談一談。
A：唔，你也知道，特殊優惠總是有期限的。
B：我了解，我下星期五前會給你我的決定。

🖐 超實用精選短句 *Useful Sentences*

» Have you decided yet?
您決定了嗎？

» When will you give me the answer?
您什麼時候給我答案呢？

» Could you make a decision by Friday?
您能在星期五以前作出決定嗎？

» I have to ask our boss before making the decision. But I will give you the answer as soon as possible.
在做決定之前我得請示一下老闆，但我會儘快給你答覆。

» I need some time to think it over.
我需要一些時間考慮。

» I haven't decided yet.
我還沒決定呢。

» Aren't you satisfied with our products?
您對我們的產品不滿意嗎？

» There is not much stock in the shop right now.
現貨存量已經不多了。

» I am afraid our special offer has an expiration date.
恐怕我們的優惠是有期限的。

» What's your decision?
你的決定是什麼？

» I will give you my decision by the day after tomorrow.
後天以前我會告訴你我的決定。

» OK. We will wait until next week.
好，那我們就等到下周囉。

⚡ 你一定要知道！⚡ *More Tips*

　　我們買東西的時候一定要注意標上的製造日和過期日，而英文就是「manufacturd date」（製造日）和「expiration date」（過期日）。

06 商談中的閒聊

📚 關鍵單字 & 片語 *Words & Phrases*

tiring	[ˈtaɪrɪŋ]	形 令人疲倦的
anywhere	[ˈɛnɪˌwhɛr]	副 什麼地方
give me a break	[gɪv mi ə brek]	片 讓我休息一下
sort of	[sɔrt ɑv]	片 有點
earn	[ɜn]	動 賺取
forget it	[fəˈgɛt ɪt]	片 算了吧

😃 情境會話 *Conversation*

Ⓐ Oh, let's stop this *tiring* discussion. We've been talking for over two hours, and haven't gotten *anywhere*.

Ⓐ Come on, *give me a break*!

Ⓑ That's true. I'm *sort of* tired after all this talking.

Ⓐ Tell me, why do we all work so hard?

Ⓑ We have to eat, you know.

Ⓐ I know, but *earning* your daily bread is not everything in life, is it?

Ⓑ Of course not.

Ⓑ *Forget* it, let's go get something to eat.

A：唉喲！停止這個累人的討論吧！我們已經討論兩個多鐘頭了，還是毫無進展。
A：拜託，休息一下吧！
B：好吧，經過這冗長的討論，我也覺得有點累了。
A：唉，告訴我，為什麼我們都得這麼拚命工作？
B：人都要吃飯過日子嘛！
A：我知道啊，可是餬口並不是生活的全部。
B：當然不是！
B：算了，我們出去找點吃的吧！

超實用精選短句 *Useful Sentences*

» How about taking a short break?
稍稍休息一下怎麼樣？

» Let's go out for dinner.
我們去吃晚餐吧。

» You look great in that skirt.
你穿那件裙子很漂亮。

» How do you think of him?
你覺得他怎麼樣？

» Why not have lunch first?
為什麼不先去吃午飯呢？

» Do you want to go clubbing tonight?
今晚想去夜店玩嗎？

» How is your project going?
那個計畫進行得如何了？

» What have you been doing lately?
你最近在幹什麼？

» How about going out for a drink?
要不要出去喝杯酒？

» I am going on a business trip next week.
我下周要出差了。

» What do you usually do in your free time?
你空閒時間通常在做什麼？

» I have to work hrd to support my family.
為了養家我不得不去拼命工作。

你一定要知道！ *More Tips*

「I had a small talk with my boss.」（我和我的老闆閒聊。）中的「small talk」就是「閒聊」的意思。當商業會議要結束的時候，你也可以說「Let's call it a day. Let's talk about the rest of it tomorrow.」（今天就到此為止吧！剩下的我們明天在談。）。

07 索取商品資料

📗 關鍵單字＆片語 Words & Phrases

website	[ˈwɛbˌsaɪt]	名 網頁
be released	[bi rɪˈlist]	片 上市
campaign	[kæmˈpen]	名 活動
flier	[ˈflaɪɚ]	名 廣告傳單
banner	[ˈbænɚ]	名 廣告橫幅、橫旗

😊 情境會話 Conversation

Ⓐ We're looking for some information on the newly released eye contact lens product line. From your **_website_**, the model we are looking for is EC2001.

Ⓐ We would like to know when this product will **_be released_**.

Ⓐ Please send the product fact sheet and other related info to us as we are trying to come up with a promotional **_campaign_** for this new model.

Ⓐ We also will need to know when we can place an order for the promotional materials, such as **_fliers_**, store **_banners_** and samples.

A：我們想找新上市的隱形眼鏡系列產品的資訊。從你們的網站上，我們要找的那一款產品是 EC2001。
A：我們想知道這個產品何時會上市。
A：請寄給我們產品介紹以及其他相關資訊，因為我們正試圖針對這個新產品提出促銷活動。
A：我們還想知道什麼時候可以訂宣傳品，像是廣告傳單、放在店面的橫旗和樣品這些東西。

超實用精選短句 *Useful Sentences*

» Could you please give me one price list?
您能給我一份價目表嗎？

» I would like a copy of your company' brochure.
我想要一份貴公司的宣傳冊子。

» Is that possible to give us more information?
可不可以給我們更多的資訊？

» I want to know more about your company.
我想更瞭解貴公司。

» Anybody can get a copy of the brochure for free.
任何人都能免費得到一份宣傳冊子。

» Could you give me your latest fall catalogue?
能否給我一份你們新的秋季商品目錄？

» Please contact us if you'd like other information.
如果您想要其他資料請聯繫我們。

» I need more information about the product.
我需要更多有關這種產品的資訊。

» Can I have a catalogue of your products?
能給我一份貴公司的產品目錄嗎？

» Could you give me a copy of your annual report?
您可不可以給我一份貴公司的年度報告呢？

» Please provide me with some related information.
請提供我一些相關資料。

» Could you offer something about your products?
你能否向我們提供一些貴公司產品的資料呢？

你一定要知道！ *More Tips*

一件產品可能有許多種不同的價格，如「retail price」指的是「零售價」、「dealer price」指的是「批發價」，而「promotional rate」指的是「促銷價」。如：「If I can buy this product at its dealer price, it will save me a lot of money.」（如果我能用批發價買到這項產品，就能省下很多錢呢。）。

08 約訪聯繫

📚 關鍵單字&片語 Words & Phrases

furniture	[ˈfɝnɪtʃɚ]	名 家具
factory	[ˈfæktərɪ]	名 工廠
sorry for	[ˈsɑrɪ fɔr]	片 抱歉
wait	[wet]	名 等候
excuse me	[ɪkˈskjuz mi]	片 不好意思
who	[hu]	代 誰
call	[kɔl]	動 打電話
Sweden	[ˈswidn̩]	名 瑞典
pine	[paɪn]	名 松木

😊 情境會話 Conversation

> **A** Hello! This is Taiwan **_Furniture_**, May I help you?
>
> **B** Hello! Taichung **_factory_**, please.
>
> **C** **_Sorry for_** the **_wait_**, this is Taichung factory speaking, may I help you?
>
> **B** May I speak to Mr. Pan?
>
> **C** **_Excuse me_**, may I know **_who_** is **_calling_**?
>
> **B** This is Chen, Zhi-Ming calling from **_Sweden Pine_**. I would like to speak to Mr. Pan.
>
> **C** Please wait a moment.

A：喂！這裡是台灣家具，您好！
B：喂！請接台中工廠。
C：讓你久等了，台中工廠，您好。
B：麻煩你接潘先生。
C：對不起，請問您哪裡找他？
B：我是瑞典松木的陳志明，想與潘先生通電話。
C：請稍待。

超實用精選短句 *Useful Sentences*

» Hello, this is she.
你好，我就是。

» Are you doing anything special tomorrow? I'd like to drop by your place.
明天你有什麼特別的安排嗎？我想順道拜訪。

» I am going to give you a product demonstration.
我要為您做產品解說。

» What have you been doing recently?
您最近在忙什麼？

» I can hold.
我可以等。

» I'd like to meet your manager.
我想見你們的經理。

» How is everything going in your company?
貴公司一切都還好嗎？

» I think we need a face-to-face discussion.
我想我們必須當面談。

» I want to show you the new layout.
我想給你看新的設計圖。

» There is an important meeting tomorrow.
明天有個很重要的會議。

» Could I stop by your office?
我可以順道拜訪嗎？

» You can stop by my office. We can have lunch together.
你可以順道過來我的辦公室，我們可以一起吃個午餐。

你一定要知道！ *More Tips*

在電話中的用語與一般的說話文法不一樣，當有人打電話來時說：「May I speak to Mr. White, please?」（我可不可以跟懷特先生說話？），若你就是懷特先生本人，那你就應該要說：「This is he.」（我就是。）或是「This is Mr. White speaking.」。

09 相約拜訪時間

📖 關鍵單字&片語 Words & Phrases

calling from	[ˈkɔlɪŋ frɑm]	片	從……打來
chat	[tʃæt]	名	談話
regarding	[rɪˈgɑrdɪŋ]	介	關於
purchase	[ˈpətʃəs]	動	購買
tomorrow	[təˈmɔro]	副	明天
o'clock	[əˈklɑk]	名	……點鐘
afternoon	[ˈæftəˈnun]	名	下午

😊 情境會話 Conversation

A Hello! This is Mr. Pan speaking.

B This is Jacky Chen *calling from* Sweden Pine.

B I would like to have a *chat* with you *regarding purchasing* pine. Will you be free *tomorrow*?

A Oh, I see. How about 2 *o'clock* tomorrow *afternoon*?

B OK, I will visit you around 2 o'clock tomorrow afternoon.

A I'll be waiting for you.

B See you then.

A：喂！我是潘先生。
B：我是瑞典松木的陳傑克。
B：有關採購松木的事，想和您談一下，您明天有空嗎？
A：原來如此，明天下午兩點左右如何？
B：可以。那麼我就明天下午兩點左右去拜訪您。
A：我等你來。
B：到時見。

超實用精選短句 *Useful Sentences*

» Could we meet tomorrow morning?
我們明天上午可以見面嗎？

» Come by my office tomorrow afternoon.
明天下午過來我的辦公室。

» Are you available sometime next week?
您下禮拜有時間嗎？

» I could come by your office and bring you the contract.
我可以帶合約過去您的辦公室給你。

» I suppose I could meet with you after lunch.
我想午餐後我可以跟你見面。

» Shall we have a talk a moment later?
待會我們能談談嗎？

» Why don't I come by your office right now?
不如我現在就過去你辦公室吧。

» I will visit you next week.
我下週將會去拜訪您。

» How about 10 o'clock?
十點如何？

» Not today. How about tomorrow?
今天不行，明天怎麼樣？

» Are you free around 3 o'clock tomorrow afternoon?
您明天下午三點左右有空嗎？

» I will be expecting you.
我會等你來的。

你一定要知道！ *More Tips*

「appreciate」是「感激、欣賞」的意思：「I really appreciate your help.」（我真的很感激你的幫忙。），「His art work is not appreciated by his classmates.」（他的藝術作品不受到同學的賞識。）。

10 通知拜訪遲到

📖 關鍵單字&片語 *Words & Phrases*

in a meeting	[ɪn ə ˈmitɪŋ]	片 開會中
forward	[ˈfɔrwəd]	動 轉達
message	[ˈmɛsɪdʒ]	名 訊息
be stuck	[bi stʌk]	片 被困住
traffic jam	[ˈtræfɪk dʒæm]	片 交通阻塞
think	[θɪŋk]	動 認為
be late	[bi let]	片 遲到

😊 情境會話 *Conversation*

A Mr. Pan's office, may I help you?

B Hello, This is Jacky Chen speaking. I would like to speak with Mr. Pan.

A I am sorry, but Mr. Pan is ***in a meeting*** now.

B Excuse me, Could you kindly ***forward*** a ***message*** to him?

A Yes, please tell me.

B I ***am stuck*** in a ***traffic*** jam, and I ***think*** I will ***be late***.

A When Mr. Pan finishes with the meeting, I will inform him.

A：潘經理辦公室，有什麼事嗎？
B：喂！我是陳傑克，想找潘先生聽電話。
A：對不起，潘先生正在開會。
B：真不好意思，能否拜託您傳話給他嗎？
A：可以，請説。
B：我遇到了塞車，大概會遲到。
A：潘先生會議結束時，我會轉達你的意思。

📣 超實用精選短句 *Useful Sentences*

» Would you like to leave any message?
  你要留言嗎？

» May I speak to Mr. Smith?
  我可以跟史密斯先生通電話嗎？

» We'll be ten minutes late.
  我們會遲到十分鐘。

» I am calling to tell you that I will be a little late.
  我打電話是想告訴您我會晚一點到。

» I got stuck in the traffic.
  我遇到大塞車了。

» I will arrive there about half an hour later.
  我大概半個小時後到那。

» I am afraid I will be late for the appointment.
  恐怕我約會要遲到。

» I got stuck in an elevator!
  我剛被困在電梯裡了。

» My car broke down on my way to your company.
  在去您公司的路上，我的車拋錨了。

» I think I can't get there in time because of traffic jam.
  由於交通堵塞我不能及時到那兒了。

» I am sorry I am a little late.
  對不起，我遲到了一點時間。

» Please tell him that I'll be a little late.
  請告訴他，我會晚點到。

✗ 你一定要知道！✗ *More Tips*

　　當你打電話找不到對方的時候你可以「leave a message」（留話），或是請人家「forward a message」（傳話）。當人家問你「Do you want to leave a message?」（你要不要留話？），你就可以說「Yes. Please tell him to call me back as soon as possible.」（要，請你要他回來後馬上打電話給我。）。

11 變更拜訪時間

📚 關鍵單字&片語 Words & Phrases

something	[ˈsʌmθɪn]	代 某事
need to	[nid tu]	片 需要
come up	[kʌm ʌp]	片 發生
cancel	[ˈkænsl]	動 取消
in the morning	[ɪn ðə ˈmɔrnɪn]	片 在早上
make it	[mek ɪt]	片 能夠出席

😊 情境會話 Conversation

B This is Jacky Chen speaking, I have *something* urgent and *need to* speak to Mr. Pan.

A I am sorry. Mr. Pan is not in now.

B I have an appointment with him at 2 o'clock this afternoon, but something urgent has *come up*. I would like to *cancel* it.

A I see.

B Is Mr. Pan available tomorrow?

A How about tomorrow at 9 o'clock *in the morning*?

B I can *make it*.

B：我是陳傑克，我有急事找潘先生。
A：對不起，真不巧潘先生正好外出了。
B：我原來和他今天下午兩點有約，但因為有別的急事，我想要取消。
A：明白了。
B：潘先生明天有空嗎？
A：明天上午九點怎麼樣？
B：可以。

超實用精選短句 *Useful Sentences*

» I have something important to tell Mr. Wang.
我有重要的事找王先生。

» I would like to cancel our appointment tomorrow.
我想要取消明天的約會。

» Can we postpone our meeting?
我們可以把會議延期嗎？

» We can meet another day.
我們可以改天再見面。

» Can we take a rain check?
我們可以改期嗎？

» I am sorry, but I can't meet with you today.
我很抱歉，今天無法和你見面了。

» I am very busy now. I'll talk to you later.
我現在很忙，等等再說。

» I will be free after 4 p.m. tomorrow.
我明天下午四點以後會有空。

» How about 10 o'clock tomorrow morning?
明天上午十點左右如何？

» Could we postpone our meeting to next Monday?
我們下禮拜一再見面怎麼樣？

» I am not available until the day after tomorrow.
我後天才有空。

» I am afraid I have to cancel the appointment this time.
我恐怕得取消這次約會了。

你一定要知道！ *More Tips*

「urgent」是緊急的意思，如「I have something urgent to tell you.」（我有一件緊急的事要告訴你。），「This is not urgent, you can finish it tomorrow.」（這並不急，你可以明天再做完。）。

12 未事先約定之拜訪

📖 關鍵單字&片語 Words & Phrases

out	[aʊt]	副 外出
expect	[ɪkˋspɛkt]	動 等待
any	[ˋɛnɪ]	形 任何
get back	[gɛt bæk]	片 回來
wait for	[wet fɔr]	片 等待
else	[ɛls]	副 另外的
How about this...	[haʊ əˋbaʊt ðɪs]	片 這樣好了……

😊 情境會話 Conversation

A Excuse me, is Mr. Chen in now? I am Chen, Zhi-Ming from Sweden Pine.

B I am very sorry, but Mr. Chen is _out_. Is he _expecting_ you?

A No, I didn't make _any_ appointment with him. When do you think he will _get back_?

B I am not sure, do you want to _wait for_ him?

A No, I have something _else_ to do.

A _How about this_, when Mr. Chen gets back, please pass on this sample to him.

B Sure, I will do it.

A：對不起，陳先生在嗎？我是瑞典松木的陳志明。
B：非常抱歉，陳先生外出了，您和他有約嗎？
A：不，沒有預先約好。他什麼時候會回來呢？
B：我不知道，您要等他嗎？
A：不，我還有事。
A：這樣好了，如果陳先生回來，請把這個樣品轉交給他。
B：好的，我會的。

超實用精選短句 *Useful Sentences*

» I am sorry, Mr. Black is not in his office now.
很抱歉，布萊克先生現在不在辦公室。

» Have you made an appointment?
您有預約嗎？

» Would you like to wait for a moment?
您願意等一會兒嗎？

» Do you know when he will get back?
您知道他什麼時候回來嗎？

» I want to meet your boss right now.
我現在想見你們老闆。

» Please make an appointment next time.
下次請先預約。

» I am afraid I must see him right now.
恐怕我現在必須見他。

» I will be happy to wait.
我很樂意等候。

» Are you willing to wait for a moment?
您願意等一下嗎？

» I'll let you know when he is available.
等他有空見你的時候，我會告知你。

» Would you please give him the documents when he gets back?
他回來的時候請您把這個文件交給他好嗎？

» I didn't make any appointment beforehand.
我沒有事先預約。

你一定要知道！ *More Tips*

「appointment」特別指較正式的「約會」：「I have an appointment with my dentist this afternoon.」（我下午和我的牙醫有約。）、「Did you make an appointment with John first?」（你有先和約翰預約嗎？）。

13 婉拒見面

📚 關鍵單字＆片語 Words & Phrases

event	[ɪˋvɛnt]	名	事件
downtown	[ˋdaʊnˏtaʊn]	名	市區、市中心
emergency	[ɪˋmɝdʒənsɪ]	名	緊急事件
regional	[ˋridʒənəl]	形	區域性的
set up	[sɛt ʌp]	片	安排
authority	[əˋθɔrətɪ]	名	權利
release	[rɪˋlis]	動	公開

😊 情境會話 Conversation

A The company has a marketing **_event downtown_** this weekend, so the rest of this week doesn't look good for me.

A If it is an **_emergency_**, I will suggest you contact the **_regional_** manager. He might be able to **_set_** you **_up_** with another sales person.

A I am sorry I don't have the **_authority_** to **_release_** any other sales persons' contact information, but I can give you our regional manager's contact info.

A I am sorry that I can't help you this time.

A：公司這週末在市中心有場行銷會，所以這星期接下來幾天我都抽不出時間。

A：如果是緊急事件，我建議您聯絡區經理。他可能可以幫您安排另一個業務人員。

A：很抱歉我不能給您任何其他業務人員的聯絡方式，不過我可以給您我們區經理的聯絡方式。

A：很抱歉我這次沒辦法為您服務。

🔊 超實用精選短句 *Useful Sentences*

» Can you come another day?
您可以改天再來嗎？

» I am afraid that I won't be able to meet with you today.
我今天恐怕沒辦法跟您碰面。

» Wait a minute. Let me check my schedule.
請稍等。讓我查查我的行程表。

» I am sorry. I am going to attend a meeting tomorrow.
抱歉，我明天要去參加一個會議。

» Perhaps we can meet some other day.
或許我們可以改天再見面。

» I would have done it, but I had no time.
我本來要辦這事的，可是沒時間。

» I want to schedule a meeting with you this Friday.
我想跟您在本週五開個會。

» I hope you could come to the party.
希望您能夠參加這個派對。

» Would you please call me if you have time?
如果您有時間的話打電話給我好嗎？

» There is something wrong with my stomach.
我的胃怪怪的。

» I am going on a business trip tomorrow.
我明天要出差。

» I wish I could help you in the near future.
希望在不久的將來能幫助你。

✏ 你一定要知道！✏ *More Tips*

告知他人未能赴約時，通常會在道歉的同時，附帶說明原因，如：
「I regret to tell you that I will be unable to meet you on the day we scheduled, because something serious happened to our factory.」（很抱歉，我將無法在我們約好的那天去與您碰面，因為我們的工廠發生了嚴重的事情。）。

14 變更會面地點

📚 關鍵單字＆片語 Words & Phrases

realize	[ˋrɪəˌlaɪz]	動 了解
be able to	[bi ˋebḷ tu]	片 可以……
come around	[kʌm əˋraʊnd]	片 過來見面
instead	[ɪnˋstɛd]	副 作為替代
close by	[klos baɪ]	片 在旁邊
block	[blɑk]	名 街區
miss	[mɪs]	動 錯過

😊 情境會話 Conversation

A Mrs. Albert, I just ***realized*** that I won't be able to meet in your office today, because there is an emergency in the office and it took longer than I thought.

A I am just wondering if you will ***be able to come around*** my office this afternoon ***instead***.

A We can meet in my office or maybe have a lunch meeting in a cafe ***close by***.

A The cafe is at the corner of 11th Street and 8th Avenue. It's just two ***blocks*** away from my office. You can't ***miss*** it.

A：亞伯特女士，因為公司有個緊急狀況，比我原來所以為的需要花更長時間來處理，因此，我想我今天是無法到您辦公室去跟您碰面了。
A：不知道可不可以改由您今天到我辦公室附近來呢？
A：我們可以在我辦公室碰面，或者也可以在附近的咖啡館開個午餐會議。
A：那個咖啡館在第十一街與第八大道的轉角處，離我公司只有兩街區。您一定會找到的。

✍ 超實用精選短句 *Useful Sentences*

» I am sorry to tell you that we have to meet in another place.
我很遺憾告訴您我們必須變更會面地點。

» I am afraid that you have to change the route.
恐怕你得改變路線了。

» Please remember the new location for our conference.
請記下我們新的會議地點。

» I am sorry that I can not meet you in your office.
抱歉我不能在您的辦公室跟您見面了。

» We have some situations here.
我們這邊出了些狀況。

» I should have got there, but something happened.
我本該到那的，但是出事了。

» I want to tell you the new address.
我想告訴你新地址。

» I still hope you could be present on time.
我仍然希望您能夠準時出席。

» Could you come here instead of going to the hotel?
可不可以請您過來而不是去飯店？

» I am sure you can find it.
我相信你能夠找到。

» I am terribly sorry for the change.
對於此次變更我感到非常地抱歉。

» Anyway, thank you very much for coming.
無論如何，非常感謝您能來。

✎ 你一定要知道！ ✎ *More Tips*

「miss」在這裡是指「錯過」，「You won't miss it.」是表示「你一定會找到那個地方的。」；「miss」也有「想念」的意思，如：「I will be missing you very much after you leave.」（你離開之後我會很想念你的。）。

15 資料準備不全

關鍵單字&片語 *Words & Phrases*

forget	[fɚˋgɛt]	動	忘記
form	[fɔrm]	名	表格
electronic copy	[ɪlɛkˋtrɑnɪk]	名	電子檔
billing address	[ˋbɪlɪŋ əˋdrɛs]	名	郵寄地址
in order to	[ɪn ˋɔrdɚ tu]	片	為了
qualified	[ˋkwɑlɪfaɪd]	形	符合條件的

情境會話 *Conversation*

A I am sorry that I *forgot* to bring the *form* that you faxed to me yesterday.

A I will try to see if anyone from the office can send me an *electronic copy* to my iPhone.

A There is some information missing in the form. We will need your client to give us his *billing address*.

A Please send the document by E-mail or fax by 2:30 p.m. tomorrow *in order to* be *qualified* as an urgent application.

A If there is any other info I need from your clients, I will contact you.

A：很抱歉，我忘記把您昨天傳真給我的那張表格帶過來了。

A：我想辦法看辦公室是否有人可以傳電子檔到我的 iPhone。

A：表格裡有些資訊漏掉了。我們需要您的客戶給我們他的帳單郵寄地址。

A：請在明天下午兩點半之前將文件以電子郵件或傳真方式寄過來，才能符合急件資格。

A：如果需要任何您的客戶的其他資訊，我會與您聯繫的。

超實用精選短句 *Useful Sentences*

» Do you have any more brochures?
你還有更多的宣傳冊子嗎？

» I am afraid that I have to get some back.
我恐怕得去拿些回來了。

» I have no more brochures at hand now.
我現在手頭沒有更多的宣傳手冊了。

» I am sorry that I left it at home.
很抱歉我把它忘在家裡了。

» Is there anybody getting some copies here?
有沒有人拿些副本到這來？

» Why not send a fax to our branch?
為什麼不發傳真去分公司呢？

» Please contact us if you want more information.
如果您想獲得更多的資訊請聯繫我們。

» I need more information about the product.
我需要更多有關這種產品的資訊。

» Could you please get more brochures here?
請您多帶些宣傳冊子過來好嗎？

» I can email the form back to you.
我可以將表格以電子郵件回傳給您。

» I will email you after going back to my office.
我回到辦公室再寄電子郵件給你。

» I will try to get some more information.
我會試著獲取更多資料的。

你一定要知道！ *More Tips*

「hard copy」指的是「列印稿」，而「electronic copy」指的是「電子檔」，如：「The printer is not working now. I can't make a hard copy of this electronic copy for you right now.」（印表機現在不能用。所以我現在無法幫您將這個電子檔印出來。）。

Part

10

接單
細節

篇

→ **Part 10 音檔連結** ←

因各家手機系統不同，若無法直接掃描，
仍可以至以下電腦雲端連結下載收聽。
（https://tinyurl.com/ejrdahcm）

01 接訂單

📖 關鍵單字&片語 *Words & Phrases*

container	[kənˋtenɚ]	名 容器
or	[ɔr]	介 或者
account	[əˋkaunt]	名 帳號
enter	[ˋɛntɚ]	動 進入
system	[ˋsɪstəm]	名 系統
quote	[kwot]	動 引用

😊 情境會話 *Conversation*

B I would like to order 1 *container* of apple juice to arrive by January 25th.

A Are you a new customer? *Or* have you had an *account* number already assigned?

B My account number is 11123.

A Thank you! Please hold on and let me check for you. Here you are. Are you Mr. Chang?

B Yes. So, have you *entered* my order into your computer *system*?

A Sure. Your order number is AD567, please *quote* the number when you have any questions regarding the order.

B：我想下一櫃蘋果汁訂單，交貨日在 1 月 25 日。
A：您是我們的新客戶嗎？或您已有我們公司的客戶編號？
B：我的客戶編號是 11123。
A：謝謝您，讓我為您查詢。有了，您是張先生嗎？
B：正是。所以我的訂單進入您的記錄系統了嗎？
A：當然，您的訂單號碼是 AD567，當您對訂單有任何問題時，請您報上該號碼。

超實用精選短句 *Useful Sentences*

» You can have 1-year warranty on our products.
我們的產品提供一年保固。

» Would you like to place an order right now?
您現在就想下訂單嗎？

» I want to buy some computer software.
我想買一些電腦軟體。

» I come here to place an order.
我來是想訂一批貨。

» What will be the earliest possible date of shipment?
最早能在什麼時候交貨呢？

» Here's your order number 1585639945.
您的訂單號碼是 1585639945。

» Delivery within three working days is guaranteed.
我們保證訂貨會在三個工作天內送到。

» Please enter my order into your computer system.
請把我的訂單錄入您的系統裡。

» When shall I receive the goods?
我什麼時候能收到這批貨？

» I want to order 5,000 units.
我想要訂 5,000 個。

» You can have a 20% discount if you order more than 10,000 units.
如果你下訂超過 10,000 個，可以打八折。

» If you have any questions, please contact us.
如果您還有任何問題，請與我們聯繫。

你一定要知道！ *More Tips*

　　專業的商業接線生，在接電話的時候，可以先報上公司的名字，再告知對方自己的名字以增加親切感：「Hello, this is the Grand Industry. I am Joyce, May I help you please?」（你好，這裡是格藍產業，我是喬伊斯，我能為你服務嗎？）。

02 缺貨通知

📚 關鍵單字&片語 *Words & Phrases*

currently	[ˋkɝəntlɪ]	副	現在、目前
out of stock	[aʊt ɑv stɑk]	片	缺貨
just	[dʒʌst]	副	剛剛、剛才
short of supply	[ʃɔrt ɑv səˋplaɪ]	片	缺貨
production	[prəˋdʌkʃən]	名	生產
surely	[ˋʃʊrlɪ]	副	當然

😊 情境會話 *Conversation*

🅐 I am sorry to inform you that the product you ordered is ***currently*** ***out of stock***.

🅑 What? I can't believe what you are saying. You ***just*** confirmed my order yesterday but now you are saying the product is ***short of supply***?

🅐 I am so sorry. We are expecting a 1-week delay. As soon as the new packaging materials arrive in our factory, we can start the ***production*** right away.

🅑 Are you sure this time you will have the product delivered on time?

🅐 ***Surely***. I will do my best.

A：我很抱歉的通知您，您所訂購的產品目前缺貨。
B：你說什麼？我真不敢相信你現在所說的，你昨天才確認我的訂單，現在你居然告訴我你的產品缺貨。
A：我真的很抱歉。我們預計將延遲 1 個禮拜。只要我們收到新的包裝材料，就可以馬上安排生產。
B：你確定這次你會準時交貨？
A：當然，我會盡力。

🔊 超實用精選短句 *Useful Sentences*

» I am sorry that this kind of mini skirts is out of stock.
我很抱歉，這種迷你裙沒有現貨。

» The product you ordered is out of stock now.
你訂購的產品目前缺貨。

» That's alright. I'll cancel my order.
沒關係，我取消訂單。

» You shouldn't have made the mistake.
你不應該出這種錯的。

» As a matter of fact, the camera has run out of stock for several days.
事實上，這種相機已經缺貨好幾天了。

» We'll replenish the stock of the dictionary.
我們會補這本字典的貨。

» The goods you ordered is short of supply.
您訂的貨暫時缺貨。

» The books have been sold out but we'll replenish our stock.
這書都賣光了，但我們會陸續進貨。

» When will you replenish your stock?
你們什麼時候會再進貨？

» We will lay in a stock of the keyboard next week.
我們下週會補鍵盤的貨。

» So when shall I receive my order?
那麼我們什麼時候能收到貨物呢？

» Are you sure this time it will be okay?
你確定這次會沒問題嗎？

⚡ 你一定要知道！⚡ *More Tips*

　　以下的幾個字都可以用來表示「缺貨」：「out of stock」、「short of supply」、「insufficient product supply」等等。

03 商品損壞處理

📚 關鍵單字＆片語 *Words & Phrases*

damage	[ˈdæmɪdʒ]	名 損壞
shipment	[ˈʃɪpmənt]	名 運送
clear	[klɪr]	形 清楚的
warehouseman	[ˈwɛrˌhausmən]	名 倉庫人員
unload	[ʌnˈlod]	動 卸貨
wet	[wɛt]	形 濕的

😊 情境會話 *Conversation*

A I am calling to complain about product ***damage*** of the ***shipment*** I received yesterday.

B I am sorry to hear that. Can I have your order number to process your complaint?

A 0022123.

B Could you give me a ***clear*** idea of the damage situation, please?

A When my ***warehousemen*** ***unloaded*** the container yesterday, the product was ***wet*** outside the shipping carton.

B That's too bad. May I know how you want us to proceed with the damaged products?

A Please exchange them for me.

A：我打電話是為了抱怨我昨天所收到的產品有損壞。
B：很抱歉。請給我您的訂單號碼以便為您處理。
A：0022123。
B：請告訴我詳細的損壞情形好嗎？
A：倉庫人員昨天卸櫃的時候，發現產品的運送外箱溼了。
B：那太糟了。請問您想要我們如何處理這些損壞品呢？
A：請換新貨給我。

超實用精選短句 *Useful Sentences*

» I demand a refund for damaged product.
對於毀損的產品我要求退費。

» I apologize for causing you unnecessary troubles.
給您造成不必要的麻煩我感到很抱歉。

» How much goods were damaged?
有多少貨物被毀損了？

» Why have some of the goods we received today been damaged?
為什麼我今天收到的一部分貨物毀損了？

» I do apologize for damaging your products during transportation.
對於運輸中毀損了您的貨品我向您道歉。

» We promise that such error won't happen again.
我們保證這樣的失誤再也不會發生。

» We will definitely exchange your goods.
我們一定會為您更換貨品。

» You may exchange the damaged goods but we won't refund the money.
你可更換毀損貨物但我們不會退錢。

» We will settle the matter as soon as possible.
我們會儘快解決此事。

» Please accept my sincere apology for our carelessness.
為我們的疏忽向您真誠地道歉。

» Is it possible to exchange them for me?
可以換新貨給我嗎？

你一定要知道！ *More Tips*

　　表示遺憾的說法有：「That's too bad.」（那真糟糕。）、「I am really sorry to hear that.」（聽到這事讓我覺得很遺憾。）、「It is really a pity.」（真得很遺憾。）等等。

04 催收帳款

📖 關鍵單字&片語 *Words & Phrases*

sunshine	[ˈsʌnˌʃaɪn]	名 陽光
week	[wik]	名 週
Letter of Credit	[ˈlɛtɚ ɑv ˈkrɛdɪt]	名（=LC）信用狀
last	[læst]	形 最後過去的
clear	[klɪr]	動 結帳、償清債務

😊 情境會話 *Conversation*

A This is Karen speaking. May I help you?

B Yes. I am calling from the *Sunshine* Company. I received your order 2 *weeks* ago, but as of today I have not received your *Letter of Credit* for payment.

A Really? But I issued it *last* Wednesday. Didn't you receive notice from the bank?

B Sorry, I didn't.

A OK, I will check with the bank right away. But it will not affect our product delivery, will it?

B I am sure the product will go on time if you have your payment *cleared* already.

A：我是凱倫。可以為您服務嗎？
B：是的。我從陽光公司打電話來，我在兩星期前收到貴公司的訂單，但是直到今天，我還沒收到您的信用狀。
A：真的嗎？但是我已經在上星期三就開了，您沒收到任何銀行的通知嗎？
B：對不起，沒有。
A：好的，我馬上與銀行聯絡，但這不會影響到我們的產品交貨吧？
B：我相信只要您付清款項，產品會準時交貨。

🔊 超實用精選短句 *Useful Sentences*

» I am afraid that we haven't received your payment yet.
恐怕我們還沒有收到您的貨款。

» It has been several weeks since we sent you our first invoice.
我們的第一份發票已經寄出有好幾個星期了。

» What we expected is nothing less than a timely payment.
及時付款正是我們所盼望的。

» Can you give me a reasonable explanation?
您能給我一個合理的解釋嗎？

» We hope you could clear the payment within three days.
我希望您能在三日內付款。

» I want to know about your payment plan.
我想瞭解一下你的付款計畫。

» This is unpleasant for both of us and is damaging your credit.
這對我們雙方都不好，同時也損害您的信用。

» The debt totals to $50,000.
你的欠款總計為五萬元。

» We will pay you as soon as possible.
我們會儘快付款。

» We are terribly sorry for delayed payment.
對於延遲付款我們感到非常抱歉。

» If not, we will take legal action to collect the money.
如果不付款的話，我們就會採取法律行動追討欠款了。

✍ 你一定要知道！ ✍ *More Tips*

當你請人家在電話上稍待一下，你可以說：「Please wait for a moment.」（請等一下。）、「Please hold on.」（請稍待。）、「Please hang on.」（請等一下。）、「Hold, please. I will make the connection for you.」（請等一下，我幫你轉接。）。

05 訂單更改

📚 關鍵單字&片語 Words & Phrases

possible	[ˈpɑsəbl̩]	形 可能的
sunscreen	[ˈsʌnˌskrin]	名 防曬霜
ml	[ˈmɪlɪˌlitɚ]	名（=milliliter）毫升
lipstick	[ˈlɪpˌstɪk]	名 唇膏、口紅
series	[ˈsiriz]	名 系列
excellent	[ˈɛksl̩ənt]	形 極好的
service	[ˈsɝvɪs]	名 服務

😊 情境會話 Conversation

A My name is Amber, and I placed an order on April 30.

A My order number is 25689.

A I would like to know if you have shipped my order.

A If it is **possible**, I would like to add some more items on that order.

A Please add two more bottles of NIVEA **sunscreen**, 100 **ml** ones, and two tubes of **lipstick** from the same **series**.

A Thank you so much for your **excellent service**.

A：我的名字叫安柏。我在 4 月 30 號那天有訂貨。
A：我的訂單號碼是 25689。
A：我想知道你們是否已經寄出我訂的貨。
A：如果可以的話，我想追加訂單。
A：請多加兩支 100 毫升的妮維亞防曬霜，還有兩條同系列的唇膏。
A：非常感謝您良好的服務。

超實用精選短句 *Useful Sentences*

» I placed an order with you on May 11th.
我在五月十一號那天有向你下訂單。

» My order number is 31168.
我的訂單號碼是 31168。

» I wonder that if you have shipped my order.
我想知道你們是否已經寄出我訂的貨。

» Can we make a change in our order?
我們的訂貨單可不可以更改？

» If you want to cancel or change your order, please contact us at once.
如果您需要刪除或更改訂單請立即通知我們。

» Why do I have to pay $20 administration fee if I change the order?
為什麼我更改訂單就必須付 20 美元的手續費呢？

» Can the fee be waived since I am adding more items?
既然我是追加訂貨，那筆費用是不是就能取消？

» No change or cancellation once order is confirmed.
確認訂單後，你無法更改或取消訂單。

» How do you process a change of order?
更改訂單的程序是怎樣的？

» We need to make a change on our last order.
上回的訂單我們需要更改。

» We need to issue an additional order.
我們需要追加訂單。

你一定要知道！ *More Tips*

「administration fee」指的是「行政費用、手續費」，也可以表示為「administrative charge」。如：「An administrative charge of $50 will be required to change your original order.」（要變更您原始的訂單，將需要收一筆 50 美元的手續費。）。

06 訂單取消

📚 關鍵單字＆片語 Words & Phrases

reason	[ˈrizn̩]	名 理由
have to	[hæv tu]	片 必須
credit	[ˈkrɛdɪt]	名 信用
pay	[pe]	動 付帳
debit card	[ˈdɛbɪt kɑrd]	名 銀行卡
cancellation fee	[ˌkænsl̩ˈeʃən fi]	名 解約金
charge	[tʃɑrdʒ]	動 收費

😊 情境會話 Conversation

Ⓐ I need to cancel an order for emergency **_reason_**. Here is my order receipt.

Ⓑ May I ask why you **_have to_** cancel this order?

Ⓐ It is because there is not enough **_credit_** in my credit card account.

Ⓐ And I can't **_pay_** with my **_debit card_** because I need to keep the cash for other expenses.

Ⓑ In that case, may I remind you that there will be a **_cancellation fee_**?

Ⓐ Yes, please **_charge_** the cancellation fee to my credit card.

A：因為緊急原因，我必須取消訂單。這是我的訂貨收據。
B：可以請問您為何必須取消這筆訂單嗎？
A：那是因為我的信用卡的額度不夠了。
A：而且我無法用我的金融卡付錢，因為我必須留著錢付其他費用。
B：那樣的話，容我提醒您得付一筆解約金喔。
A：好的，請用我的信用卡刷這筆解約金。

超實用精選短句 *Useful Sentences*

» We have to cancel the order for some reason.
由於某種原因我們不得不取消訂單。

» Can you tell me why you want to cancel this order?
請您告訴我為什麼想取消這筆訂單呢？

» If you fail to make the shipment soon, we will cancel the order.
如果你們不能近期發貨，我們將取消訂單。

» We insist on immediate delivery.
我們要求立即發貨。

» Can we cancel the order?
我們可以取消訂貨嗎？

» We request you to compensate for the loss caused by the cancellation of the order.
我方要求貴公司賠償由於取消訂單造成的損失。

» No cancellation is allowed after payment remittance.
匯款後，不能取消訂單。

» If you want to cancel your order, please contact us.
如果您需要取消訂單請及時通知我們。

» Can you tell me how to cancel the order?
請告訴我如何取消訂單好嗎？

» You cannot cancel the order unilaterally.
你們不能單方面取消訂貨。

» Please make a payment within three days, or we will cancel the order.
請於三天內匯款，否則我們將取消訂單。

你一定要知道！ *More Tips*

「debit card」就是「金融卡」，有刷卡功能，卻是刷自己帳戶裡的錢。而「bank card」則是單純的「提款卡」。如：「I'm afraid that I can't pay for the MP3 player with my debit card because there isn't enough money in my bank account.」（我恐怕不能用金融卡買這個 MP3 播放器，因為我的帳戶裡錢不夠。）

07 索取發票／收據

📖 關鍵單字&片語 *Words & Phrases*

bought	[bɔt]	動（buy 的過去式）買
bicycle	[ˈbaɪsɪk̩l]	名 腳踏車
apply for	[əˈplaɪ fɔr]	片 申請
paper	[ˈpepɚ]	名 文件
as long as	[æz lɔŋ æz]	片 只要
claim expense	[klem ɪkˈspɛns]	片 報帳

😊 情境會話 *Conversation*

A I *bought* a Knell *bicycle* from your store yesterday, but I didn't get a receipt from you.

A I will need a receipt to *apply for* the company expense.

A I don't have any other purchased *papers* provided by you for that purchase.

A But I paid with my credit card, and I do have the credit card charge slip here.

B Is the purchase price $1595?

A Yes, *as long as* the price and the item are shown on the receipt, I can use them to *claim* this *expense* from my company.

A：我昨天在你們店裡買了一台尼爾腳踏車，不過我忘了跟你們拿收據了。
A：我需要收據才能向公司報帳。
A：我並沒有其他你們所提供購買這件東西的購買單據。
A：不過我是用信用卡付帳的，我這裡的確有信用卡簽單。
B：購買的價格是 1595 元嗎？
A：是的，只要收據上有價格和品項，我就能跟公司請款了。

超實用精選短句 *Useful Sentences*

» I hope you could give me the receipt for my payment at once.
我希望您立即為我的付款開具收據。

» I haven't got the receipt from you yet.
你還沒給我收據。

» I have called you several times to request the receipt.
我已經給你打了好幾次電話索要收據。

» I need a receipt to claim expense from my company.
我需要收據去跟公司報帳。

» I am terribly sorry for not giving you the receipt.
非常抱歉忘記給您發票了。

» Could I see your receipt, please?
我能看看你的發票嗎？

» Please make out a receipt for these goods.
請開一張這些貨的發票。

» Thank you for your cooperation.
謝謝您的合作。

» I forgot to ask for a receipt for my purchase yesterday.
我昨天忘記索取此次購物的發票了。

» Please write out a receipt so that I can apply for the company expense.
請寫一張收據給我，讓我可以跟公司報帳。

» There you go.
給你。

» This is exactly what I need.
這就是我所需要的東西。

你一定要知道！ *More Tips*

　　若是交易已完成，而對方尚未開立發票，則可去電：「I will be needing a receipt for tax purposes. Can you send it to me by express delivery today?」（我需要收據做報稅之用。能否請你今天將收據快遞給我？）。

Part

11

處理糾紛／狀況篇

→ Part 11 音檔連結 ←

因各家手機系統不同，若無法直接掃描，
仍可以至以下電腦雲端連結下載收聽。
（https://tinyurl.com/2zxek7mk）

01 延遲交貨

📚 關鍵單字&片語 Words & Phrases

receive	[rɪ`siv]	動 收到
notice	[`notɪs]	名 通知
sincere	[sɪn`sɪr]	形 誠摯的
apology	[ə`pɑlədʒɪ]	名 道歉
packaging	[`pækɪdʒɪŋ]	名 包裝
delay	[dɪ`le]	名 延遲

😊 情境會話 Conversation

A I should have *received* my product by today, but I have not received anything from your company.

B But according to the computer records, your product was not ready until today. I am terribly sorry.

A I do not think it is my problem. You should have given me a *notice* in advance.

B Please accept my *sincere* *apology*. Our *packaging* material has been in short supply for three days. I am sure it is the main reason for the *delay*.

A：我應該在昨天收到我所訂購的產品，但是直到今天我卻什麼都沒有收到。

B：但是根據電腦記錄，您的產品要到今天才會準備好。我真的很抱歉。

A：這不是我的問題。你應該在事前就通知我。

B：請接受我誠摯的歉意。我們的包裝物料已經缺貨三天，我想這是延誤交貨的主要原因。

超實用精選短句 *Useful Sentences*

» The goods should have been delivered the day before yesterday.
這批貨物本應前天就該送達的。

» Please deliver the goods we ordered immediately.
請立即發送我們訂購的貨物。

» I am so sorry for delaying the goods.
延遲為您送貨我感到非常抱歉。

» How do you explain the delay?
對於交貨延遲您作何解釋呢？

» How long will the delay last?
會延遲多久？

» The delivery will take three extra days.
貨物會晚三天到達。

» I am sorry to tell you that we can't deliver on schedule.
很抱歉告訴你我們無法準時送貨。

» The next shipment will arrive on time.
下次送貨會準時。

» The next shipment won't be late.
下次送貨不會延遲了。

» I hope there won't be a next time.
我希望不會再有下次了。

» We are terribly sorry for delayed shipment.
對於交貨延遲我們感到非常抱歉。

» We promise this won't happen again.
我們保證這種事情不會再發生。

你一定要知道！ *More Tips*

　　對不起的說法，除了「I'm sorry.」之外，還可以說：「Please accept my sincere apology.」（請接受我真誠的歉意。）、「I really do apologize for the inconvenience that we have caused you.」（我對我們所造成的不方便感到抱歉。）等等。

02 產品有瑕疵

📖 關鍵單字&片語 *Words & Phrases*

charger	[ˈtʃɑrdʒɚ]	名 充電器
broken	[ˈbrokən]	形 壞的
arrive	[əˈraɪv]	動 到達
exchange	[ɪksˈtʃendʒ]	動 交換
return	[rɪˈtɜn]	動 退回
defective	[dɪˈfɛktɪv]	形 有缺陷的
deduct	[dɪˈdʌkt]	動 扣除

😊 情境會話 *Conversation*

A I received my cellular phone yesterday but I found the *charger* did not work.

B I see. Was the package *broken* when you received the product?

A I do not think so. It was well packed when it *arrived*.

B OK, then I can have it *exchanged*.

B I will send you a new one but please *return* the *defective* charger to our company. I will have the delivery charges *deducted* from your bill.

A That would be great. Thank you very much.

A：我昨天收到我的行動電話產品，但是我發現充電器不能用。
B：我了解了。您收到產品時是否有發現包裝破損呢？
A：沒有，當它抵達時包裝是完好的。
B：好的，我可以為您換貨。
B：我會寄個新的給您，但是請協助將有瑕疵的充電器退還給我們，我會在帳單中扣除退貨運費。
A：那太好了，非常感謝您。

超實用精選短句 *Useful Sentences*

» I am so sorry for delivering the defective goods.
非常抱歉寄送了有瑕疵的貨物。

» I found a big flaw in these goods.
在這些貨物中我發現了個很大的瑕疵。

» The air conditioner I bought yesterday doesn't work.
我昨天買了冷氣不能用了。

» We feel that there are too many defective items.
我們覺得瑕疵品太多了。

» We have to return these products. There are too many defects.
我們必須退回這些產品，瑕疵太多了。

» Of course. We will accept the return of these items.
我們當然接受退貨。

» One fourth of the products are defective.
四分之一的產品有瑕疵。

» Since the product is faulty, we have no choice but to withhold the payment.
既然產品有瑕疵，我們不得不扣住貨款。

» We found that nearly 20% of the package is broken.
我們發現有將近 20% 的包裝已破損。

» Can you replace all the defective items for us?
你能替我們更換所有的瑕疵品嗎？

» You can get refunds on any defective merchandise.
任何瑕疵商品都可以退款。

» I'd like to exchange a new one for you.
我願意換一個新的給你。

你一定要知道！ *More Tips*

　　產品有瑕疵的時候，可以打電話到「Customer Service」（客戶服務中心）去詢問換貨事宜：「The video player that I bought does not work. Can I exchange it ?」（我買的錄放影機壞了，我可以換新的嗎？）。

03 請求賠償

📚 關鍵單字&片語 *Words & Phrases*

case	[kes]	名	箱子
debit note	[`dɛbɪt not]	名	欠款單
loss	[lɔs]	名	損失
extremely	[ɪk`strimlɪ]	副	極度地
fill out	[fɪl aʊt]	片	填寫
complaint form	[kəm`plent fɔrm]	名	申訴表

😊 情境會話 *Conversation*

Ⓐ I received your product on October 12th, but found some of the shipping *cases* were broken.

Ⓑ Really? May I know how many of the cases you received were broken?

Ⓐ About 35.

Ⓐ The product quality was affected by the broken cases.

Ⓐ I will send you a *debit note* to claim my *loss*.

Ⓑ I am *extremely* sorry. Can you help me *fill out* the *complaint form*? It will speed up the processing of your claim.

Ⓐ OK. Just send the form to me.

A：我在 10 月 12 日收到您的產品，卻發現部份外箱破損。
B：真的嗎？可否告訴我有多少箱在您收到的時候是破損的？
A：大約有 35 箱。
A：產品品質因為外箱破損而受到影響了。
A：我會寄份帳單給您索取賠償。
B：我真的很抱歉。你可以幫忙我填寫申訴表嗎？這樣會加速我們對於您的賠償處理。
A：好吧，把它寄給我。

超實用精選短句 *Useful Sentences*

» Why don't you claim for compensation?
為什麼不要求賠償呢？

» Since the problem is on the goods, I have to claim my loss.
既然問題在貨物本身，我不得不提出索賠了。

» How do you solve the problem?
您要如何解決這個問題呢？

» We accept your claim for compensation for the delay of the shipment.
我們接受你們對於延遲發貨的賠償要求。

» You should pay compensation for our loss.
你們應該賠償我們的損失。

» How do you plan to deal with it?
你打算怎麼處理這件事呢？

» We accept your claim for compensation.
我們接受您的賠償要求。

» What do you like us to do?
您希望我們怎麼做呢？

» We will certainly compensate for you.
我們一定會對您作出賠償的。

» If you don't carry out the contract, you have to pay us compensation.
你如果不履行合同就得向我們作出賠償。

» You can accept compensation as well as return goods.
您既可以退貨也可以接受賠償。

你一定要知道！ *More Tips*

「speed up」是「加速」的意思：「Could you speed up the car? I am really late.」（你可不可以開快一點？我已經遲到很久了。）、「I really have to speed up. I should have finished this yesterday.」（我真的應該快一點，我昨天就應該把這個做完了。）。

04 抱怨客服

📖 關鍵單字&片語 *Words & Phrases*

time	[ˈtaɪm]	名	次數
question	[ˈkwɛstʃən]	名	問題
orientation	[ˌorɪɛnˈteʃən]	名	（對新人的）情況介紹
line	[laɪn]	名	線路
related	[rɪˈletɪd]	形	相關的
mailing address	[ˈmelɪŋ əˈdrɛs]	名	聯絡地址
change	[tʃendʒ]	動	改變

😊 情境會話 *Conversation*

A I have called your customer service 4 *times* but no one answered my *question*.

A They just kept me waiting and waiting.

B Oh, please accept my sincere apology. We just had 2 new staff members join the department and they are still in *orientation*. I am sure they did not know how to connect your *line* to the *related* department.

A I just want to have my *mailing address changed*.

B Sure. I will do it for you now.

A：我已經打了 4 次電話給你們的客服部門，但是卻找不到任何人可以回答我的問題。
A：他們只是一直讓我等。
B：喔！請接受我的道歉。我們部門最近來了兩個新員工，正在訓練中，我想他們一定是不知道如何幫你接線至相關部門。
A：我只是要改變我的聯絡地址。
B：當然，我馬上幫您辦。

超實用精選短句 *Useful Sentences*

» Hello, this is Customer Service, may I help you?
您好，這裡是客服部，我可以為您效勞嗎？

» I want to complain about one of your salespersons.
我要投訴你們一位店員。

» Can anybody answer my questions?
有人可以回答我的問題嗎？

» I have a complaint to make.
我有事要投訴。

» May I ask what you are dissatisfied with?
請問你對什麼不滿意呢？

» Can you tell me why my problem is still unsolved?
為什麼我的問題還沒有解決？

» Please accept our apology.
請接受我們的道歉。

» We will solve it as soon as possible.
我們會儘快處理此事。

» Could you tell me what you want us to do?
能否告訴我您想要我們怎麼做呢？

» We are terribly sorry for the fault.
對於我們的失誤我們感到很抱歉。

» I got no response after sending a complaint email.
我寄了投訴信之後都沒有回應。

» I appreciate your consideration.
我感謝您的體諒。

你一定要知道！ *More Tips*

當客人打電話抱怨的時候，好的服務客戶的態度就是要有耐心的聽客人抱怨，並盡速幫客人解決問題：「We will solve the problem for you right away.」（我們馬上幫你解決問題。）、「We will do it for you instantly.」（我們馬上幫你辦。）、「We will deal with it instantly.」（我們馬上為你處理。）。

05 副作用處理

📖 關鍵單字&片語 Words & Phrases

side effect	[saɪd ɪˋfɛkt]	名 副作用
surgical	[ˋsɝdʒɪkl̩]	形 外用的
gather	[ˋgæðɚ]	動 收集
recall	[rɪˋkɔl]	動 召回
stage	[stedʒ]	名 階段
proof	[pruf]	名 證據
occurrence	[əˋkɝəns]	名 發生

😊 情境會話 Conversation

🅐 We have a few complaints from the customers that there are some *side effects* after they use our *surgical* tapes.

🅐 From the reports I *gathered*, those side effects include rashes, itchiness and blisters.

🅐 Before we *recall* this product, I need the testing department to do a few more tests.

🅐 At this *stage*, we will accept a refund if a customer can provide *proof* of the *occurrence* of side effects, such as a doctor's note.

A：我們接獲一些顧客的抱怨，説他們使用我們的醫用膠帶之後出現了一些副作用。
A：我這邊收集到的報告説，那些副作用包含了疹子、發癢還有水泡。
A：在我們回收這項產品之前，我需要試驗部門多做點試驗。
A：現階段，如果顧客能提供發生副作用的證據，如醫生證明，我們就會退款。

📖 超實用精選短句 *Useful Sentences*

» Every drug has possible side effects.
每一種藥都可能有副作用。

» These medicines have severe side effects.
這些藥物具有嚴重的副作用。

» The side effects of the drug are as yet unknown.
這種藥的副作用尚未發現。

» One of the side effects of this drug is you get addicted easily.
這種藥的副作用之一就是容易上癮。

» We received a lot of complaints from the customers.
我們收到了很多消費者的投訴。

» Why didn't you tell me that the drug had side effects?
你為什麼沒告訴我這個藥有副作用？

» Do you know that if the medicine has side effect?
你知道這種藥物有沒有副作用呢？

» It is rare for any drug to be free from side effects.
對任何藥物來說，全然沒有任何副作用是極其罕見的。

» I feel sick after taking that medicine.
吃完那個藥之後我就覺得噁心。

» The management has decided to stop the production of this product.
管理部已經決定停產這項產品。

» We won't ship out any of these surgical tapes until further notice.
在進一步公告出來之前，這些醫用膠帶不會再出貨。

⚡ 你一定要知道！⚡ *More Tips*

　　「doctor's note」指的是「醫生證明」，如：「If you want to excuse from work, you will need to provide a legal document, such as the doctor's note.」（如果你想離開辦公室，你必須提出正式文件才行，例如醫生證明。）

06 要求退貨

📚 關鍵單字&片語 *Words & Phrases*

policy	[ˈpɑləsɪ]	名 政策
receipt	[rɪˈsit]	名 發票
warranty	[ˈwɔrəntɪ]	名 保固
repair	[rɪˈpɛr]	名 修理
cost	[kɔst]	名 花費
issue	[ˈɪʃjʊ]	動 核發
store credit	[stor ˈkrɛdɪt]	名 抵用券

😊 情境會話 *Conversation*

🅐 Mr. Lee, is there any reason why you need a refund for this slow cooker?

🅐 We do have a 30-day refund *policy*. Do you have a purchase *receipt* with you?

🅐 I am sorry, but you purchased this item on March 1st. It has passed the 30-day period.

🅐 But this item is still under *warranty*. We can send this back for *repair* at no *cost*.

🅐 Our store manager agreed to *issue* you *store credit* for this item. You can use it to purchase anything in this store.

A：李先生，請問您要退這個慢燉鍋的理由是什麼呢？
A：我們的確有三十天內退貨政策。您有帶購買收據嗎？
A：很抱歉，您是在三月一日購買這項商品，已經超過三十天的期限了。
A：但這項商品仍享有保固。我們可以把它送回去免費修理。
A：我們經理同意為此商品核發給您本店的抵用券。您可以用來購買本店的任何東西。

超實用精選短句 *Useful Sentences*

» I'd like to refund this washing machine.
我想退掉這台洗衣機。

» If it does not work well, may I bring it back later?
如果它不好用，我可以拿回來退貨嗎？

» May I take a look at your receipt?
我可以看一下收據嗎？

» Sorry, things on sale are not allowed to be refunded.
對不起，折扣商品不退貨。

» What appears to be wrong with the printer?
這台印表機出什麼問題了嗎？

» I'm sorry, I lost my receipt.
對不起，我弄丟了收據。

» Can you look up the sale details for me?
您能不能幫我查查銷售記錄？

» We don't accept returns for bargains.
我們不接受特價商品的退貨。

» You can call our customer service if you have any questions.
有任何問題請您撥打我們的客服電話。

» The return of most items is accepted within 30 days.
大部分商品可在 30 天內退貨。

» Domestic appliances have special returns policies.
家用電器有特別的退貨政策。

» Please check our manual book for more information.
請您查看我們的手冊來瞭解更詳細的資訊。

你一定要知道！ *More Tips*

辦理退貨時，最常見的理由：「We are not satisfied with the quality of the machine.」（我們不滿意這台機器的品質。），若要提出具體理由，可以說：「This vacuum cleaner's suction performance is fairly disappointed.」（這台吸塵器的吸力實在差強人意。）。

07 運送中遺失

📖 關鍵單字&片語 Words & Phrases

ground	[graʊnd]	**名** 地面
ETA	[i ti e]	**縮寫字** (=estimated time of arrival) 預計到達時間
tracking	[ˋtrækɪŋ]	**名** 追蹤
distribute	[dɪˋstrɪbjʊt]	**動** 分配
depot	[ˋdipo]	**名** 儲藏處
undeliverable	[ˌʌndɪˋlɪvərəbl̩]	**形** 未送達的
replacement	[rɪˋplesmənt]	**名** 代替物

😊 情境會話 Conversation

A It was shipped by UPS ***ground*** and the ***ETA*** is February. Do you need the ***tracking*** number?

A I just checked the UPS website. Looks like this item is still sitting in the UPS ***distribution depot***. The record shows ***undeliverable***.

A Can I confirm the shipping address with you?

A That was the address that you have on the purchase order.

A In this case, we will send you a ***replacement*** right away, but you will be responsible for the shipping cost.

A：它是以 UPS 陸運方式寄送的，預計到達時，時間是二月二日。您需要貨品追蹤號碼嗎？

A：我剛剛查過 UPS 網站了，看來這項貨品還在 UPS 的收發站。紀錄顯示尚未送達。

A：我可以跟您確認一下寄送地址嗎？

A：那的確是您採購訂單上的地址沒錯。

A：這樣的話，我們會立刻補寄一份給您，但是您將要自行負擔運費。

超實用精選短句 *Useful Sentences*

» Are you sure you've sent them to us?
你確定您已經將它們寄給我們了嗎？

» We will send you a replacement right now.
我們會馬上補寄一批貨過去。

» Could you tell me the reason for the loss?
你能告訴我遺失的原因嗎？

» Don't forget to send me a replacement next week.
別忘了下周補寄一份給我。

» Can I confirm the address with you again?
我可以再次跟您確認一下地址嗎？

» I guess they might be lost.
我猜它們可能被弄丟了。

» Could you help me confirm that again?
請幫忙冉確認一下好嗎？

» If you can find them, we would be grateful.
如果您能找到它們，我們將不勝感激。

» These materials are of great importance to me.
這些資料對我相當重要。

» I am sure the address is correct.
我確信地址是正確的。

» We look forward to receiving the goods soon.
我們期待盡快收到貨物。

» We will need the order ID to look into your order.
我們得有你的訂購證明才能查閱您的訂單。

你一定要知道！ *More Tips*

　　當有送貨延遲的情形發生時，最好主動打電話向對方詢問，如：「I haven't received the items I ordered from your company. Please confirm the status of my order #1234 dated March 28.」（我還沒收到向你們公司訂購的貨品。請確認我在三月廿八日所訂，編號1234 貨品目前的狀況。）。

08 退貨寄送

📖 關鍵單字&片語 *Words & Phrases*

dead on arrival	[dɛd ɑn əˋraɪvl̩]	片	貨到即損
original	[əˋrɪdʒənl̩]	形	原始的
slip	[slɪp]	名	紙條
along with	[əˋlɔŋ wɪð]	片	與……在一起
apologize	[əˋpɑləˏdʒaɪz]	動	道歉
inconvenience	[ˏɪnkənˋvinjəns]	名	不方便

😊 情境會話 *Conversation*

A Mr. Wang, we have received your request of returning a ***dead on arrival*** product.

A If you prefer a refund, we will need you to provide us with the ***original*** purchase receipt and the shipping ***slip***.

A Either way, we will also need you to send the defective item back to us ***along with*** related documents.

A We ***apologize*** for the ***inconvenience***, and if you have any questions, please feel free to contact us.

A：王先生，我們已經收到您要退回貨到即損產品的要求了。
A：如果您比較想要退款，我們會需要您提供原始購貨單據以及送貨單。
A：不管您選擇哪一種，我們都需要您將瑕疵品連同相關文件一起寄回來給我們。
A：在此為造成的不便向您致歉，如果您有任何問題，請儘管與我們聯繫。

超實用精選短句 *Useful Sentences*

» I would like to return the goods which have just arrived today.
我想要退還今天剛到的貨物。

» I want to claim compensation for the damage of the goods.
我想要求貨物毀損的賠償。

» May I know why the goods were damaged?
我能知道貨物毀損的原因嗎？

» Because they were seriously damaged.
因為他們嚴重損毀。

» We cannot refund your deposit unless you return the goods within a week.
除非你們在一星期內退貨否則我們不退還訂金。

» I will replace goods for you.
我將為您換貨。

» Would it be possible to change another product?
我能換成其他的產品嗎？

» If you can replace the goods, we would be grateful.
如果您能換掉這批貨物，我們將不勝感激。

» I feel so sorry for bringing inconvenience to you.
非常抱歉給您帶來不便。

» If the goods were damaged, you will get a full refund.
如果貨物毀損了，您會得到全額退款。

» Please contact us if you have any more questions.
如果你還有任何問題請聯繫我們。

你一定要知道！ *More Tips*

「dead on arrival」是表示「貨到即損」，商業文件中常以 DOA 來表示。「Our order arrived timely, but unfortunately, most of our commodities were dead on arrival.」（我們訂購的東西準時送達了，但是很不幸地，我們的商品大部分都是貨到即損。）。

採購
下單
篇

→ Part 12 音檔連結 ←

因各家手機系統不同，若無法直接掃描，
仍可以至以下電腦雲端連結下載收聽。
（https://tinyurl.com/mpbvkt4v）

01 索取樣品

📚 關鍵單字&片語 *Words & Phrases*

innovative	[ˈɪnoˌvetɪv]	形	創新的
reasonable	[ˈriznəbl]	形	合理的
flavor	[ˈflevɚ]	名	口味
take	[tek]	動	需要、花費

😊 情境會話 Conversation

A I was very impressed by your ***innovative*** cookie packaging.

B Our company is very pleased to provide free samples for interested customers, but you may need to pay for the delivery charges, is that ok?

A That sounds ***reasonable***. I'll pay the shipping fees.

B So, what ***flavors*** would you like? We have orange, vanilla, and chocolate.

A If you can give me all of them, I would appreciate it very much.

B Sure. I will arrange for 1 carton of each flavor and mail them at the post office for you to sample. It ***takes*** an estimated 1 week to arrive.

A：我非常喜歡貴公司餅乾具創意的包裝。
B：我們公司非常高興能提供免費樣品給予有興趣的客戶，但是您可能需要自行負擔運費，可以嗎？
A：這聽起來相當合理，我會付運送費用。
B：需要哪些口味呢？我們有柳橙、香草與巧克力。
A：如果您可以給我全部的口味，我會非常感謝。
B：當然可以。我會安排每種口味 1 箱並經由郵局郵寄給您，約須 1 星期到達。

🔊 超實用精選短句 *Useful Sentences*

» Could you send me a free sample?
您可以給我一個免費的樣品嗎？

» I have compared several samples of silk.
我已經比較過好幾種絲綢樣品。

» I think I need a full range of samples.
我認為我需要全套的樣品。

» Could you show me some other sample?
其他樣品拿給我看看可以嗎？

» This is our sample and product catalogue.
這是我們的樣品和產品目錄。

» I am really impressed by your product.
我滿喜歡你們的產品。

» You will receive the samples within a week.
你一個禮拜內會收到樣品。

» Is it for sale or only a sample?
這是用來賣的，還是僅僅是樣品？

» May I know if the sample is free of charge?
請問樣品是免費的嗎？

» Have you received our samples?
您收到我們的樣品了嗎？

» Which sample do you want?
您想要哪個樣品呢？

» I need to take the sample to show the dealer. Could you provide some?
我要帶樣品回去給經銷商看看。你可以提供一些嗎？

✏ 你一定要知道！ ✏ *More Tips*

在商業上若是有人說：「We will share the market, fifty fifty.」（我們平分市場，各佔一半。），你就可以說：「That sounds reasonable.」（聽起來合理。），或是「That sounds fair.」（聽起來很公平。）。

02 確認商品包裝方式

📚 關鍵單字&片語 *Words & Phrases*

standard	[ˈstændəd]	形 標準的
ensure	[ɪnˈʃur]	動 確保
plastic	[ˈplæstɪk]	形 塑膠
tray	[tre]	名 托盤
breakage	[ˈbrekɪdʒ]	名 破損
reliable	[rɪˈlaɪəbl̩]	形 可靠的

😊 情境會話 *Conversation*

A What is your *standard* export packaging?

B To *ensure* the product's quality, we use *plastic trays* to separate each level of cookies, and then we have the cookie trays wrapped in plastic bags, and finally we use paper cartons.

A That sounds good. But how about the shipping carton? Do you have any specific way to secure cookies from *breakage*?

B Yes. We use double-thick cartons, which have been specially designed for export. They have proven *reliable* for our customers in Japan.

A：貴公司的產品標準出口包裝是什麼呢？
B：為了保障產品品質，首先我們會使用塑膠盤分開各層餅乾，然後再用塑膠袋將餅乾盒包裝起來，最後使用紙盒再包裝。
A：那聽起來很好。但是運送外箱呢，您們是否有特殊方式來保護餅乾不會破損？
B：當然。我們使用為出口特別設計之雙重厚度的紙箱，而該紙箱已被我們在日本的客戶認同非常可靠。

🖋 超實用精選短句 *Useful Sentences*

» What are your packing methods?
你們的包裝方式是什麼？

» Does the packing meet market criteria?
包裝是否符合市場標準？

» We have no objection to the packing.
我們同意這種包裝方式。

» How are you going to pack the goods?
這批貨你們會怎麼包裝？

» We appreciate your recommendations on improving packing methods.
我們很高興您能推薦更好的包裝方式。

» We can also pack according to your requests.
我們也可以按照你們的要求包裝。

» Our products are always beautifully packed.
我們的產品總是包裝得非常精美。

» Have the goods been packed yet?
請問貨物包裝好了嗎？

» Excessive packaging is also a problem of the products.
這些產品還存在過度包裝的問題。

» It's absolutely unnecessary to pack excessively.
過度包裝是完全沒有必要的。

» We have put plenty of wrappings round the china when packing it.
我們在包裝瓷器時已經在周圍放很多包裝材料。

» The foil packets can seal the flavor in.
用錫紙包裝可以保持原味。

✒ 你一定要知道！ ✒ *More Tips*

「export」（輸出、出口）的相反詞就是「import」（輸入、進口）：「Our company exported umbrellas.」（我們的公司出口雨傘。）；「We imported coffee from Brazil.」（我們從巴西進口咖啡。）。

03 商品下單

📚 關鍵單字&片語 *Words & Phrases*

blank	[blæŋk]	形	空白的
lead-time	[ˈlidtaɪm]	名	產品設計與實際生產間相隔的時間
working day	[ˈwɜkɪŋ de]	名	工作天
preparation	[ˌprɛpəˈreʃən]	名	準備
shorten	[ˈʃɔrtn̩]	動	縮短

😊 情境會話 *Conversation*

A I am calling to place our first order. I would like to know if I need to fill out any specific order form?

B You need to fill out our order form. Can I fax a ***blank*** copy to you?

A Yes, please. By the way, what is your production ***lead-time***?

B Normally we require 45 ***working days*** for product ***preparation***.

B But if you need an urgent delivery, we can check if the production lead-time can be ***shortened*** by up to 30 days.

A：我打電話來是為了下第一次訂單。我想知道我是否需要填特殊的訂購單嗎？

B：您需要填寫訂購單，我可以傳真一份空白的給您嗎？

A：是的。麻煩您。對了，您公司產品生產準備需要多久呢？

B：通常需要 45 個工作天。

B：但是如果您要求緊急訂單，我們可以幫您查詢縮短生產時間至 30 天。

超實用精選短句 *Useful Sentences*

» I'd like to place an order for some electronic equipment.
我想從貴公司訂購一些電子設備。

» Are you going to place an order now?
您現在就下訂單嗎？

» Can I place an order for 200 suits of school uniforms?
我可以向您訂購兩百套校服嗎？

» This is my first time to order your product.
這是我第一次訂你們的產品。

» How long will it take to produce 100 cars?
生產一百輛車要多久？

» Could you please shorten the delivery time?
你可以縮短交貨日期嗎？

» There won't be enough time for us to prepare your goods.
這樣我們會不夠時間準備你們的貨。

» Do I need to fill out a order sheet?
我需要填寫訂購單嗎？

» I can place an order right away if your price is agreeable.
如果你們提供的價格合適我可以立即下訂單。

» Please fill out the order form carefully.
請仔細填寫訂貨單。

» I am wondering if you take special order.
我想知道你們是否接受特殊訂貨。

你一定要知道！ *More Tips*

「place」在這裡是當動詞是「訂購」的意思，而它還有「放、整頓」的意思：「I placed the books on the table.」（我把書放在桌上。）、「I placed the books in alphabetical order.」（我把那些書依字母順序排列好。）。

04 催貨

📚 關鍵單字&片語 Words & Phrases

normally	[ˋnɔrmḷɪ]	副 正常地
previous	[ˋpriviəs]	形 先前的
speed up	[spid ʌp]	片 加速
reply	[rɪˋplaɪ]	名 答覆
news	[njuz]	名 消息

😊 情境會話 Conversation

A I am very sorry, but I am afraid that your order was placed only 30 days before the delivery date. We **_normally_** do not accept orders under 45 days.

B Yes, I understand that. But your company confirmed an on-time product shipment as per my **_previous_** contact with you. Can you help **_speed up_** the production procedures for me?

A Yes, I will talk to our shipping department people to see if there is any way we can have the product delivered on time. Can I ring you later when I have the confirmed **_reply_**?

B Yes, please do so. I will wait for your good **_news_**.

A：我很抱歉。但是您所下的訂單距交貨期僅 30 天，通常我們不接受低於 45 天交貨期的訂單。

B：是的，我了解。但是在我先前與貴公司的聯繫時你們已經確認準時交貨。可不可以請您協助加速處理此訂單？

A：我當然會為您聯繫我們的送貨部門，看看是否可以準時為您送貨，我可以等到有確認答案後給您回電話嗎？

B：是的。請如此作，我會等您的好消息。

超實用精選短句 *Useful Sentences*

» Please deliver the goods we ordered at once.
請立即發送我們訂購的貨物。

» Is something wrong with the delivery?
運送出了什麼問題嗎？

» Why haven't I received the goods?
為什麼我還沒收到貨？

» There's a problem with delivering.
運送出了點問題。

» Please reconfirm the delivery date for me.
請再幫我確認出貨日。

» I have to say it's a terrible mistake.
我必須説這是個很嚴重的錯誤。

» The earliest delivery is greatly desired.
希望您能儘早發貨。

» We will send your goods as soon as possible.
我們會儘快發送您訂購的貨物。

» Would you accept delivering separately over a period of time?
你們能不能接受在一段時間裡分批交貨？

» I am sure the order will be ready next Monday.
我確定你的訂單下禮拜　會準備好。

» We would thank you to execute the order as soon as possible.
感謝您能儘快處理我們的訂單。

你一定要知道！ *More Tips*

「confirm」是「確認」的意思，當你要確認訂單或是機票，用的就是這一個動詞「I would like to confirm my order.」（我想要確定我的訂單。）、「I am calling to confirm my ticket to Canada on Monday.」（我要確定我星期一去加拿大的飛機票。）

05 詢問庫存量

📚 關鍵單字&片語 *Words & Phrases*

notice	[`notɪs]	動 注意
drop	[drɑp]	動 下降
headset	[`hɛd͵sɛt]	名 耳機
inventory	[`ɪnvən͵torɪ]	名 庫存
at once	[æt wʌns]	片 馬上
back order	[bæk `ɔrdɚ]	名 未交訂單

😊 情境會話 *Conversation*

Ⓐ We have ***noticed*** the recent ***drop*** in price for ***headset*** model AC201, so we would like to order 1000 units for our ***inventory***.

Ⓐ Do you have 1000 units of AC201 available?

Ⓐ If we order 1000 units ***at once***, do we get a 10% discount from the new price?

Ⓐ If there is a ***back order***, how long will it take for the order to come in?

Ⓐ You don't have to ship alle 1000 units at once because they are for our inventory. You can ship what you have to us first.

A：我們發現 AC201 這款耳機最近價格有下降，所以我們想訂 1000 台做庫存。

A：你們有 1000 台 AC201 可以賣嗎？

A：如果我們立刻訂購 1000 台，能拿到新價格打九折的優惠嗎？

A：如果有不足的貨，要多久才會補貨進來？

A：你們不需要馬上就把全部的 1000 台都送過來，因為那些是要用來庫存的。只要先送出你們現有的貨就可以了。

超實用精選短句 *Useful Sentences*

» The demand for these goods exceeds the supply.
這些貨物供不應求。

» We want to place a large order.
我們想大量訂貨。

» Do you have any of these items in stock?
你們有這些貨的庫存品嗎？

» If possible, we need fifty more machines.
如果可能的話，我們想再購買五十台機器。

» We are very interested in your products.
我們對貴公司產品非常感興趣。

» Can we get some discount if we order more?
如果我們訂貨多可以拿到些折扣嗎？

» It depends on how much you order.
這要看你訂貨多少。

» Our stock's is running short owing to increase in order.
由於訂貨增多，我們的存貨快銷完了。

» Actually, we have run out of stock for a few weeks.
事實上，我們已缺貨幾個星期了。

» We need to replenish our stocks of it.
我們需要補貨。

» When will you replenish stocks?
您什麼時候補充庫存？

» At present, we have only a limited stock of goods.
目前，我們的貨物庫存有限。

你一定要知道！ *More Tips*

「inventory」指的是「庫存、存貨」。有些店會舉行特賣會以出清存貨，如：「The store is having a sale again to reduce their inventory.」（那家商店又要舉行特賣來出清存貨了。），另一個表示「存貨」的方式是「in stock」，如：「We don't have many of this product in stock.」（我們這件商品存貨不多。）。

06 運費議價

📚 關鍵單字 & 片語 Words & Phrases

label	[ˈlebḷ]	名	標籤
letterhead	[ˈlɛtɚˌhɛd]	名	印在信紙的信頭
by air	[baɪ ɛr]	片	空運
by ground	[baɪ graʊnd]	片	陸運
understanding	[ˌʌndɚˈstændɪŋ]	名	理解
restriction	[rɪˈstrɪkʃən]	名	限制、約束

😊 情境會話 Conversation

A We are going to order 20,000 address *labels*. How much will that cost to ship to us?

A We are also thinking about purchasing some *letterhead*. If we order 10 cases, can you ship them with the labels without extra shipping charge?

A I understand that shipping *by air* is very expensive. I will talk to our office manager and see if we can have them all shipped *by ground*.

A Thank you for your help. I appreciate your *understanding* of our *restrictions*.

A：我們想訂兩萬個地址標籤貼紙。寄過來給我們要多少錢？

A：我們還打算買一些信頭紙，如果我們訂十盒，你們可以跟標籤一起寄過來而不加收運費嗎？

A：我知道空運非常貴。我會跟我們經理談談，看看是不是可以讓它們都用陸運寄送。

A：謝謝您的幫忙。非常感謝您體諒我們的難處。

超實用精選短句 *Useful Sentences*

» The seller should be responsible for all the shipping charge.
貨物的運費應由賣主負責。

» The cost and the freight are on your account.
成本和運費由你們負責。

» How do you usually move your machines?
你們出口機器通常用哪種運輸方式？

» You should pay the freight if you buy less than 50 sets.
如果你買 50 套以下就自己負責運費。

» I wonder that who will be responsible for the shipment charges?
我想知道運費由誰來負責呢？

» I am afraid that the transportation cost is too high.
恐怕運輸費太高了。

» Does the price include shipping freight?
這個價格包含運費了嗎？

» The shipping freight is an important factor we should not ignore.
運費是一個我們不應該忽視的重要因素。

» We want our goods to be shipped by air as a dispatch.
我們想要貨物以空運急件的方式寄過來。

» We have arranged to transport the goods by rail.
我們已安排好了用火車運輸這批貨物。

» Sometimes sea transport is a problem for us.
海運有時候很麻煩。

你一定要知道！ *More Tips*

訂貨時，最好詢問清楚對方的送貨方式，如：「I'd like to inquire how my merchandise will be delivered, by express delivery or by fright?」（我想詢問一下我的商品將以何種方式寄送，快遞還是貨運？）。

07 產品試用操作

📚 關鍵單字&片語 Words & Phrases

fax machine	[fæks məˈʃin]	名 傳真機
insert	[ɪnˈsɝt]	動 插入
flash drive	[flæʃ drɪv]	名 隨身碟
print	[prɪnt]	動 列印
cartridge	[ˈkɑrtrɪdʒ]	名 墨匣
select	[səˈlɛkt]	動 選擇
tryout	[ˌtraɪˈaʊt]	名 試用

😊 情境會話 Conversation

A We are really interested in this 5-in-1 *fax machine*. Before we purchase it, can you show us more functions? And we'd like to try it out too.

A I can just *insert* my *flash drive* to *print* documents from the machine directly.

A How do I change the *cartridges*?

A The touch screen is great. I can *select* the documents that I want to print.

A I wish you had a *tryout* program, because this is not a cheap printer.

A：我們真的對這個五合一傳真機感到很有興趣。在我們購買之前，可以請你向我們展示它更多的功能嗎？而且我們也很想試用看看。

A：我只要插入隨身碟，就可以直接從機器印出文件來了呢。

A：我要怎樣換墨匣呢？

A：觸控式螢幕真是太棒了。我可以選擇我想列印的文件。

A：我真希望你們有試用方案，因為這實在不是一台便宜的印表機呢。

🖎 超實用精選短句 *Useful Sentences*

» Would you like to try it yourself?
你想不想自己試試呢？

» Looks like it is very easy to use.
看起來似乎很容易操作呢！

» Can you show me how to operate it?
您能不能演示一下怎樣操作它呢？

» First of all, you should connect the power.
首先你應該連接上電源。

» I don't think it is so difficult to operate.
我認為它沒那麼難操作。

» Do you understand how to operate the machine?
你懂得如何操作這部機器嗎？

» You should read the user's manual before using it.
在使用之前，你應該先閱讀使用說明書。

» Is that so easy as you said?
它真有您說的那麼簡單嗎？

» Please do not hesitate to do it. Just do it.
請別猶豫。直接做吧。

» We want to try it out.
我們想試用看看。

» Just operate the machine according to the procedure.
只要按照程式操作機器就好了。

» I believe that you can handle it.
我相信你能做好的。

⚡ 你一定要知道！⚡ *More Tips*

　　「try out」是用來表示「試用（產品）」的片語，如：「We'd be interested in trying out your new multi-function printer.」（我們很想試用看看你們新的多功能印表機。），這裡要注意不要把「try out」誤用為「test out」（充分檢驗）了。

Part

13

議價／交涉談判

篇

→ **Part 13 音檔連結** ←

因各家手機系統不同，若無法直接掃描，
仍可以至以下電腦雲端連結下載收聽。
（https://tinyurl.com/3hbb8h6m）

01 提出條件

📖 關鍵單字＆片語 *Words & Phrases*

sole	[sol]	形	唯一的
support	[sə`port]	名	支持
fund	[fʌnd]	名	專款
overseas	[`ovɚ`siz]	形	海外的
rebate	[`ribet]	名	退佣
invoice	[`ɪnvɔɪs]	名	發票

😊 情境會話 *Conversation*

A As we are the **_sole_** agent of your company in Asia, I believe you can provide us with some promotional **_support_**.

B Yes, our company does provide special **_funds_** for promotional activities in the **_overseas_** market.

B Annual **_rebates_** on a basis of the total **_invoice_** value. If you reach our target sales goal by the end of this year, we will provide a 5% rebate based on your total invoice value.

A So, what is your sales goal for this year?

B 10,000 cartons.

A：我們是貴公司在亞洲地區的獨家代理商，我相信公司可以提供我們促銷贊助。
B：是的。我們公司的確有提供特殊促銷贊助給海外市場。
B：以年度退佣方式並以總發票金額為計算基準。如果您在年底之前達到我們目標銷售，我們會依據您的總發票金額提供 5% 退佣。
A：所以您今年的銷售目標為多少？
B：1 萬箱。

超實用精選短句 *Useful Sentences*

» That's the lowest price we can offer you.
這是我們能提供給你的最低價格了。

» Could you bring the price down?
您能降低價格嗎？

» We can't make a profit at that price.
以那樣的價格我們無法獲利。

» We are sure we can achieve the goal this year.
我們確信今年一定能達成這個目標。

» I wonder who will pay the freight.
我想知道運費由誰來付。

» Air freight and insurance fee will be paid by your company.
空運費用及保險費將由貴公司支付。

» I think it's necessary to make it clear.
我認為很有必要弄清楚這個。

» Who will pay for the carriage of goods?
由誰支付貨物運輸的費用呢？

» It's difficult for me to accept this price.
我很難接受這個價格。

» Can you offer us twenty thousand units at thirty dollars each?
你們可以出貨兩萬個，每個單價 30 元嗎？

» The wouldn't be possible.
不可能的。

» I think that is not acceptable.
我認為無法接受。

你一定要知道！ *More Tips*

「grant」在這裡是當「發放」的意思，而它還有「准許、允許」的意思：「They were granted some money for their good deeds by the king.」（他們因為他們做的好事，而國王准予了一些錢給他們。）。

02 詢問底線

📚 關鍵單字&片語 *Words & Phrases*

continue	[kənˋtɪnju]	動 持續
raw material	[rɔ məˋtɪrɪəl]	名 原料
profitable	[ˋprɑfɪtəbl̩]	形 有利的
balance	[ˋbæləns]	動 平衡
at least	[æt list]	片 至少

😊 情境會話 Conversation

A I am sorry but we can't agree to *continue* the price discounts next year.

A Our *raw material* cost has increased since the beginning of this year. The price we gave you this year will not be *profitable* for next year.

B So what price are you planning to quote?

A A 10% increase to *balance* our cost increase.

B Ouch! It is much higher than expected.

B So, may I have an idea of your bottom-line increase?

A *At least* 7%.

B I see.

A：我很抱歉，但是我們明年不能沿用今年的折扣。

A：我們的原料自今年起已經調漲，我們今年的報價在明年已不能獲利。

B：所以您的報價是？

A：調漲 10% 以彌補我們的成本調漲。

B：喔！這實在高過我們的預期。

B：我可以知道您調價的最底限嗎？

A：最少 7%。

B：我知道了。

超實用精選短句 *Useful Sentences*

» Raw material price has risen.
原料漲價了。

» I think the price is still a little too high.
我認為這個價格還是有點太高。

» I have already lowered the quotation by 10%
我已經降低一成報價了。

» You can think it over and answer me tomorrow.
你可以考慮一下，明天答覆我。

» How about giving us a special price?
給我們特別優惠價怎麼樣？

» It is the best I can do.
最多只能這樣了。

» Your price is higher than other suppliers'.
你的價格比其他供應商還高。

» Please quote us your rock bottom price.
請向我們報最低的價格。

» I am afraid that it is a little higher than I expected.
恐怕它比我預期的稍微高了些。

» Is it possible for you to increase the quantity of your order?
你能提高訂貨量嗎？

» Could you sweeten the deal for us?
你可以給我們提供點優惠嗎？

» So, is that your bottom price?
那麼，這就是您的價格底線了嗎？

你一定要知道！ *More Tips*

「ouch」是個發語詞，當你撞到椅子或是受傷的時候你都可以發出「Ouch!」（喔！）的聲音，而「ouch」在這裡有「心痛」的意思：「I spent $20000 on the new bike. Ouch!」（我花了兩萬元買這部新單車，喔！真心痛。）。

03 重新洽談條件

📚 關鍵單字&片語 *Words & Phrases*

approval	[ə`pruvl]	名 贊成
exclusive agent	[ɪk`sklusɪv `edʒənt]	名 獨家代理商
import	[ɪm`port]	動 進口
severe	[sə`vɪr]	形 嚴峻的
except	[ɪk`sɛpt]	介 除……之外

😊 情境會話 *Conversation*

A I am sorry to let you know that we are not able to grant you *approval* as our *exclusive agent* in Taiwan due to our internal policy.

A We already have an exclusive agent in Hong Kong who takes charge of the Mainland China and Taiwan markets.

B But if we can't be your sole agent, we are afraid that other companies will *import* your product into Taiwan and then we will face *severe* price competition.

A You are right to be concerned. But I can give you our word that we will not sell products to other companies in Taiwan *except* you.

A：我很抱歉讓您知道，基於內部政策因素，我們無法給貴公司我們產品在台灣的獨家代理權。

A：我們在香港已經有代理商，他的業務範圍包括大陸與台灣。

B：但如果不能成為你的代理商，我們擔心其他公司也會進口貴公司產品到台灣，藉時我們會遭逢激烈的價格競爭。

A：你的擔心是有道理的。但是我們可以保證在台灣除了貴公司以外，我們將不會銷售產品給其他的公司。

超實用精選短句 *Useful Sentences*

» I am afraid that we still can't accept your quotation.
恐怕我們還是不能接受您的報價。

» I suppose you could accept our quotation this time.
我想這次的報價你們應該可以接受了吧。

» I think we should find a middle ground.
我想我們應該折衷一下。

» You have to deliver our order by the end of the month.
你們必須月底交貨。

» Could you pay Net 30?
你們能在到貨後 30 天付款嗎？

» We can pay Net 10 if you can give an additional one percent discount.
如果你再多給百分之一的折扣，我們可以到貨後 10 天付款。

» If so, you have to pay the freight.
如果這樣的話，您必須支付運費了。

» So you can't find other dealers, can you?
那麼您不能再找其他的經銷商了，可以嗎？

» I still think that you should not miss the opportunity.
我始終認為您不應該錯過這次良機。

» I believe it will be easy for you to sell our products.
我相信我們的產品你們會很好賣。

» When can you confirm the delivery date with us?
你什麼時候能跟我們確定交貨日？

» Once we receive your order, we will confirm the delivery date.
只要一接到你們的訂單，我們就會確定交貨日。

你一定要知道！ *More Tips*

「exclusive」在這裡是當「獨家的、專用的」，但它也有「代理商、專賣店」的意思，如：「This news is exclusive.」（這是獨家的新聞。），「This room is exclusive for the queen.」（這房間是女王專用的。）。

04 簽訂合約

📖 關鍵單字&片語 *Words & Phrases*

discounted	[ˈdɪskaʊntɪd]	形 打折的
format	[ˈfɔrmæt]	動 格式化
draft	[dræft]	名 草稿
pleasure	[ˈplɛʒɚ]	名 榮幸
stress	[strɛs]	動 強調

😊 情境會話 *Conversation*

A I am glad to inform you that we are ready to sign the annual contract with you. We really appreciate your *discounted* price offer.

B That's great. If you all agree with the pricing, we should start to *format* the detailed contract, right?

A Surely. Could you please give me a *draft* of the contract?

B It would be my *pleasure*. Is there anything you need to address regarding the contract?

A Please *stress* that we are your exclusive agent in Taiwan.

A I think that's all. Thanks a lot.

A：我很高興的通知您我們已經準備好與貴公司簽訂年度合約。我們非常感謝您提供的折扣價格。

B：那太好了。如果您們都同意價格，我想我們應該開始寫詳細的合約，對不對？

A：當然，可否請你給我一份合約草稿？

B：我很樂意。您是否有任何事需要在合約內特別強調的嗎？

A：請特別標明我們為貴公司在台灣獨家代理商。

A：應該就是這些了，非常謝謝。

🔊 超實用精選短句 *Useful Sentences*

» I think we can sign a contract now.
我想我們現在可以簽訂合約了。

» What payment terms do you accept?
你們接受哪種付款方式？

» I haven't gone over the contract yet.
我還沒有從頭到尾看過合約。

» You'd better have the contract amended as soon as possible.
您最好儘快修改合約。

» We finally reached a consensus.
我們終於達到共識了。

» Has our lawyer read this contract yet?
我們的律師看過這份合約了嗎？

» You'd better have a close study of the contract.
你最好仔細研究一下合約。

» I will start to draft a new contract.
我將會開始擬定一份新合約。

» I've made the changes you asked for.
我已經照您要求的修正過了。

» Please sign on the dotted lined.
請在虛線上簽名。

» I consider this a win-win agreement.
我認為這是一個雙贏的協議。

» If you can accept the price, we can sign the contract now.
如果您能接受這個價格，我們現在就可以簽約。

✒ 你一定要知道！✒ *More Tips*

「draft」是「草稿」的意思，如：「This is just a draft of my idea.」
（這只是我的主意的一個草稿。）、「Can you give me a rough draft of your writing?」（你可不可以給我你文章的一個大略的草稿？）。

05 以退為進

📚 關鍵單字&片語 Words & Phrases

software	[ˈsɔftˌwɛr]	名 軟體
module	[ˈmɑdʒul]	名 模組
bundle	[ˈbʌndl̩]	名 大推、大批
reduction	[rɪˈdʌkʃən]	名 降低
be willing to	[bi ˈwɪlɪŋ tu]	片 願意
re-evaluate	[ˌriˈvæljuˌet]	動 重新評估

😊 情境會話 Conversation

A I'm really interested in purchasing the full suite of **_software_**, except for the reporting **_module_**.

A I was hoping you could reduce the price on the **_bundle_** as the reporting module is a large part, but we don't need it.

A I think a **_reduction_** of $500 off the $2000 price is fair.

A If you **_are_** not **_willing to_** move at all on the price, I think I will need to **_re-evaluate_** our options.

A Even at $1800, I still think I will go with the alternative vendor.

A：除了那個報告模組之外，我真的有意購買這整套軟體。
A：我原本希望你這組可以賣我便宜一點，因為那個報告模組就佔了一大部分，而我們卻不需要那個東西。
A：我認為這兩千美元要降個五百美元才合理。
A：如果你一點都不願意調整售價，那麼我就得重新評估我們的選擇。
A：即使你賣一千八百美元，我想我還是會去找其他的攤位。

超實用精選短句 *Useful Sentences*

» We are very interested in your product.
我們對您的產品非常感興趣。

» Could you offer us a cheaper price?
您能給我更便宜一點的價格嗎？

» I think there is still room for a further reduction.
我認為還有進一步降價的餘地。

» There is not much room for further reduction.
沒有多大的餘地進一步降價。

» I think a reduction of $300 off the $1000 price is reasonable.
我覺得這一千美元要降個三百美元才合理。

» I can give you a 10% discount.
我可以給你九折的優惠價。

» However, I still hope for a price reduction.
儘管如此，我還是希望能降價。

» What about a compromise?
折衷一下怎麼樣？

» Can we sign a deal if we make a concession?
如果我們作出讓步能簽下這筆生意嗎？

» If we have reached an agreement, can you formalize it in a quote and we can sign a deal.
如果我們已經達成協議了，你可以正式報價讓我們簽下這筆生意嗎？

你一定要知道！ *More Tips*

　　「compromise」做名詞解時，指「折衷辦法；妥協」，如：「If we can't come into a compromise, I'll have to turn to another booth.」（如果我們沒辦法達成妥協，我只好去詢問另一個攤位了。）作動詞解時，指「妥協、讓步」，如：「The salesman refused to compromise with the customer over the price.」（該業務拒絕在價格上和那個顧客妥協。）。

06 解約／違約

06 解約／違約

📖 關鍵單字 & 片語 *Words & Phrases*

be aware of	[bi əˈwɛr ɑv]	片 了解、知道
penalty	[ˈpɛnl̩tɪ]	名 處罰
clause	[klɔz]	詞 條款
waive	[wev]	動 撤回
recover	[rɪˈkʌvɚ]	動 彌補

😊 情境會話 *Conversation*

A I would like to cancel my cell phone contract.

A Yes, I *am aware of* the fact that I still have 6 months left on the contract; however, I would like to cancel anyway.

A Could you please let me know how all the *penalty clauses* will be applied in my situation?

A Is there a way in which you could *waive* some of those charges?

A I understand the need for a couple of these charges to *recover* the cost of the phone itself.

A However, I am troubled by the extra $150 charge for the cancellation itself.

A：我想取消我的手機合約。
A：是的，我知道我合約還有六個月，不過我無論如何還是想解約。
A：麻煩您告訴我，我的情況會適用什麼處罰條款？
A：有什麼方法可以取消那個費用呢？
A：我明白這些收費項目中，為了彌補手機的成本，有幾項是必須的。
A：然而，我對於光是解約就要加收一百五十美元的費用這部分感到很困惑。

超實用精選短句 *Useful Sentences*

» I am afraid we have to cancel the contract.
恐怕我們不得不取消這份合約。

» I want to know how you will explain it.
我想知道你要如何作出解釋。

» You are technically in breach of contract.
嚴格按照法律條文來講您違約了。

» I am afraid you have to pay penal sum.
恐怕您必須支付違約金。

» Is there any way to reduce the loss?
有沒有什麼方法可以減少損失？

» I am afraid we can not go on fulfilling the contract.
恐怕我們不能繼續履行這份合同了。

» Can you give me a reasonable explanation?
您能給我個合理的解釋嗎？

» Would you like to solve the problem in peace?
您願意和平的解決這件事嗎？

» It's obvious that you must be responsible for the loss.
顯然你們要對這次的損失負責。

» You cannot break the contract without any good reasons.
如果沒有什麼正當理由，你們不應毀約。

» Anyway, we have to break the contract.
無論如何，我們不得不毀約。

» We request compensation from your company.
我們要求貴公司做出賠償。

你一定要知道！ *More Tips*

「cancellation fee」指的是「解約金」，是與對方解除合約時支付給對方的手續費，如：「It doesn't seem reasonable to me that we have to pay a cancellation fee of $150.」（我們必須支付 150 美元的解約金，我認為這似乎並不合理。）。

07 終止合約

📖 關鍵單字&片語 Words & Phrases

subscription	[səbˋskrɪpʃən]	名 訂閱
break a contract	[brek ə ˋkɑntrækt]	片 毀約
advertise	[ˋædvɚˌtaɪz]	動 廣告
technician	[tɛkˋnɪʃən]	名 技術人員
interfere	[ˌɪntɚˋfɪr]	動 干擾
signal	[ˋsɪgnl̩]	名 訊號

😃 情境會話 Conversation

🅰 I want to end my home internet ***subscription***.

🅰 While I am aware I will be ***breaking a contract***, the service has never worked as ***advertised***.

🅰 I have contacted your support line 16 times in the past month and had two visits from your ***technicians***.

🅰 After all of that, the issue has still not been resolved. Clearly there is something at my location that ***interferes*** with the ***signal***.

🅰 From my point of view, there is no reason to still have the service.

A：我想終止租用我的居家網路連線。

A：雖然我知道我會毀約，但是你們的服務從來就不如你們廣告上所說的那樣好。

A：過去一個月期間，我已經聯絡你們的支援專線十六次了，但是你們的技術人員只來過兩次。

A：在那之後，問題依然沒有獲得解決。顯然我這裡有東西干擾了訊號。

A：從我的立場看來，實在沒有理由繼續使用這個服務。

🔊 超實用精選短句 *Useful Sentences*

» I have already paid for the service to date, but am unwilling to pay any more.
我已經付了到今天的費用，不過不想再繼續付了。

» If you are unable to waive the penalty clause on the contract, could you let me speak to someone who is able to discuss this?
如果你無法撤銷合約上的處罰條款，能不能讓我跟可以討論這件事的人談呢？

» I want to terminate this contract.
我想要終止合約。

» The contract can be terminated unconditionally by the customer within the trial period.
在試用期，客人可以無條件地終止合約。

» Sorry, but you have no right to terminate the contract.
很抱歉，你沒有權力終止合約。

» We might take legal action against you.
我們會對你採取法律行動。

» We are unwilling to perform the contract any more.
我們不願意再履行合同了。

» I am afraid that you must be responsible for our loss.
對於我們的損失恐怕你們必須承擔。

» Why do you want to terminate the contract?
你們為什麼想終止合約呢？

» You must give us compensation for the loss.
對於我們的損失你們必須做出賠償。

⚡ 你一定要知道！⚡ *More Tips*

「break a contract」指「解約」，也可以表示為「rescind a contract」（取消合約），如：「I am calling to rescind our contract with you because we have moved to another city.」（我是打來取消我們和貴公司的合約，因為我已經搬到另一個城市了。）。

08 付款條件

📖 關鍵單字&片語 *Words & Phrases*

payment	[`pemənt]	名 付款
term	[tɝm]	名 條件
irrevocable	[ɪ`rɛvəkəbl̩]	形 不可撤回的
freight	[fret]	名 運費
exchange rate	[ɪks`tʃendʒ ret]	名 匯率
recently	[`risn̩tlɪ]	副 最近

😊 情境會話 *Conversation*

A I am very interested in your product, and wondering what ***payment terms*** you accept?

B Thank you for your interest. We usually accept D/P, T/T, and (***irrevocable***) L/C.

A Can I have your quotation in FOB terms for our review? I have received your pricing in CIF terms but I think we can get a cheaper sea ***freight*** fee.

B Sure. I will send it to you later today.

A By the way, can you quote in Australian dollars since the ***exchange rate*** for US dollars has been strong ***recently***?

A：我對於貴公司的產品非常有興趣，想知道貴公司常用的付款條件為何？

B：非常感謝您的詢問。我們通常接受到單付款，電匯，或是不可撤銷信用狀。

A：我可以請您以 FOB 報價嗎？我已經收到貴公司的 CIF 報價，但是我想我們可以得到更便宜的海運運費報價。

B：當然可以，我等會會寄給您。

A：另外，可否請您以澳幣報價，因為最近美元匯率較高。

🔊 超實用精選短句 *Useful Sentences*

» We insist on paying by Letter of Credit.
我們堅持用信用狀付款。

» How would you like to deal with the payment terms?
你們想怎麼處理付款條件？

» We always pay by L/C for our imports.
我們的進口一向以信用狀付款。

» What do you think of the terms of payment?
關於付款條件你們有什麼意見？

» We promise to open the letter of credit at sight.
我們答應會按時開狀。

» We agree on your terms of payment.
我們同意你的付款方式。

» How do you like us to pay?
你們希望我們怎麼付款？

» What are your terms of payment?
你們的付款條件是什麼？

» Would you pay by check, credit card or cash?
請問您使用什麼付款方式？支票、信用卡還是現金？

» Payment by D/A is out of the question.
用承兌交單的付款方式是不可能的。

» We pay by L/C.
我們採信用狀付款。

» Payment in installments is okay for us.
我們可以接受分期付款。

🖊 你一定要知道！🖊 *More Tips*

D/P 在這裡代表的是「Documentary Payment」（到單付款）；T/T 是「Telegraphic Transfer」（電匯）；L/C 是「Letter of credit」（信用狀）；FOB 是「Free on Board」（船邊交貨）；CIF 則是「Cost, Insurance and Freight」（貨價、保險和運費）。

09 議價／殺價

📖 關鍵單字＆片語 Words & Phrases

unprofitable	[ʌn'prɑfɪtəbl]	形	賺不到錢的
premium	[ˋprimɪəm]	名	優質的
difference	[ˋdɪfərəns]	名	不同、差異
afford	[əˋford]	動	提供
superior	[səˋpɪrɪəˋ]	形	優秀的
free of charge	[fri ɑv tʃɑrdʒ]	片	免費

😊 情境會話 Conversation

A Your price is 5% higher.

B But it is **_unprofitable_** for me to lower my quotation by 5%. Please understand our product is **_premium_** quality.

A What's the **_difference_**?

B We use the best materials to produce all the products. Also, we provide a 3-year warranty.

A Oh? But 5% is more than we can **_afford_**.

B Please take our **_superior_** customer service into consideration. We can give you technical support anytime. And it is **_free of charge_**.

A：你的價格比其他公司貴出 5%。
B：但是如果我降價 5% 是沒有利潤的，請了解我們的產品有非常高級的品質。
A：有什麼分別嗎？
B：當然。我們使用最高級的原料來製造所有的產品，另外，我們提供高達 3 年的保固期。
A：喔？但是 5% 實在太高，我們無法接受。
B：請再把我們優質的客戶服務列入您的考慮。我們隨時可以提供技術支援，而且這是免費的。

🔊 超實用精選短句 *Useful Sentences*

» Don't you plan to lower a little bit?
您就不打算再降價一些嗎？

» You'd better quote me the reasonable price.
你最好能報個合理的價格給我。

» What price are you willing to pay?
您願意出多少錢呢？

» I won't pay more than 200 dollars.
我出價不會高於兩百美元。

» I am afraid that your price seems too high.
恐怕你們的報價似乎太高了。

» I don't think your price is reasonable enough.
我覺得你們的價格還是不夠合理。

» The price of coffee is running up all over the world.
Our costs have risen.
全世界的咖啡價格正迅速上漲，我們的成本提高了。

» I am afraid that it's our best price.
這恐怕是我們的最低價了。

» If we lower the price again, we will have no profit.
如果我們再降價就不賺錢了。

» US$3,000 is the lowest price we can give without loss.
3000 美元是我們的保本價格。

» Your price is 3% higher than other companies'.
你的價格比其他公司高了 3%。

» We provide a 2-year warranty.
我們提供兩年的保固期。

⚡ 你一定要知道！⚡ *More Tips*

「premium quality」指的是「最好的品質」，當然，還可以用「best」、「promised」、「champion」、「first class」等字來表示「最好的」。

10 最終出價

📖 關鍵單字&片語 *Words & Phrases*

already	[ɔl`rɛdɪ]	副 已經、先前
lower	[`loɚ]	動 降低
significant	[sɪg`nɪfəkənt]	形 重大的
carton	[`kɑrtn̩]	名 箱
volume	[`vɑljəm]	名 數量
final	[`faɪnl̩]	形 最後的
bid	[bɪd]	名 出價

😊 情境會話 *Conversation*

A I greatly appreciate your discounted price offer, but it still seems too high.

B But I have *__already__* had the quotation lowered by 10%!

A I believe you should be able to *__lower__* your price further due to our *__significant__* quantity order.

B I see. If you can increase your order quantity by, let's say 5,000 *__cartons__*, I can offer a *__volume__* discount of another 2%.

A Only 2%?

B It is my *__final bid__*. I can't offer any more.

A：我很感謝您的降價，但是這個價格還是太高了。
B：但是我已經降價達 10% 了！
A：以我們這麼高的訂購量，我相信你應該能夠再降價一些吧。
B：我知道了。如果您可以再增加 5000 箱的訂購量，我可以給予您額外的 2% 的折扣。
A：只有 2% 嗎？
B：這是我最後的出價。我不能再退讓了。

🔊 超實用精選短句 *Useful Sentences*

» I think the price is still a little high.
我覺得這個價格還是有點高。

» It's our final bid.
這是我們最後的出價了。

» I have already cut down the price by 20%!
我已經降價 20% 了。

» Ok, $80, but that is my last offer.
好吧，80 美元，但那是我最後的出價。

» I am sorry. We can't make any reduction.
很抱歉，我們不能再降價了。

» This is my last offer and it must be paid within 10 days.
這是我的最後出價，而且必須在十日內付款。

» We can't do more than a 8% reduction.
我們只能降價 8%，不能再多了。

» How about reducing the price by 5%?
您看將價格下調 5% 怎麼樣？

» We can't give you more discount. It's the tourist season.
我們不能再降價了，現在可是旅遊旺季。

» This is our lowest price. We cannot make further concession.
這是我方最低報價，不能再降價了。

» The price has already been cut as low as possible.
價格已降到不能再降。

» This amount is my last offer. I can't go down anymore.
這是我最後的出價，不能再低了。

⚡ 你一定要知道！⚡ *More Tips*

在客戶要求廠商再壓低價錢的時候，廠商可以說：「This is the final bid.」（這是我最後的出價。）、「I can't offer any more.」（我不能再降價了。），或是「This is the best price that I can give you.」（這是我所能給你最好的價格了。）。

11 獲客戶認同

📚 關鍵單字&片語 Words & Phrases

acceptable	[əkˋsɛptəbl]	形 可接受的
trust	[trʌst]	動 相信
satisfaction	[ˌsætɪsˋfækʃən]	名 滿意
give one's word	[gɪv wʌns wɝd]	片 保證
satisfied	[ˋsætɪsˌfaɪd]	形 令人滿意的
place an order	[ples æn ˋɔrdɚ]	片 下訂單

😊 情境會話 Conversation

A I am calling to know if our quotation is **_acceptable_** at your end.

A You can **_trust_** us that our product quality has **_satisfaction_** guaranteed. We have sold 10,000 cartons of the same model products to Japan with a much higher price.

B Really?

A I can also **_give_** you **_my word_** that if you are not **_satisfied_** with what you receive, you can return it anytime.

B Hum..., OK, I'll take your offer. I will **_place an order_** today.

A：我打電話來是為了了解您是否能夠接受我們的報價。
A：您可以相信我們的產品品質是保證滿意的。我們已經銷售 10,000 箱至日本，而且價格甚至較高。
B：真的嗎？
A：我還可以保證您如果對於收到的產品不滿意，隨時可以退貨。
B：好吧，我接受你的報價，我會在今天就下訂單。

超實用精選短句 *Useful Sentences*

» We are confident of our product's quality.
我們對產品的品質非常有信心。

» You can return the product if you are not pleased.
如果你不滿意隨時可以退貨。

» Our products are the best in the market.
我們的產品是市面上最好的。

» It is both good and cheap. Why not take it?
它物美價廉。為什麼不買呢？

» I am sure you'll be very satisfied with our product.
我相信您會對我們的產品非常滿意的。

» I am quite satisfied with your products.
我對你們的產品很滿意。

» I'd like to buy a large quantity of your goods if your price is competitive.
如果你們的價格很有競爭力，我們願意大量訂貨。

» High quality is guaranteed to the customer.
向客戶保證產品的高品質。

» Although our price is a little higher, we guarantee the highest quality.
雖然我們的價格有比較高，但保證品質是非常好的。

» Since you've given me a favorable price, I'll place an order at once.
既然您已經給了我優惠價，我馬上下訂單。

你一定要知道！ *More Tips*

為了贏得客戶的信任，我們可以說「I can give you my word that you can return it if you don't find it satisfying.」（我向你保證你若是不滿意可以退還它。）、「I guarantee you that this is the best price.」（我保證這是最好的價格。）、「You can trust me on this.」（這個你可以相信我。）。

12 議價表達

📚 關鍵單字&片語 *Words & Phrases*

player	[ˋpleɚ]	名 播放器
store	[stor]	名 店家
range	[rendʒ]	名 範圍
match	[mætʃ]	動 符合
mind	[maɪnd]	動 介意
somewhere	[ˋsʌmˏʍɛr]	副 某個地方

😊 情境會話 *Conversation*

A What is the price for that MP3 *player* that is with your *store* promotion plan?

A We have been looking for this model for a while and the price *range* is around $10 to $25.

A Will you be able to *match* the price?

A Do you *mind* talking to the manager and see if he can give us a better price?

A If you can't match the price with other stores, I might have to buy this MP3 player *somewhere* else. But still, thank you for you time and efforts.

A：那台 MP3 播放器搭配你們店裡的優惠專案是多少錢呢？
A：我們找這款商品已經找好一陣子了，價格範圍大概是在 10 美元到 25 美元之間。
A：你們能賣這個價格嗎？
A：你介意去跟經理談一下，看看他能否給我們一個較好的價格嗎？
A：如果你不能賣跟其他家一樣的價錢，我可能就必須去其他地方買這台 MP3 播放器了。不過還是很感謝你花了時間和精神。

超實用精選短句 *Useful Sentences*

» I wonder what the lowest price you can offer is.
我想知道你們能提供的最低價是多少。

» Will you please tell me how many you want?
能告訴我你想買多少嗎？

» I am afraid that it's the best price we can offer.
這恐怕是我們所能提供的最低價了。

» If you can't lower the price, I'll go somewhere else to buy it.
如果你不能降價，我就去別的地方買。

» I am afraid we can't accept the price you offer.
恐怕我們不能接受您提供的價格。

» I don't think your price is competitive enough.
我覺得你們的價格還是不夠有競爭力。

» The price is much higher than other places.
這個價格比其他地方都貴。

» There is not any price reduction for this product.
這個產品我們不做任何的降價。

» I can't make a decision until I report it to my boss.
我要跟我的老闆報告之後才能決定。

» We can't accept your last price all the same.
我們仍然不能接受您最後的價格。

» The price seems higher than some other stores.
這價格似乎比其他店家要貴呢！

» Are you sure this is a promotion rate?
你確定這是促銷價嗎？

你一定要知道！ *More Tips*

議價時，讓對方知道你已經比過價了是很有效的方法：「I have shopped around the entire hypermarket and noticed that you are selling this cellphone at a much higher price than others.」（我已經逛過整個賣場，並且發現你們這隻手機賣得比其他家貴多了。）

13 分期付款

📖 關鍵單字&片語 *Words & Phrases*

save	[sev]	動 省
percent	[pɚˋsɛnt]	名 百分比
down payment	[daʊn ˋpemənt]	名 頭期款、訂金
interest rate	[ˋɪntərɪst ret]	名 利率
pay off	[pe ɔf]	片 付清
credit card	[ˋkrɛdɪt kɑrd]	名 信用卡

😊 情境會話 *Conversation*

A This dining set is exactly what we are looking for. But the price is a bit higher than what we expected.

A The discount really won't **_save_** us any money. We would like to go for the payment plan.

A What **_percent_** do we have to put down for the **_down payment_**? What is the **_interest rate_**?

A If there is no penalty if we **_pay off_** early, I think we will take this dining set.

A Here is our form that you want us to fill out for the payment plan and our bank and **_credit card_** information is all on it.

A：這套餐桌椅的確就是我們要找的那一套。不過價格比我們預計的要高了一些。

A：這個折扣實在不能幫我們省到什麼錢。我們想用分期付款。

A：我們必須支付多少比例的頭期款？利率是多少呢？

A：若我們提早付清不用罰款，我想我們就買這套餐桌椅了。

A：這是你要我們填的分期付款方案表格，我們的銀行和信用卡資料都在上面了。

🔊 超實用精選短句 *Useful Sentences*

» Could you give me any discount?
您可以給我一些折扣嗎？

» You can pay 400 dollars for down payment and the rest in monthly installment.
您可以先付四百美元訂金，其餘的按月分期付款。

» Is there any payment plan for that?
它有沒有分期方案呢？

» How much do we have to pay for the down payment?
我們訂金要付多少呢？

» I am afraid I'll be broken after make the down payment.
恐怕付了訂金我就沒錢了。

» You can pay on a twelve-month installment plan.
你可以分十二個月來分期付款。

» I think you'd better pay in monthly installment.
我認為你最好按月分期付款。

» The full payment is too much for me.
全部付款對我來說太多了。

» I can't afford it if I don't go for the payment plan.
如果我不用分期方案的話就買不起它。

» I have to discuss it with my husband.
我得跟我的先生商量一下這件事。

» Installment payment can reduce your economic pressure.
分期付款可以減少你的經濟壓力。

» If I were you, I will buy it by installment.
如果我是你，我就會以分期的方式買下它。

✏ 你一定要知道！✏ *More Tips*

「down payment」指「分期付款的頭款」。要求以分期付款的方式購物時，可以説：「Is it possible that we pay for this DVD player by installments?」（我們可以用分期付款的方式購買這台 DVD 播放器嗎？）。

14 催款

📖 關鍵單字&片語 Words & Phrases

monthly	[ˈmʌnθlɪ]	副 每月
outstanding	[ˈautˈstændɪŋ]	形 未償付的
shut off	[ʃʌt ɔf]	片 關掉
automatically	[ˌɔtəˈmætɪklɪ]	副 自動地
resend	[riˈsɛnd]	動 再送
updated	[ʌpˈdetɪd]	形 更新的、最新的
invoice	[ˈɪnvɔɪs]	形 發票

😊 情境會話 Conversation

A Mrs. Chu, I am calling to inform you that you have missed two payments of your *monthly* bill.

A Currently you have a 109 dollar *outstanding* balance in your account.

A Our system *shuts off* the service *automatically* if there is no payment shown in the account for 3 months.

A I will make a note on your account here that we changed your billing address today and we will *resend* the *updated invoice* to your new address.

A：朱太太，我是打來通知您，您已經兩期沒有付款了。
A：目前您帳戶中有未償付的款項 109 美元。
A：如果帳戶中顯示有三個月未付款，我們的系統會自動切斷服務。
A：我會在您的帳號上註明我們今天更改了您的帳單寄送地址，並且
會重新寄發最新的發票收據到您的新地址去。

超實用精選短句 *Useful Sentences*

» I have to tell you that you have missed three payments of your monthly bill.
我必須告訴您，您已經三期沒有付款了。

» I come to remind you that your bill come due again.
我來是告訴您，您的帳單又到期了。

» How much do I have to pay at least?
我至少要付多少錢呢？

» I have to remind you that the rent is due.
我得提醒您房租已經到期了。

» Our record shows that you have not paid your bill yet.
我們的記錄顯示您尚未付款。

» I found an unpaid bill on my table.
我桌上發現一張未付的帳單。

» Please kindly make the relevant payment as soon as possible.
請您儘快支付相關費用。

» Please contact us if you have any questions.
如果您有任何疑問請聯繫我們。

» Please be sure you make your payment by August 7th.
請您務必在八月七日之前支付款項。

» Thank you very much for your cooperation!
非常感謝您的合作！

你一定要知道！ *More Tips*

以「分期付款」的方式購買商品後，如果忘記繳款期限而漏繳，通常必須繳納所謂的「late payment penalty」（逾期付款罰金），如：「May I remind you that the late payment penalty will be in effect if you miss the deadline for the monthly payment.」（容我提醒您若您錯過每月繳款期限，就會產生逾期繳款的罰金。）。

Part

14

國際參展篇

→ Part 14 音檔連結 ←

因各家手機系統不同，若無法直接掃描，
仍可以至以下電腦雲端連結下載收聽。
（https://tinyurl.com/3f2p2z5b）

01 報名參展

📚 關鍵單字&片語 *Words & Phrases*

trade show	[tred ʃo]	名 貿易展
application	[ˏæpləˋkeʃən]	名 申請
deadline	[ˋdɛd͵laɪn]	名 最後期限
booth	[buθ]	名 攤位
show room	[ʃo rum]	名 展示間
area	[ˋɛrɪə]	名 地區
deposit	[dɪˋpɑzɪt]	名 訂金

😊 情境會話 *Conversation*

A We would like to participate in this year's International Communication *Trade Show*.

A When do you start taking *applications* and when is the *deadline* for the applications?

A We will need two *booths*. One will be used as a *show room*, and the other will be used as the sales and customer service *area*.

A Here is our application form. Can you take a look and see if there is anything missing?

A Here is our company's *deposit* check. Please give me a receipt for the deposit.

A：我們想參加今年的國際通訊貿易展。

A：你們何時開始接受申請，還有何時截止申請呢？

A：我們將會需要兩個攤位，一個要用來做展示間，另一個會用來做銷售和顧客服務區。

A：這是我們的申請表。能否麻煩你看一下，看看是不是有哪裡漏掉了？

A：這是我們公司的訂金支票。請給我一張訂金收據。

超實用精選短句 *Useful Sentences*

» Many companies have applied for the book fair.
已有許多公司報名參加此次書展。

» Could you tell me when the deadline is?
請您告訴我截止日期是什麼時候？

» What are the requirements of registration?
具備什麼條件才能報名？

» Please take your business card when you attend the conference.
出席會議時請攜帶您的名片。

» If you want to join the competition, you must fill in these forms.
假如想報名參賽，您必須填寫這些表格。

» When will you start taking applications?
您什麼時候開始接受報名？

» You must pay the fee within five days after application.
報名後五天之內必須繳費。

» How many companies have applied for this exhibition?
有幾家公司報名參加這次的展覽了呢？

» Please hand in a photocopy of your business license.
請提供您的營業執照副本。

» Anything missing on the application form?
報名表上有任何遺漏的地方嗎？

» Thank you for your interest and participation.
謝謝您的關注和參與。

你一定要知道！ *More Tips*

「application」是「申請；申請書」的意思。如：「The organizer started taking the application two days ago.」（主辦單位兩天前就開始接受申請了。），或是：「The deadline for the application was two days ago.」（截止申請的時間是兩天前。）。

02 企業簡介

📚 關鍵單字&片語 *Words & Phrases*

top	[tɑp]	形 最重要的、最高的
solution	[sə`luʃən]	名 解決方法
specialize in	[`spɛʃəˌlaɪz ɪn]	片 專門於……
intranet	[`ɪntrənɛt]	名 企業內部的網路
transmission	[træns`mɪʃən]	名 傳輸

😊 情境會話 *Conversation*

A I am glad I have this chance to introduce our corporation to you all.

A Speed Connect is one of the world's *top* 5 communication *solutions* companies.

A We have branches all over the world. Our Asian division headquarters is based in Taipei, which currently has a staff of 230 people.

A We *specialized in* helping corporations set up the communication systems, such as the company's *intranet*, Internet connections, voice and data *transmissions*.

A Our customer service is also highly valued by our existing clients.

A：我很高興有這個機會向各位介紹我們的公司。
A：速聯是全世界五大通訊技術方案公司之一。
A：我們的分公司遍及全球。我們的亞洲總部位在台北，目前有 230 位員工。
A：我們專門協助公司行號設立傳訊系統，例如公司內部網路、網路連線、聲音及資料的傳輸。
A：我們的顧客服務也得到目前客戶極高的評價。

超實用精選短句 *Useful Sentences*

» I am very interested in getting to know your company.
我很有興趣瞭解貴公司。

» Could you provide me with detailed information about your company?
您能為我提供公司的詳細資訊嗎？

» Is there further information about your company available on your website?
公司網站上有貴公司的詳細資訊嗎？

» Is it possible to give me a copy of your annual report?
您可不可以給我一份貴公司的年度報告？

» We are one of the biggest exporters of medical devices in our country.
我們公司是我們國家最大的醫療設備出口商之一。

» We specialized in futures trading.
我們專門從事期貨貿易。

» Thank you for inquiring about our company.
感謝您對我們公司的垂詢。

» Please visit our website for further information about our company.
關於我們公司的詳細資訊請登陸我們的網站。

» Our company has more than 20 years of experiences in the field of electronic trade.
我們公司在電子貿易領域擁有二十多年的經驗。

» We are looking forward to serving you in the near future.
希望在不久的將來能為您服務。

你一定要知道！ *More Tips*

　　做公司的推介時，通常會加入顧客的評價或是提出公司信譽良好的保證，如：「We have enjoyed a good reputation among our customers.」（我們一直在客戶間享有良好的信譽。），或「We are considered to be one of the most reliable agents.」（我們是公認最可靠的代理商之一。）。

03 招呼新客

📚 關鍵單字 & 片語 *Words & Phrases*

browse	[braʊz]	動	瀏覽
take your time	[tek jʊɚ taɪm]	片	慢慢來
exhibition	[ˌɛksəˈbɪʃən]	名	展示
actually	[ˈæktnʊəlɪ]	副	事實上
local	[ˈlokl̩]	形	當地的、本地的
no wonder	[no ˈwʌndɚ]	片	難怪
be familiar with	[bi fəˈmɪljɚ wɪð]	片	熟悉
get acquainted with	[gɛt əˈkwentɪd wɪð]	片	認識

😊 情境會話 *Conversation*

A Hi. Is there anything I can help you with?

B Oh! Just *browsing*, thanks for asking!

A That's ok, *take your time*.

B Is this your first time attending this *exhibition*?

A *Actually*, yes, it is. In the past, we only focused on *local* exhibitions.

B *No wonder* I *am* not *familiar with* you.

A Here is our brochure, it'll help you *get acquainted with* our company and products.

A：嗨，有什麼可幫你忙的地方嗎？
B：哦，只是隨便看看，謝謝！
A：沒關係，慢慢看。
B：看起來你們好像是第一次參加這個展覽？
A：事實上，是的。以往我們只參加國內展。
B：難怪，對你們公司沒什麼印象。
A：這是我們的簡介，它將會幫你對我們公司和產品有更深的了解。

超實用精選短句 *Useful Sentences*

» Good morning, what can I do for you?
早安，有什麼能為您效勞嗎？

» Thank you for coming to our booth.
感謝參觀我們的攤位。

» We will show you how this product works.
我們會向你示範這個產品怎麼使用。

» I am just looking around.
我只是隨便看看。

» Here's our information brochure. Please take a look.
這是我們的資訊手冊，請看一下。

» May I have your name so that I can follow up with you?
可以給你的名片以方便進一步和你聯繫嗎？

» It's a large International Trade Show, isn't it?
這是個大型的國際商展，不是嗎？

» Can you give me some brochures?
能給我一些宣傳冊嗎？

» This is our first time to join the International Trade Show.
這是我們第一次參加國際商展。

» I am sure you will like our products.
我相信您會喜歡我們的產品的。

» It there anything that you're interested?
您想要看點什麼呢？

» Do you mind leaving your contact information?
您介意留下您的聯繫方式嗎？

你一定要知道！ *More Tips*

「browsing」這個字的意思就是「翻閱、瀏覽」的意思，當你在逛服飾店的時候，店員問你說：「Can I help you?」（我可以幫你嗎？），你可以說：「I am just browsing.」（我只是逛逛。）；而當你只是翻閱一本書的時候，你可以說：「I was just browsing through it.」（我只是翻閱了一下。）。

04 介紹自家商品

📖 關鍵單字&片語 *Words & Phrases*

particular	[pəˈtɪkjələ]	形 特別的
prototype	[ˈprotəˌtaɪp]	名 原型
early stage	[ˈɝlɪ stedʒ]	名 早期階段
technology	[tɛkˈnɑlədʒɪ]	名 技術
behold	[bɪˈhold]	動 注視

😊 情境會話 *Conversation*

A Anything in **_particular_** that you're interested in?

B Show me this one. Is this your new product?

A It's a **_prototype_** of our new improved product. This one will have more functions than the first models did.

A According to our schedule, it will be released next month.

B So soon? This one seems to be in the **_early stages_**.

A Recently we've developed better **_technology_**. The finished product will be a pleasure to **_behold_**.

A：有沒有什麼特別感興趣的東西？
B：讓我看看這個東西。你們的新產品？
A：這裡擺的是我們新進改良產品的原型。新一代產品比起第一代多了更多功能。
A：根據我們的計劃，它將於下個月上市。
B：這麼快？看起來好像尚未很成熟。
A：最近我們已研發出更優良的技術。成品將會使你的眼睛為之一亮。

超實用精選短句 *Useful Sentences*

» One of our main strengths is the great quality of the products.
我們的主要優勢之一是產品品質。

» There will be a large market opportunity for the products.
這種產品在市場上會大有商機。

» I believe you will be interested in our new product.
相信您對本公司新產品會感興趣。

» Let me introduce our latest product for you.
讓我為您介紹我們最新的產品。

» I believe you will be interested in our newly released product .
我們的新產品剛剛上市，相信您會感興趣。

» The computer comes with a two-year warranty.
這台電腦保固期為兩年。

» You have to admit that the feature will attract many clients.
您不得不承認這一特點會吸引很多客戶。

» You can save 34% for buying them together.
如果你一起買就可以享 66 折優惠。

» We commit to provide professional after-sales service to our customers.
我們承諾為用戶提供優質的售後服務。

» Our products can stand the competition.
我們的產品是經得起競爭的。

✔ 你一定要知道！✔ *More Tips*

　　當你去店家的時候，店員都會親切的説：「May I help you?」（我可以幫你嗎？）、「Is there anything that you are interested in?」（你對什麼比較有興趣？）、「Is there anything I can do for you?」（有沒有我可以幫你做的？）。

05 讓客戶下試用訂單

📖 關鍵單字＆片語 *Words & Phrases*

user manual	[ˋjuzɚ ˋmænjuəl]	名 使用手冊
trouble	[ˋtrʌbl̩]	動 麻煩
sell	[sɛl]	動 賣
especially	[əˋspɛʃəlɪ]	副 特別是
hot cakes	[hat kek]	副 很好賣的貨物
trial	[ˋtraɪəl]	名 試用

😊 情境會話 *Conversation*

A This is this product's data sheet. Shall I show you its ***user manual***?

B No, don't ***trouble*** yourself!

A After an introduction, you'll find our products are easier to operate than our competitor's.

B How is this product ***selling***?

A It's selling well, ***especially*** in Taiwan, It's selling like ***hot cakes***. Would you like to place a ***trial*** order?

B That would be great. We'll order once we try this sample.

A Please fill out this order form. We'll send our sample and invoice to you soon.

A：這是這項新品的規格表。需要看使用手冊嗎？
B：不必麻煩了。
A：經過介紹，您會發現我們的產品比競爭者的容易操作。
B：這項產品賣得如何？
A：賣得很好，尤其在台灣很暢銷。您要不要下個試用訂單？
B：這樣很好，試過樣品後我們會訂購。
A：請填寫這張訂購單，我們將儘快把產品和帳單寄給您。

超實用精選短句 *Useful Sentences*

» We've heard lots of good things about your products.
我們聽過很多關於你們產品不錯的評價。

» How about placing a trial order?
您為什麼不下個試用訂單呢？

» It is quite popular in Europe and America.
它在歐美非常暢銷。

» You can try it free for two weeks.
您可以免費試用兩個星期。

» We don't give customers free samples.
我們是不提供免費樣品的。

» We'll make a sample discoumt of twenty percent if ypu want to try our products.
這個試用樣品我們可以打八折。

» You can place a trial order instead.
您可以改下個試用訂單。

» If you're satisfied with the quality, we can discuss the order in detail later on.
如果您滿意這個品質，我們可以隨後再來討論訂單事宜。

» You can have this sample free of charge.
你可以拿這個免費的樣品。

» You can place a trial order before buying it.
購買前您可以下個試用訂單。

» You have to pay $100 for this sample.
這個樣品必須收費一百元。

» We'll send our product to you as soon as possible.
我們會儘快給您寄出我們的產品。

你一定要知道！ *More Tips*

「hot cake」是「暢銷」的意思。當美國人剛移民到美國的時候，以玉米粉做成的餅，特別是剛出爐的，是最好吃的，所以引申為最好的、最受歡迎的意思。「His records sells like hot cakes.」（他的唱片賣得很好。）。

06 聯繫客戶親臨展場

📖 關鍵單字&片語 *Words & Phrases*

next	[ˋnɛkst]	形 下一個
around	[əˋraʊnd]	介 在……附近
corner	[ˋkɔrnə]	名 角落
hard	[hɑrd]	形 困難的
probably	[ˋprɑbəblɪ]	副 可能

😃 情境會話 *Conversation*

A Mr. Brown, we'll have a booth in the exhibition *next* week.

B Sounds good.

A We'll release our new product there. Would you like to visit our booth and see this new product?

B Sure, when is the exhibition?

A From next Tuesday to Saturday, 9 a.m. to 4 p.m..

B And your booth number?

A It's B-612, *around* the *corner* on your right-hand side.

B It shouldn't be *hard* to find. OK, let's see, I'll *probably* be there next Wednesday morning.

A：布朗先生，我們在下禮拜的展覽中有設一個攤位。
B：聽起來不錯啊！
A：我們將會在那裡展出我們的新產品。到時要不要來看看？
B：當然，展覽期間為何時？
A：從下個星期二到星期六，早上 9 點到下午 4 點。
B：攤位號碼呢？
A：在 B-612 號，在你進來後右手邊的角落附近。
B：應該不難找，好吧，我看一下，我大概在星期三早上去。

超實用精選短句 *Useful Sentences*

» We have a booth in the International Exhibition Center.
我們在國際展覽中心有一個攤位。

» Our new product will be put on display then.
到時候我們的新產品將會展出。

» It would benefit your company to attend the trade show.
參展會對你們公司很有益處。

» When will the exhibition be held?
展覽將什麼時候舉行啊？

» Could you tell me your booth number?
可以告訴我您的攤位號碼嗎？

» Welcome to visit our booth next week.
歡迎下周來參觀我們的攤位。

» We will be happy to see you then.
到時候看到您我們會很高興的。

» From next Monday to Saturday 10: 00 a.m. to 5 p.m..
從下個星期一到星期六，早上十點到下午五點。

» Our booth is at the right side of the exhibition room.
我們的攤位在展覽廳的右邊。

» I am sure you won't miss it.
我確信您一定會找到的。

» Your booth is arranged very nicely.
你們的攤位佈置得非常好。

» I think I might be there next Wednesday afternoon.
我想我大概下週三下午去參觀。

你一定要知道！ *More Tips*

「booth」除了是表示在展覽會上或是市場的攤子之外，還是選舉時隔離的小投票所、看歌劇表演的雅座，或是「telephone booth」（電話亭）。

07 拜訪新買家

📚 關鍵單字&片語 *Words & Phrases*

meet	[mit]	動 見面
during	[ˋdjʊrɪŋ]	介 在……的整個期間
remember	[rɪˋmɛmbɚ]	動 記得
so	[so]	介 所以
sometime	[ˋsʌmˏtaɪm]	副 某一時候
show	[ʃo]	動 展示
anytime	[ˋɛnɪˏtaɪm]	副 在任何時候

😃 情境會話 *Conversation*

A Good Morning, Mr. Smith, this is Jack from ABC Company. We **_met_** at our booth **_during_** the exhibition.

B Yes, I remember you.

A Thank you for visiting our booth. I **_remembered_** you said you are interested in our products, **_so_**... Could I see you **_sometime_** this week to **_show_** you more information?

B How about Tuesday at 3 p.m.?

A **_Anytime_** you say.

A：史密斯先生早，我是 ABC 公司的傑克，展覽期間在我們的攤位上見過面。

B：是的，我記得你。

A：謝謝您的來訪參觀，我記得您說對我們的產品頗有興趣，所以，我想……是不是可以在這個禮拜的某個時候見見您，再向您補充多一點資料？

B：禮拜三下午 3 點如何？

A：您說什麼時候都可以。

超實用精選短句 *Useful Sentences*

» May I know if you are Mr. Robert?
請問您是羅伯特先生嗎？

» I am Mike from NEC Company. Do you remember me?
我是來自 NEC 公司的麥克，你還記得我嗎？

» I would like to visit you next week.
我想要下禮拜去拜訪你。

» Sorry, but I am going on a business trip.
不好意思，我要出差。

» You can come here after I get back.
你可以等我回來再過來。

» I'd like to give you some information about our product.
我想給您一些有關我們產品的資料。

» Is it possible for me to visit you some day?
改天我可以去拜訪您嗎？

» I would love to listen to your opinion about our products.
我想聽聽你對我們產品的意見。

» What about 4 p.m. this Friday?
那麼本週五下午四點如何呢？

» I wonder when is convenient for you.
我想知道您什麼時候方便呢。

» Thank you for inquiring about our product.
謝謝您詢問我們的產品。

» Not at all. Please come again soon.
不用謝，歡迎再次光臨。

你一定要知道！ *More Tips*

　　當你送走你的客人，不管他們是否買了你的產品，你都該禮貌的說期待他們下次的光臨：「I will be expecting you.」（我期待你下次再來。）、「I hope you will be stop by soon.」（希望你將很快的再次光臨。）、「Please come again soon.」（歡迎再度光臨。）。

Part

15

海外考察／出差

篇

→ **Part 15 音檔連結** ←

因各家手機系統不同，若無法直接掃描，
仍可以至以下電腦雲端連結下載收聽。
（https://tinyurl.com/57xt6ck3）

01 預訂機位

📚 關鍵單字&片語 *Words & Phrases*

date	[det]	名 日期
seat	[sit]	名 座位
check in	[ˈtʃɛk ˌɪn]	片 報到
airport	[ˈɛrˌport]	名 機場
got it	[ɡɑt ɪt]	片 知道了、了解

😊 情境會話 *Conversation*

A China Airlines Reservations. May I help you?

B Yes, I'd like to make a reservation for one person to San Francisco.

B My name is Li-Li Wang.

A OK, what *date*, please?

B October 27th.

A OK, Miss Wang, your *seat* is confirmed on flight 0662, leaving at 7 p.m. Please *check in* at the *airport* two hours before the flight. Please also don't forget to confirm your ticket 3 days before you leave.

B *Got it*, thank you.

A：中華航空公司訂位組，有什麼可以效勞的嗎？
B：是的，我想預訂一張去舊金山的機票。
B：我的名字是王俐俐。
A：好的，時間是哪一天呢？
B：10 月 27 日。
A：好的，王小姐，你的機位確定 OK，班機號碼為 0662，晚上 7 點起飛，請記得提早 2 個小時到機場辦理登記。並且不要忘了在 3 天前再一次確認妳的機位。
B：知道了，謝謝你。

🖐 超實用精選短句 *Useful Sentences*

» I would like to book a flight ticket to London tomorrow.
我想預訂一張明天去倫敦的機票。

» I need to change my flight date.
我需要更改班機日期。

» May I have your name?
請問您貴姓大名？

» Which date are you flying on?
您哪一天要搭機？

» What can I do for you, sir?
先生，有什麼能為您效勞的？

» I want to confirm my ticket to Tokyo this Friday.
我要確認本週五到東京的票。

» Would you prefer a window or aisle seat?
您想靠窗的還是靠走道的位子？

» An aisle seat, please.
請給我一個靠走道的位子。

» I want a first class ticket.
我要一張頭等艙機票。

» Could you tell me how to spell your name?
可不可以告訴我怎樣拼寫您的名字？

» Your flight number is AB123.
您的班機號碼是 AB123。

» Please take care of your ticket.
請保管好您的機票。

⚡ 你一定要知道！⚡ *More Tips*

　　當你預定機票，在出國前一定要記得打電話去「confirm」（確認），「I would like to confirm my ticket to Paris this Sunday.」（我要確認這禮拜日到巴黎的票。），還可以要求：「I need to order a vegetarian meal and make sure that I have an aisle seat.」。（我要訂素食餐，而且要靠走道的座位。）。

02 預訂飯店

📖 關鍵單字 & 片語 *Words & Phrases*

book	[bʊk]	動 預訂
single room	[ˈsɪŋɡḷ rum]	名 單人房
party	[ˈpɑrtɪ]	名 一行人
depart	[dɪˈpɑrt]	動 出發

😊 情境會話 *Conversation*

A Room Reservations, may I help you?

B Yes, this is Li-Li from Taiwan. I'd like to **book** a **single room** for October 28th.

A For how many nights? And how many guests will be in your **party**?

B Just one night is fine. Only me, one person!

A May I have your name, please?

B Li-Li Wang.

A May I also have your airline and flight number?

B China Airlines, the flight number is 0662 **departing** from Taiwan on October 27th, arriving in San Francisco the next day.

A：訂房組，有什麼可效勞的嗎？
B：是的，我從台灣打來的，我想在 10 月 28 日晚上預約一間單人房。
A：要住幾晚呢？會有多少人？
B：一個晚上就夠了，只有我一人。
A：請告訴我你的名字。
B：王俐俐。
A：請順便告訴我您搭乘的航空公司及班機號碼，好嗎？
B：中華航空公司，班機號碼 0662，10 月 27 日從台灣起飛，隔天抵達目的地。

超實用精選短句 *Useful Sentences*

» Reservations, what can I do for you?
訂房部，有什麼能為您效勞的？

» Can you reserve a double room for me?
可以幫我訂一間雙人房嗎？

» How long will you be staying?
您準備住多久？

» Which kind of room do you like?
您想要什麼樣的房間？

» A single room will be OK.
一間單人房就夠了。

» Would you please tell me the room rate?
您能告訴我房價是多少嗎？

» US$150, including tax.
一晚 150 美金，含稅。

» I want to make a reservation for two nights.
我想要訂兩個晚上的房間。

» I prefer a suite.
我想要一間套房。

» How can I get to your hotel from the LAX airport?
我要怎麼從洛杉磯國際機場到你們飯店？

» We offer a 10% discount for group reservation.
團體訂房的話打九折。

» Wish you a happy stay here.
祝您住得愉快！

你一定要知道！ *More Tips*

「book」當作名詞的時候是「書」的意思，「I like to read a book before I go to bed at night.」（我在晚上睡覺前喜歡讀書。）；當作動詞就是「預訂」的意思：「I would like to book a table for two.」（我想要訂一個兩人的座位。）。

03 約定拜訪客戶時間

📚 關鍵單字&片語 Words & Phrases

in detail	[ɪn ˋditel]	片 詳細地
absolutely	[ˋæbsəˌlutlɪ]	副 當然
get	[gɛt]	動 到達
far	[fɑr]	形 遠的
Union Square	[ˋjunjən skwɛr]	名 聯合廣場

😊 情境會話 Conversation

🅐 Hello, Mr, Johnson, this is Li-Li. Just to inform you, I'll be in San Francisco on October 28th. Could we meet later that day to discuss this matter **_in detail_**?

🅑 **_Absolutely_**, when is it convenient for you?

🅐 How about October 29th, 3 o'clock in the afternoon?

🅑 OK, then I'll be waiting for you.

🅐 Mr. Johnson, could you tell me how to **_get_** to your office?

🅑 We are not **_far_** from **_Union Square_**, it's easy for you to find.

A：哈囉！強生先生，我是俐俐，想通知您，我將會於 10 月28 日抵達舊金山。我們能不能在稍後碰個面，討論一下這件事的細節？
B：當然，那妳何時比較方便呢？
A：那麼就 10 月 29 日，下午 3 點，如何？
B：好，那我就等你來。
A：強生先生，您可否告訴我如何到您公司那裡？
B：我們這兒離聯合廣場不遠，很容易找得到的。

🔊 超實用精選短句 *Useful Sentences*

» Will you be in your office next Friday?
你下個禮拜五會在公司嗎？

» I will arrive in Frankfort on May 12th.
我將於五月十二號抵達法蘭克福。

» I wonder when it is convenient for you.
我想知道您什麼時間比較方便呢。

» Would you like me to come up to your office?
你要我上去你們公司嗎？

» Shall we get together that day?
我們那天可以碰個面嗎？

» I'm afraid I will not be in the office that day.
恐怕我那天不會在公司。

» How about we meet at your hotel?
在你的飯店見面如何？

» I will stop by your hotel at six.
我六點會到你的飯店。

» I would like to make an appointment with you.
我想和您約個時間見面。

» I can schedule you for three.
我可以安排在兩點。

» Any time is good for me.
我什麼時候都可以。

» I am looking forward to meeting you soon.
期待儘快見到您。

⚡ 你一定要知道！⚡ *More Tips*

　　與客戶約定時間除了問：「When is it convenient for you?」（你何時比較方便呢？），或是「When will it be a good time for you?」（什麼時間對你比較好？）、「Is five o'clock all right with you?」（五點對你說可以嗎？）等等。

04 拜訪客戶公司

📖 關鍵單字&片語 *Words & Phrases*

get lost	[gɛt lɔst]	片	迷路
as usual	[æz ˋjuʒuəl]	片	跟平常一樣
thought	[θɔt]	名	想法
organized	[ˋɔrgənˏaɪzd]	形	有組織的
thoughtful	[ˋθɔtfəl]	形	體貼的
environment	[ɪnˋvaɪrənmənt]	名	環境

😊 情境會話 *Conversation*

A Hi, Mr. Johnson.

B Hi, Li-Li... Did you find us all right?

A Yes, I didn't have any trouble. I didn't **get lost**.

B Good! Well, haven't seen you for a long time. How's everything?

A Everything is the same **as usual**, thanks!

B Please come with me.

B What are your **thoughts** concerning our company?

A Well, wonderful. It is a very **organized** company and a **thoughtful environment**!

A：嗨，強生。
B：嗨，俐俐……妳是順利找到我們的嗎？
A：是，一點困難都沒有。我沒有迷路。
B：那就好，好久不見了，你一切可好？
A：一切和往常一樣，謝謝關心。
B：請跟我來。
B：對我們公司感覺怎麼樣？
A：嗯，很好。很有組織的公司，而且環境非常舒適。

超實用精選短句 *Useful Sentences*

» My name is Michael. I represent IBM.
我是 IBM 的代表，麥克。

» I'm so glad to see you here.
真高興能在這裡見到你。

» Welcome to our company!
歡迎蒞臨敝公司！

» Did you have a nice flight?
一路上還好吧？

» This is my first time to come to your company.
這是我第一次來你的公司。

» Let me show you around.
讓我帶您去參觀一下吧。

» It's been a long time.
好久不見了。

» I have an appointment with Mr. Wang at ten.
我想見這裡的王先生。

» How do you feel about our company?
你覺得我們公司怎麼樣？

» I brought you a present.
我帶了禮物來給你。

» Well, let's get down to business.
那麼，讓我們言歸正傳吧。

» This is an impressive office.
好氣派的辦公室啊！

你一定要知道！ *More Tips*

若是有客人到公司參訪你可能會需要用到以下的句子：「Let me take you for a tour around the office.」（我到你到公司參觀一下。）、「Let me introduce you our company.」（讓我來為你介紹我們公司。）、「I will be the guide to lead you around our office.」（我當導遊帶你在公司看看。）。

05 交換市場心得

📚 關鍵單字&片語 Words & Phrases

be proud of	[bi praud ɑv]	片 以……為傲
force	[fors]	名 力量
so far	[so far]	片 目前
strategy	[ˈstrætədʒɪ]	名 策略
totally	[ˈtotḷɪ]	副 完全地

😃 情境會話 Conversation

A How were your sales of our products over the past three months?

B Our sales were up 12% compared to last year.

A It seems you've done quite well!

B We'*re proud of* our sales *force*. I thought we could be better than that.

A So is your present sales area still the Western United States?

B *So far*, Yes! We plan to expand our business to the East. However, you know, its market style and the *strategy* we require are *totally* different.

A：你們過去 3 個月代理我們產品銷路如何？
B：與去年同時比較，銷售量提升了 12 個百分點。
A：看來您做得不錯嘛！
B：我們非常以我們的銷售力量為傲，其實我以為我們應該成長更多的。
A：所以，你目前的銷售區域還是仍然集中於美國西半部？
B：目前是的。我們有計劃要去開拓東部市場，不過你也知道，那是一個完全不同的市場型態，要用的策略也不同。

🔊 超實用精選短句 *Useful Sentences*

» How is that new marketing strategies?
那個新的行銷策略如何啊？

» We have increased 5% of the market share in the first half year.
上半年我們已經增加了 5% 的市場份額。

» Would you like to go on expanding foreign market?
您想繼續開發國外市場嗎？

» How are sales of new products for the first quarter?
第一季的新產品銷售狀況如何？

» Have you gone over the proposal?
你有看完整個提案嗎？

» We should pay more attention to the quality control techniques.
我們應該更關注品質控管技術。

» I'd welcome any comments you have.
歡迎你有任何的評論。

» Did my method work in your management?
我的方法在你的管理中奏效嗎？

» I think advertisement is the key to our success.
我認為廣告是我們成功的關鍵。

» Is there something you're not satisfied?
有什麼地方你不滿意的嗎？

» Most buyers have withdrawn from the market because of unstable prices.
由於價格不穩定，大多數買主已退出市場。

» We look forward to having a long-term relationship.
我們希望保持長久的合作關係。

✐ 你一定要知道！ ✐ *More Tips*

「expand」是「擴展」的意思：「Our company has expanded rapidly over the years.」（這幾年我們公司急速拓展。）。

06 回報公司出差事宜

📚 關鍵單字&片語 *Words & Phrases*

explore	[ɪkˋsplor]	動 開拓
advertise	[ˋædvɚˌtaɪz]	動 廣告
popular	[ˋpɑpjələ]	形 受歡迎的
supply	[səˋplaɪ]	動 提供
promise	[ˋprɑmɪs]	動 答應

😊 情境會話 *Conversation*

B How's Mr. Johnson and his business?

A He is fine. His business is great. Over the past three months, sales have increased a lot.

A To increase sales and *explore* a new market, he hoped we could *advertise* in some *popular* magazines and *supply* him with some promotional materials.

B Did you *promise* him?

A No, not yet. I told him I needed to discuss it with you first.

B Right, we need to evaluate it and check the advertising budget.

B：強生先生和他的公司都好嗎？
A：強生先生人很好。公司生意也不錯，光是過去三個月業績成長很多。
A：為了因應業績成長並加速開拓新市場，他希望我們能夠多在當地暢銷雜誌上做廣告，並支援一些其它的促銷用品。
B：你承諾他了嗎？
A：還沒有，我告訴他我必需先和你商量一下。
B：沒錯，我們必須評估一下可行性和我們的廣告預算。

超實用精選短句 *Useful Sentences*

» Hello, this is Catherine and I am going back tomorrow.
喂，我是凱薩琳，我明天就回去了。

» I have signed the contract with them.
我已經和他們簽約了。

» I found that their company has some financial problems.
我發現他們公司有些財務問題。

» Mr. Robert rejected our proposal.
羅伯特先生拒絕了我們的提議。

» Can you tell me what I should do next?
能告訴我下一步該怎麼做嗎？

» I got something urgent to tell you.
我有急事要告訴你。

» What's his position on this issue?
他對這個議題持什麼態度？

» I will keep you updated.
我會隨時報告你最新消息。

» If anything comes up, let me know immediately.
有任何事發生，馬上讓我知道。

» Please keep me up-to-date.
請隨時告知我最新狀況。

» We will discuss that when you get back.
等你回來我們再討論。

» Let's leave it till I get back to Taiwan.
就把這個問題留到我回台灣再說囉。

⚡ 你一定要知道！⚡ *More Tips*

「evaluate」是「評估」的意思，如：「We have to evaluate the plan before carrying it out.」（我們在執行這計劃之前要先評估它。）。

07 租車詢問

📖 關鍵單字&片語 *Words & Phrases*

reward	[rɪˋwɔrd]	名 獎勵
option	[ˋɑpʃən]	名 選擇
vehicle	[ˋviɪkl̩]	名 車輛
full-size	[fʊl saɪz]	形 標準大小的
sedan	[sɪˋdæn]	名 轎車
insurance	[ɪnˋʃʊrəns]	名 保險
benefit	[ˋbɛnəfɪt]	動 獲益
driver	[ˋdraɪvɚ]	名 駕駛人

😊 情境會話 *Conversation*

A Hi, my name is Justin. I am a member of your *rewards* program. I will be in Beijing on the 15th and require a car for one week.

A What are the different *options* of *vehicles* you have available?

A How much will it cost for the *full-size sedan* including all *insurance* for one week.

A Is there any free upgrade or promotion that I can *benefit* from?

A What are the requirements for more than one *driver*?

A：嗨，我叫賈斯汀。我是你們獎勵計畫的會員。我在本月15 日會到北京，需要一輛車，要租一星期。
A：你們現在可租的車輛中有哪些不同的選擇？
A：標準大小的轎車含保險，租一星期要多少錢？
A：有沒有對我有利的免費升級或優惠方案？
A：如果有超過一個駕駛人要開車，必要條件是什麼？

🔊 超實用精選短句 *Useful Sentences*

» I want to rent a car for a couple of days.
我需要租幾天車。

» How much will it cost for three days?
租三天要多少錢？

» How long will you need it?
你要租多久呢？

» Is there any discount if I rent it longer?
如果我租久一點可以有折扣嗎？

» I am wondering if I need to return it with a full tank.
我想知道還車時是否要加滿汽油。

» Does the price including tax and insurance?
這個價格包括稅和保險嗎？

» I'd like some information about renting a car.
我想瞭解一下有關租車的事宜。

» Do you offer insurance on this rental car?
租這台車有提供保險嗎？

» What do you charge for car rentals?
租車費用你們怎麼計算？

» Is there car rental service near the hotel?
請問旅館附近有沒有可以租車的地方呢？

» Do you offer car rental service?
您那裡提供租車服務嗎？

» What is the charge for dropping the vehicles off in Shanghai instead of Beijing?
如果車子要在上海還車，而不是北京，要怎麼收費？

✒ 你一定要知道！✒ *More Tips*

　　租車時，很重要的一點就是要問清楚費用是否含稅或保險，如：
「Are tax and insurance included in the rates?」（費用有包含稅及保險嗎？），此外還要問清楚：「Do I have to return it with a full tank?」
（還車時是否要加滿汽油？）也是很重要的。

語研力 **E087**

國際職場溝通專書 商用英語：
從自我介紹到海外考察，通通難不倒！

作　　者	Luna
顧　　問	曾文旭
出版總監	陳逸祺、耿文國
主　　編	陳蕙芳
文字校對	翁芯琍
美術編輯	李依靜
法律顧問	北辰著作權事務所

印　　製	世和印製企業有限公司
初　　版	2023年10月
出　　版	凱信企業集團-凱信企業管理顧問有限公司
電　　話	（02）2773-6566
傳　　真	（02）2778-1033
地　　址	106 台北市大安區忠孝東路四段218之4號12樓
信　　箱	kaihsinbooks@gmail.com

定　　價	新台幣349元／港幣116元
產品內容	1書

總 經 銷	采舍國際有限公司
地　　址	235 新北市中和區中山路二段366巷10號3樓
電　　話	（02）8245-8786
傳　　真	（02）8245-8718

國家圖書館出版品預行編目資料

國際職場溝通專書 商用英語：從自我介紹到
海外考察，通通難不倒！／Luna著. -- 初版. --
臺北市：凱信企業集團凱信企業管理顧問有限
公司, 2023.09
　面；　公分
ISBN 978-626-7354-03-2(平裝)

1.CST: 英語 2.CST: 職場 3.CST: 讀本

805.18　　　　　　　　　　　　112011701